DATE DUE

MAY 2 2 '15	
JUN 0 8 '15	
JUN 1 8 '15	
AUG 2 8 '15	
AUG 1 6 2021	
NOV 0 6 2021	

STRAND OF DECEPTION

Center Point
Large Print

Also by Robin Caroll and available from
Center Point Large Print:

Justice Seekers Series
  Injustice for All
  To Write a Wrong

Evil Series
  In the Shadow of Evil

**This Large Print Book carries the
Seal of Approval of N.A.V.H.**

STRAND OF DECEPTION

ROBIN CAROLL

CENTER POINT LARGE PRINT
THORNDIKE, MAINE

This Center Point Large Print edition is published
in the year 2013 by arrangement
with B & H Publishing Group.

The text of this Large Print edition is unabridged.
In other aspects, this book may
vary from the original edition.
Printed in the United States of America
on permanent paper.
Set in 16-point Times New Roman type.

ISBN: 978-1-61173-690-8

Library of Congress Cataloging-in-Publication Data

Caroll, Robin.
Strand of deception : a Justice Seekers novel / Robin Caroll. — Center
Point Large Print edition.
pages cm
ISBN 978-1-61173-690-8 (Library binding : alk. paper)
1. United States. Federal Bureau of Investigation—Fiction.
2. Murder—Investigation—Fiction. 3. DNA fingerprinting—Fiction.
4. Tennessee—Fiction. 5. Large type books. I. Title.
PS3603.A7673S77 2013
813'.6—dc23

2012050823

For Momma . . . because when I grow up,
I want to be just like you.

ACKNOWLEDGMENTS

If I searched throughout the publishing industry, I could not ask for a better editor than the one I've been blessed to work with—Julee Schwarzburg. She is so amazingly talented and works extremely hard to make my novels the best they can be. My heartfelt thanks to you, Julee. Your friendship is so valued.

My thanks to the whole Pure Enjoyment team at B&H for helping the Justice Seekers series see the light of day. I truly appreciate each of you for extending your talent and skill on my behalf. It's been a fun journey.

Special thanks to Kristin Helm at the Tennessee Bureau of Investigation. Your input was invaluable and your willingness to answer my millions of questions was so appreciated.

This book dealt with minute details. Huge thanks to the following people for sharing their knowledge with me: Timothy D. Kupferschmid, MBA, MFS; Melissa Myhand with the Arkansas Crimelab; Cara Putman; and Jill Spriggs, CA DOJ Bureau Chief, Bureau of Forensic Services. Any mistakes in the representation of details are mine, where I twisted in the best interest of my story.

Special thanks to Cara Putman for reading this

book (fast) before I turned it in. You are amazing!

As always, there are many in the writing community who help me in so many ways, I can't even begin to list them. My heartfelt thanks to Colleen Coble, Pam Hillman, Tosca Lee, Dineen Miller, Cara Putman, and Cheryl Wyatt.

My most sincere thanks to my awesome agent, Steve Laube (HP), who keeps me focused and on task, as well as remaining the steady calm when I need it. THANK YOU.

My extended family members are my biggest fans and greatest cheerleaders. Thank you for ALWAYS being in my corner: Mom and Papa, BB and Robert, Bek and Krys, Bubba and Lisa, Brandon, Rachel, and Aunt Millicent.

I couldn't do what I do without my girls—Emily Carol, Remington Case, and Isabella Co-Ceaux. I love each of you so much! Thank y'all so much for your support and encouragement when I needed to write. And my precious grandsons, Benton and Zayden. You are joys in my life.

There aren't enough words to express the love and gratitude for my husband, Case. Thank you for everything you do. You truly are my rock . . . my true North . . . my partner in this life. I could not do this without you and I love you with all my heart.

Finally, all glory to my Lord and Savior, Jesus Christ. *I can do all things through Him who gives me strength.*

Glossary of Acronyms

AFIS—*Automated Fingerprint Identification System*

ALS—Alternate Light Source

BOLO—Be On the LookOut

CI—Confidential Informant

CODIS—Combined DNA Index System

CSU—Crime Scene Unit

DOC—Department of Corrections

IAFIS—*Integrated Automated Fingerprint Identification System*

MO—Modus Operandi

NIBIN—National Integrated Ballistics Information Network

PCR—DNA strand identifiers test

RFLP—Restriction Fragment Length Polymorphism

TBI—Tennessee Bureau of Investigation

"For it is with your heart that
you believe and are justified,
and it is with your mouth that
you profess your faith and are saved."
ROMANS 10:10

PROLOGUE

The stack of photographs slipped to the floor, splaying across the wood planks like wildflowers over a grassy meadow. Her hands trembled as tears flowed down her cheeks. This wasn't real. This couldn't be happening.

Yet the pictures proved otherwise. This was real, very real.

Her knees weakened. She slumped into the leather chair behind the desk. Even the familiar *whoosh* couldn't comfort her now. The proof of his betrayal assaulted her. On the floor. On the desk. In her hand.

Photographs of him in another woman's arms. How could he do this to them, his family? To her? Surely he knew this would destroy them, but he cheated anyway. She didn't understand. Did they mean so little to him?

Her heart ached in a way she never thought possible. Like someone shredded her insides. Another sob escaped her clenched lips. It bounced off the walls and rattled her ears. She never imagined betrayal like this would hurt so badly. So deeply.

She held her head in her hands, her elbows digging into the unyielding wood of the desk. Her lungs fought to push air in and out. Her legs wouldn't stop quaking.

The morning sun beat past the curtains and

flooded the loft with light. How dare such a symbol of joy invade when her entire life had just been destroyed?

Swallowing against a dry mouth, she bit her bottom lip and stared at the photographs. All of a sudden, she felt physically ill. This would destroy not only their family, but his career. His future. Was that why the pictures were taken?

Her heart slammed against her ribs as another thought raced through her mind . . . Why were the pictures *here?* Everything in her didn't want to believe what stared her right in the face. But there was no other explanation. The photos were here . . . for what? Money? A favor?

Blackmail?

Bile burned the back of her throat. This was all wrong. Everything.

Her mind struggled to comprehend. She'd let him into the family. Trusted him. Thought she loved him and he loved her. Apparently, she was wrong.

Dead wrong.

The pictures mocked her from all sides. This was her fault. She didn't have a choice now—she'd have to confront him and hear his excuse, not that she'd believe any lie he told. She'd destroy the photographs, all of them, and demand the negatives. Then she'd shut him out of their lives forever, even though it would kill her.

Her legs barely supported the weight of her decision as she ran for the bathroom.

CHAPTER ONE

"Adversity is sometimes hard upon a man; but for one man who can stand prosperity, there are a hundred that will stand adversity."
ELVIS PRESLEY

Two Weeks Ago

"We call Ms. Madeline Baxter to the stand."

Maddie wiped her hands on her skirt and stood. She'd testified at various trials over the years, but never one like this. Only a handful of people sat in the stuffy courtroom, the heat turned too high. She took the oath to tell the truth amid little fanfare before taking her seat in the witness stand.

She glanced over the few people sitting on the very hard, very uncomfortable pews. The judge had closed the hearing to the media, but the hounds waited just outside the oversized doors of the Shelby County Courthouse. Those allowed inside were legal figures, police, family members, and of course, the defendant.

"Ms. Baxter, will you please state your name and occupation for the court record?"

She leaned forward to the microphone. "Madeline Baxter. I'm a forensic scientist specializing in serology and DNA."

"And you are currently employed by the Tennessee Bureau of Investigation, correct?"

Maddie licked her lips. "In the Forensic Services Division, yes."

The defense attorney shuffled through pages on the legal pad he held. "Can you tell us a little about your professional background and qualifications, Ms. Baxter?"

Standard questions, but for the first time in her career, she felt like she was in the hot seat. "I hold a bachelor's degree in chemistry, as well as one in forensic science from the University of Tennessee. I graduated magna cum laude ten years ago and have been working for the TBI ever since. As such, I am a commissioned law-enforcement officer."

"Would you be described as an expert in your field, Ms. Baxter?"

They always asked the same question, just worded in various ways. Getting it on the record. "Yes."

"And the lab where you conduct your tests . . . is it accredited?"

"The TBI forensic lab is accredited by the American Society of Crime Laboratory Directors/ Laboratory Accreditation Board."

"Good." The lawyer paused for effect, Maddie was sure, returning to the table where the defendant sat, back straight and shoulders squared. "Now, Ms. Baxter, I'd like to direct you to a recent DNA test you conducted at the request of my office, regarding the defendant, Mr. Mark Hubble."

And here we go. Maddie licked her lips again. "Yes."

"You recall performing this test?"

"Yes."

"Can you give the court a brief overview for the record?"

"Our lab was supplied a saliva sample taken nine years ago from a crime scene involving a sexual assault. The sample was well preserved. I initially made tests, presumptive tests, for the presence of blood, which is ortho-tolidine. I utilized hydrogen peroxide as the tests reagents. I conducted testing for acid phosphatase, testing for P30 protein and for amylase, which is an enzyme found in saliva in high concentrations."

"Go on." The attorney nodded, as if he understood everything she said. He didn't. Most people didn't. All they wanted to know was what she would testify to next.

"We were also supplied, by the Shelby County Sheriff's Office, a saliva sample of the defendant."

"And you ran these same tests on that sample?"

"I did."

The lawyer paced slowly in front of the courtroom, paused, then moved beside her. "And you compared the two results?"

"Yes."

"And what was your conclusion?"

Maddie sat up straighter. "That Mr. Hubble is excluded as a match for the saliva sample."

The attorney smiled as he faced her. "So, in your *expert* opinion, Ms. Baxter, the tests you ran on the samples concluded the samples were from a different person, right?"

She nodded, then remembered she was in court. "Yes."

"Are you positive?"

"Yes. Science doesn't lie."

The defense attorney smiled broadly. "Thank you, Ms. Baxter." He grinned at the judge. "I have no further questions, Your Honor."

The judge glanced at the opposing table. The prosecutor jumped to his feet. "We have no questions, Your Honor."

"You may step down." The judge excused her.

She marched from the witness stand, catching the defendant's stare as she did. His eyes were dark, lifeless as he stared through her. A chill settled over her as she rushed past him.

The victim had stood in court, faced the man, and testified that Mark Hubble had sexually assaulted her. He'd been found guilty and sentenced to fifteen years. He'd served six already when his appellant lawyer discovered the saliva sample sitting in evidence and the order for DNA testing came through.

Looking at him now, Maddie's stomach knotted. He gave her the creeps, but DNA didn't lie. She had run the tests twice and gone over the results multiple times, twice with the head of the crime lab. The samples weren't from the same person—she was 100 percent positive of that fact. She stood behind the science over eyewitness testimony. How had the victim identified the wrong man?

Within moments, the judge had overturned the conviction and set Mr. Mark Hubble free with the court's humble apology. Right . . . Maddie could see the defense attorney's eyes shining with visions of dollar signs as he would prepare a civil suit for wrongful incarceration and try to get rich off sensationalizing this case. The media would grab hold of the details like pit bulls, locking their jaws on the story and not letting loose until the next big one surfaced.

Maddie shoved open the courtroom door and ducked behind the marshal as he held up his hands to ward off the vultures waiting in the hall. Flashes snapped.

She rushed down the hall, trying to ignore the reporters tailing her. Turning, she let the music soothe her as it had for years. *"If you're looking for trouble—"*

"Ms. Baxter, is it true Hubble's DNA wasn't a match to the saliva sample?" Yes. She kept walking at a fast clip. *Daa-da-da-da-da.*

"Is it possible your lab contaminated the samples?" No. *"You came to the right place."*

Gritting her teeth to stop the retort on the tip of her tongue, Maddie stomped toward the exit. While most of the media stayed behind at the courtroom to hound Mark Hubble, a few industrious reporters dogged her heels.

"Ms. Baxter, a statement, please?"

No way. *Daa-da-da-da-da.*

"How do you feel about your results freeing a man?"

If only the man didn't give her the creeps . . . if only she could believe he was innocent.

"What would you say to Mark Hubble's victim right now?"

Maddie stumbled at the last question. How *did* she feel toward the victim? The woman had to have mistakenly identified Hubble, right? But how would she feel when she heard the news that Hubble was free?

Dear God, please be with that poor woman. Wrap her in Your arms and comfort her in the way only You can.

Maddie regained her footing and broke free out the doors. She paused, gulping in the cool February air. The midday sun shot through the sky but didn't offer much heat against the breeze. She rushed down the stairs to the street corner, then turned back to the courthouse.

Her sword at her side, the statue of Lady Justice

with her blindfold permanently in place stared back at Maddie. The marble she was carved from as cold as Maddie's heart.

Science didn't lie.

Present Day, Friday

"Sir, is it possible your daughter might have stayed the night at a friend's and just overslept today?" Special Agent in Charge Nick Hagar peered into the man's face, gauging even the slightest nuance for possible deception.

"No, it's not." The man's stance tightened, his Adam's apple bobbing.

Nick sighed. Missing children were the worst cases—parents distraught, scared, and rightly so, no matter the child's age. The enormous emotional toll on parents when they didn't know what happened to their child . . . he knew all too well what that looked like. Memphis kept her secrets—always had, always would.

"Gina is well aware of the immediate consequences if she misses a check-in." Les Ford's public expression usually hid well his fifty-nine years. Today, every year weighted the lines of his ebony face. His tensed shoulders seemed out of place against the smooth lines in the formal living room. "Especially in light of that girl last week."

"I understand that, sir, and I mean no disrespect.

I must ask these hard questions to find your daughter. If there's even a remote chance she's merely out of touch . . ."

Despite her father's prominent position, Gina Ford was a college student. One who could've stayed at a party and crashed with a friend. Or stayed somewhere she didn't want her father to know about. Several other reasons she was just out of touch. So far, nothing indicated she'd been taken hostage to manipulate her father or she was a victim of foul play. Nick made brief eye contact with Darren, motioning him over to the couch.

The distraught father ran a trembling hand over the top of his head. The ends of his closely cropped black hair were tipped with white. "I apologize, Agent Hagar." He let out a long, slow breath. "Call it a gut feeling or father's intuition, whatever, but my daughter's in trouble."

"Okay, let's back up. I know you've already told the police everything, but I'm going to ask you to tell me so I have all the details." Nick sat forward on the high-back chair, taking in every movement, nuance, and gesture Les Ford made. "This is Agent Timmons, who'll be taking notes for our investigation."

Nodding at Darren, Ford flexed, then relaxed his fingers dangling in front of him. "Last night, Gina had study group and didn't plan to get home until after midnight."

"Do you know the names of those in her study group?" Darren asked, pen poised over his notebook.

"Rebecca Dragon, Cynthia Mantle, Lisa Trainer, and Rachel Boxer. But Rachel wasn't feeling well last night so she called to tell them she wouldn't be able to join them." Gina's father shot Darren a look that indicated he knew everything about his daughter's life. Or thought he did. He turned his piercing black eyes to Nick. "The group usually meets every Thursday evening in the McWherter Library from eight until eleven, then they go out for pizza at Garibaldi's."

Darren scribbled while Ford continued. "Last night, Gina returned to her room early. She told me she didn't feel like pizza and had some stuff to do before her workout in the morning. So she planned on going to bed as soon as we hung up. That was at eleven fifteen last night. I haven't heard from her since." His voice cracked.

Nick waited, understanding the father needed a moment to recompose. Nick cleared his throat. "What time did you realize she was out of contact?"

"Ten thirty this morning. She always calls when she arrives at the university's fitness center, and we walk half an hour on the treadmill together every weekday."

Nick glanced at his watch—closer to one than noon. The silent ticking of every second falling off the clock skidded down his spine. "And when she didn't call?"

"I called her cell. It went straight to voice mail. I called her room. No answer. I went to her apartment. She wasn't there, but I saw evidence that she'd slept there last night."

"You have a key to your daughter's place?" Darren asked.

Ford shot him a look full of disdain. "I'm her father. Of course I have a key to her apartment." He pushed to his feet and dug out a key ring from his front pocket. His hands trembled as he pulled a single key off the ring and passed it to Nick. "Here's her key. Her car wasn't there."

This was feeling less and less like a kidnapping and more and more like . . . what? Nick swallowed the sigh and stood, staring out the expansive window overlooking a private garden. "And your wife? Is it safe to assume she has no idea where your daughter could be?"

"Mrs. Ford hasn't heard from Gina. Of course, she is extremely upset at the moment. I ordered her to take a sedative to calm her nerves and to lie down for a bit." He gave a slight shrug. "She had a minor medical procedure performed a few days ago and needs her rest."

Oh, yeah, Nick understood all right. He'd seen video clips of Jennifer Ford on the news recently, leaving the dermatologist's office. Rumors floated around that she'd had some lightening done. Without intent, his gaze settled on the framed photos adorning the marble mantel. Jennifer's skin looked like smooth mocha as she smiled at the camera.

Nick stopped at the photograph of Gina. "May I?" He pointed at the frame and raised a single brow to Ford.

"Certainly." Ford nodded. "That was taken a few months ago."

The girl was beautiful, there was no doubt about that. Her skin was even lighter than her mother's, her chocolate eyes wide, but not as wide as her smile showing off perfectly straight and white teeth. There was a freshness to her face . . . a reflection of genuine passion for life. Nick's chest tightened at the mere word— *passion*. How long had it been since he'd felt passionate about much of anything?

He shook off his thoughts and directed his attention to Gina's father. "Did she mention what *stuff* she needed to do this morning before her workout?"

Ford shook his head. "I assumed it had to do with schoolwork."

Nick sat back on the chair. "We'll get her schedule later. Right now, tell me about Gina. What are her interests? Hobbies? Special people in her life?"

Ford's eyes glistened as his voice warbled uncharacteristically. "Gina is kind and loving, a wonderful daughter and person." He cleared his throat, staring off into space. "She loves the ballet and art. Takes after her mother that way." A gentle smile was affixed on his face and he swallowed hard. For a moment, Nick forgot who the man was and saw only a scared father.

The Tennessee afternoon sun settled over the garden just on the other side of the wall. Various flowers extended and poised toward the warmth of the rays against the February chill. A gust shoved against stems, swaying them.

"Gina is an excellent student. Takes pride in her work. All of her professors tout how much they enjoy her being in their class."

Which could just be lip service to an important man, who happens to sit on the University of Memphis's board.

"She's active in various community-volunteer positions, mainly through my office. My assistant can give you a list of them."

Nick nodded. "What about the people she spends the most time with?"

"Gina's best friend is Cynthia Mantle. They've been close since high school. They were on the dance squad together back then."

They're also in the same study group. Nick would definitely speak with Ms. Mantle.

Darren tapped against the notebook. "What about a boyfriend?"

The senator frowned. "Gina understands it's

not prudent to become serious with anyone while she's so young."

Surely Ford didn't believe his daughter didn't date.

"She has, however, begun seeing a young man. A David Tiddle."

Nick leaned forward again. "I mean no disrespect, sir, but I'm sure you've had him checked out, so I'd like to see your report, if I might."

Ford stared down his nose. "She's not serious about him. He's only been to the house a couple of times for dinner." He shrugged. "Seems like a nice enough young man."

And Nick would just bet Ford had a nice, fat dossier on Tiddle. "Sir, I'm not judging you or your family, but anything you can provide will help us to find your daughter."

Ford stood and moved to the desk in the corner of the room. He opened a drawer and withdrew a thin manila envelope he passed to Nick. "That's all the initial query gathered. I haven't authorized more digging. Hadn't planned on it unless Gina felt like the relationship was turning exclusive."

Nick slipped the file under his arm and stood. "Thank you. One last thing . . . can you think of anyone who would want to harm your daughter?"

"Considering my position? I have many enemies, Agent."

"Anybody in particular recently?"

"Let me get you a list of those on our current threat-watch."

Interesting they had to keep a current list. Nick paused at the door while Ford returned to the desk. Nick turned to Darren. "I'm going to question Ms. Mantle. You check out the other members of the study group. And pull Gina's phone records."

Darren nodded as Ford returned and passed a piece of paper to Darren.

Nick moved to the hallway and addressed the senator. "Is there anything else you can think of? Even if it's remote and seems unimportant at the moment?"

Ford's fear flickered across his face. "Please, find my daughter."

Chest tightening, Nick nodded. "I'll do my best, Senator."

CHAPTER TWO

"Ambition is a dream with a V8 engine."
ELVIS PRESLEY

"Cynthia Mantle?"

The svelte young woman walking with two other girls turned and flipped her shoulder-length, blond waves over her shoulder. Her gaze roamed over Nick before locking stares and smiling. "How can I help you?"

Ridiculous. She had to be all of what—twenty-three, twenty-four at most?—and she was hitting on him, who looked every bit of his thirty-nine years? He didn't have time for women. Not after Joy. Nick shook his head as he pulled his badge and flashed it.

Her smile slipped from her face. "This about Gina?"

How did she—?

"Her dad called, told me you'd probably be by to speak to me." Cynthia waved the other girls on, then gestured to the Carpenter Student Housing Complex. "Would you like to come inside?"

Nick nodded and followed her up the stairs. If Les Ford interfered in his investigation, influential or not, Nick would go ballistic.

"I don't know what I can tell you, but the senator asked me to assist you in any way I can." She stopped at the door on the right at the top of the landing and slipped a key in the knob. "He's really worried about Gina." She motioned Nick inside. "Have a seat. Can I make you a cup of coffee? Or something to eat? We were just heading out to lunch."

"No, thanks. I'll make this as quick as possible so you can get on with your plans." Nick hunkered down on the couch, an obvious hand-me-down with its baring threads, but it was a lot more comfortable than the chair at Senator Ford's. He waited until Cynthia sat on the opposite end

27

before he started. "You said Gina's father was worried about her. Are you?"

She shrugged. "It's not like her to ignore her dad and all, but . . ."

Nick sat up straighter. "But what?"

"I don't know. I think he puts too many demands on her. Where she can and can't go. Who she can and can't hang out with. The pressure she's under . . ." Cynthia shook her head. "The way he's always checking up on her. It's enough to drive anyone nuts. Maybe she decided just to disappear for a little while."

"He's always checking up on her?"

She nodded. "Calling all the time. Making sure she's where she says she is." Cynthia gave a half snort, half laugh. "He even asks her what she eats. It's crazy."

Sounded like. "So you think she's . . . what, hiding out?"

"Maybe she just wanted to get away. Have some time for herself. Spend some alone-time with her boyfriend without Daddy breathing down her neck."

"Her boyfriend, David?"

"Yeah." Cynthia's eyes widened as she nodded. "He's a keeper. I saw him first, you know, but he wasn't interested." Her gaze dropped to the floor.

Nick pulled out his notebook and jotted down notes. "Is he a student here?" Although the dossier

Ford had compiled on Tiddle reflected he wasn't, Nick wouldn't take anything at face value.

"Not hardly. I think Gina said he was thirty or something."

"Do you know how they met?" That wasn't something in the dossier.

"Our reading club was out to dinner. I saw him sitting in the back booth when we entered, but he wouldn't even make eye contact with me for more than a second. He bumped into Gina when she went to the ladies' room. Lucky dog. He asked her out and they've been dating ever since."

"How long?" Ford indicated the relationship wasn't serious, so they couldn't have been dating too long.

"About seven months or so."

Whoa. Seven months? In this day and age, that was a long time to be dating. Apparently Gina *didn't* tell her father everything. "Are they exclusive?"

Cynthia tilted her head. "Dude, they're practically engaged."

Gina definitely didn't tell Daddy everything. "That serious? And her father approves?"

"Are you kidding? Gina just told her dad about meeting David a month ago. She knew her dad would get all weird and ask a lot of questions, and Gina didn't want to go through all that until she knew if she and David were going to have a relationship instead of just casually dating."

Not that Nick blamed her, but seven months and practically engaged?

"And she was right. After she told her dad about David, the senator started asking all sorts of questions about him . . . inviting them to dinner or brunch. Just sticking his nose in their relationship, if you ask me."

"Do you know where I can get in touch with David?" Although the dossier listed a home address and phone number, he wanted to know what Gina had told her best friend.

"He lives in an apartment in Germantown, I think. He's like a photographer's apprentice or something cool like that."

Nick would use the information Ford had compiled to fill in the blanks. "I understand you were with Gina last night?"

Cynthia nodded. "Study group. But she didn't go out for pizza with us afterward like usual."

Breaking routine. "Did she say why?"

"Said she had something important she had to do in the morning. But she'd been acting weird all night."

Nick sat up straighter. "Weird how?"

Cynthia shrugged. "Like she was upset about something. I asked her what was wrong, and she blew me off. Didn't want to talk about it, I guess."

"Do you have any idea what could have been bothering her?"

"Maybe she got a poor grade on a test. Her dad

stayed on her about making great grades. Like if she got even a B, it would cost him votes."

Sounded oppressive. He shifted his position on the couch to better face Cynthia. "Can you think of anyone who doesn't like Gina? Someone who might want to hurt her?"

Cynthia's face paled. "You think something's happened to her? Like Hailey Carter? Campus security is giving us all kinds of safety information and warnings."

"I'm just getting all the information I can to find Gina, but you should heed the cautions." Nick paused, waiting and watching the girl's face. "Were you and Gina friends with Hailey?"

She shook her head. "I'd never seen her before. She didn't hang out with us."

No obvious connection between the two girls —good. "About Gina . . . anyone she was having problems with recently?"

"Everybody likes Gina. She's kind and generous. Smart. Funny. Nobody I know would have anything against her." Honesty sat in the contours of her face. "Do you think she's okay? You don't think—?"

Nick stood and plastered on his most reassuring expression. "Thank you for your time, Ms. Mantle. I'll be in touch." He handed her his business card. "If you hear from Gina, please give me a call."

"Sure."

After giving a final nod, Nick left the apartment and headed to his car. The late-afternoon sun split the blue sky. A gust of wind tickled the back of his neck.

Years of experience told him something was off. Maybe it was the oddness of the senator and his daughter's relationship. Maybe it was Cynthia's comment about Gina acting weird the night she went missing. Maybe it was the peculiar feeling sitting in his gut like a proverbial lead balloon. Whatever it was, Nick had the sensation this case would be different.

His cell rang as he slipped behind the wheel. "Nick Hagar."

"It's Timmons, sir."

"Finished at the senator's?"

"Yes, sir. Just got back to the office. That BOLO we put out on Ms. Ford's car?"

They'd put out the "Be On the LookOut" immediately upon notification of Gina and her vehicle missing. "Yeah?"

"Someone just called it in to Memphis PD. Body reported found inside the car. TBI investigator is on its way."

"What's the address?" Nick started his car's engine as Darren rattled off the street and number—in the same area they'd found Hailey Carter's body, close to where he was now. If he hurried, he'd probably arrive right behind the Tennessee Bureau of Investigation representative. "I'm on my way. Meet me there." He disconnected the call and pulled onto Poplar Avenue.

Just because there was a body in the car, just like Carter's, and that it was found in the same area didn't mean it . . . No, they didn't even know if the body was Gina or not. He would stick to the established facts thus far.

As he drove, Nick mentally reviewed the dossier on David Tiddle. Thirty years old. Parents died when he was ten. No other living relatives could be located, so he was put into care of the state. Bounced around foster homes, making appearances in juvie a handful of times, then dropped out of the system's paperwork trail at sixteen.

Nick took a sharp right onto South Goodlett Street, then slammed on his brakes as a truck pulled out in front of him. Tiddle didn't show back up on the report until his late twenties. A couple of pleas for minors, but all probation or warnings. Nothing serious. Work record read sketchy, at best. Waiter. Maître d' at several restaurants. Assistant to various professions. No stability. No permanency. Hit or miss.

Two turns later and Nick parked his unmarked car behind a local patrol cruiser on Norriswood Avenue. The two uniformed officers paused in their discussion with a young couple diagonal to Gina Ford's car.

Nick flashed his badge. "Special Agent Nick Hagar." He shoved the shield back into its place on his hip. "We put the BOLO out on this one."

One of the uniforms stepped away from the couple. "Officer Layton. TBI will be here soon." He nodded at the couple talking with the other officer. The girl cried behind her hand, streaks of bluish-black makeup running down her face. "They were heading into the Engineering Tech building and saw the car with the door left open, came over to investigate. Saw the body and called it in."

Nick made his way to the driver's open door. Little drops of blood stained the floorboard. At least, that's what he assumed they were. A female figure hunched over the steering wheel. All he could tell about the victim was it appeared to be a young African American woman. "Did they touch the body?"

Officer Layton nodded. "He says they moved her back to see if she was alive, saw that she was dead, and let her fall back over the steering wheel, then called us. We've verified they are, in fact, usually here at this time every week doing independent work. Not many others are here on this day and time as no professors hold classes in these buildings on Fridays."

Great. If this was Gina Ford, and Nick suspected it was, the crime scene had already been contaminated. Senator Ford would breathe down the bureau's neck. Down Nick's neck.

He wouldn't touch the body further. Vital

forensic evidence could be lost forever. "Call the TBI director and ask that he get his best forensic team out here to collect evidence. Per FBI request."

Officer Layton moved to his cruiser while Nick joined the local officer finishing the initial interview of the couple.

"I'll see her face in my nightmares." The girl sniffed.

"Did you recognize her?" Nick interrupted.

"No." The girl didn't ask who he was, which suited him just fine.

The boy wouldn't make eye contact with him.

"What about you?" Nick took a step toward the kid, invading his personal space, making him uncomfortable. "Did you recognize her?"

The kid shrugged. "She looked kinda familiar."

"Familiar in you might have a class with her? Familiar in you might have seen her at a party?"

"I dunno." He toed a loose rock with his sneaker. "She might be somebody famous. Like been on TV or something."

Ah. He didn't know who she was but recognized enough. "I see." Nick nodded at the officer. "This nice man here will finish taking your information and then will ask you to report to the police station to sign your statements. You're not to discuss anything about this with anyone. Not family, not friends, and not media. Understood?"

"Yes, sir." The boy's bottom lip quivered for a

split second. "Is this like the other girl? Reports all over campus was that she was stabbed three times in the chest and left in her car, right around here. Right?"

"No comment. That's what you are to say about this: no comment." Nick turned and headed back to his car. The last thing he needed was for the media hounds to get wind of this and blast it everywhere before Nick could get official confirmation of the body's identity.

He sat behind the wheel while he waited for Timmons and the TBI agent, staring at the crime scene. If the body was truly Gina Ford, Nick would have the horrible duty of informing the senator and his wife. It was moments like this that Nick missed the innocent faith of his youth. Missed being able to believe that everything happened for a reason.

But Nick was older now and remembered all too well how it felt to be on the receiving end of that kind of news. Life and faith shattering.

"You running RFLP on the sample that came in this morning?" Eva Langston waltzed into the lab as she usually did—with a lot of drama and flair.

"Nope. Sample was too degraded to run a restriction fragment length polymorphism. Running a PCR." Maddie looked up from the table and smiled. "Aren't you chipper this far into the afternoon? Have a lovely lunch?"

Eva tossed her purse into her locker and donned her blue lab coat. "As a matter-of-fact, I did. I had a date with Lance."

"Where'd y'all eat?" Maddie went back to work on entering DNA strand identifiers into the computer.

Now more than ever, doing her job flawlessly was of the utmost importance. Recently approved funding for the lab's expansion and new equipment had been put on hold. Rumor in the wind was the money just wasn't there. If the money didn't come through, the crime lab would have to cut corners where it could—and salaries or employees were always the first heads on the chopping block.

"Oh, honey . . . we didn't eat. We made out the whole time."

"Eva!"

"Oh, c'mon, Maddie. There ain't a thing wrong with kissing a man instead of eating. Goodness knows I don't need the calories."

Maddie shook her head and frowned at her friend. "You barely know Lance."

"So? Isn't that the point of dating, to get to know someone?"

"Dating, yes. But how do you get to know someone better by making out for an hour?"

"You can learn a lot about a man by kissing him." Eva grinned and waggled her finely manicured eyebrows. "C'mon, admit it—you enjoy making out just as much as I do."

"Of course I enjoy making out." The heat surged to Maddie's cheeks. She ducked her head behind the computer monitor. "With someone I've gotten to know and care about."

Eva plopped on the edge of the desk. "When was the last time you went out on a date?"

"Um." Maddie scrambled to think. "I've had a lot going on."

"Yeah. Going to see your little sister. Making sure the sale of your brother's house went through with no problems. Helping your future sister-in-law pick out a wedding gown." Eva jumped to her feet. "But when was the last time you did something for you?"

"I had my nails done just last week." And they still looked good, Maddie noted.

"I meant, romantic. Something with a man. You know, a member of the opposite sex."

The phone rang, startling them both. Eva recovered first and, while laughing, lifted the receiver. "Forensics Lab."

Maddie continued her work on the computer but monitored Eva's half of the conversation while she sang under her breath. *"Love me tender—"*

"Yes, sir. I understand. What's the address?"

Lovely, a call. Just when she'd been looking forward to an early night with a good book, but her team was on call this month. *"Love me sweet—"*

Eva scribbled on a notepad. "Yes, sir. We will." She hung up the phone and stared at Maddie with wide eyes. "That was the director."

Interesting. The man never contacted their unit himself. "What's up?"

"Seems a potential high-profile case is brewing. Body found in a car. Whole violent crime response team is being called out. Peter and the rest of the team will meet us there."

Maddie automatically shrugged out of her lab coat and reached for the team's royal blue vest with the yellow TBI AGENT on the back. She slipped her holster housing her gun around her waist. "Not multiple victims?" She grabbed her badge and secured it on her hip before donning the blue baseball-style cap.

Eva shook her own cap-clad head. "Director said just one. Over by the campus." She, too, wore the team's vest.

"Must be somebody famous." Maddie recalled the headlines of the paper just this morning. "Or related to the girl they found last week." *Please, no.* Serial murders were the hardest to deal with. No sense. No logic. Just evil and hatred.

Eva opened her desk drawer and grabbed her holster and badge. "Director's called in the other team members. We're to take the truck and meet at the scene."

"The director bypassed Peter and called in the team himself? Must be something serious." One that if they messed up, it'd be *their* heads on the chopping block.

Eva lifted her notepad and stared at her scribble. "The team is to liaise with an FBI agent at the scene. And his name seems so familiar. You probably know him."

Maddie raised an eyebrow. Her brother was an FBI agent but relocated to Arkansas. His best friend, and one of Maddie's, Darren Timmons, was in the bureau here. She knew lots of the local agents.

"A Special Agent in Charge Nick Hagar."

"Nick?"

Eva cocked her head as she reached for the truck keys. "Wait a minute . . . that's the guy you had a date with before you went to Louisiana, isn't it?" She smiled and her eyes lit up. "The hunky biceps one."

"Darren set us up." She still couldn't believe she'd let Darren fix her up with Nick. Of all people.

"Darren, now there's a man." Eva grinned. "Have you talked to this Nick Hagar since you got back?"

She led the way out of the lab. "I haven't had time. Let's go." She had told him she'd call after she returned from Louisiana. Yet since returning, she hadn't gotten up the nerve to pick up the phone. What did *that* mean?

"Maddie! That was weeks ago. Why haven't you called him?" Eva wasn't ready to let it go either as she pushed open the doors into the parking lot. "He's single, has a good job, is handsome as all get-out, and you said he was a perfect gentleman."

"He's also my brother's former boss."

"Key word there being *former*."

Maddie let out a puff of air. Her breath showed in the cool February afternoon as she hoofed it to the crime scene-investigation truck and slipped in the passenger's seat.

How could she explain to Eva what she didn't understand herself? Nick Hagar made her nervous, that was the only way she could put her feelings into words. His intense, dark eyes that probed through the walls of protection she'd built around her heart. The way he made her feel things, it reminded her too much of Adam and . . . well, she just knew he was a threat to her. That was it, plain and simple.

Eva shoved the key into the ignition and turned over the engine. "This is fate shoving you together."

"Maybe. So, when are you going to see Lance again?"

Eva smiled and her cheeks pinked. "He's picking me up at six, so we need to finish up the testing for the day. I can't be late. He's taking me for a picnic."

Maddie blew on her hands. "It's quite chilly, in case you haven't noticed."

41

"He said he'd keep me warm." With Eva's blond hair, blue eyes, and legs that seemed to never end, she never had much problem getting a man. Staying interested in them for longer than a couple of months, however, was a totally different subject.

While Eva rambled about the virtues of dating and making out, Maddie's mind went to the upcoming case, the one she'd have to work with Nick on. Her thoughts raced from one possible scenario to the next. *"We're caught in a trap"*— she hummed under her breath.

Was this victim going to be another young college girl, her life cut short by some sicko?

Eva made a sharp turn, knocking Maddie against the truck's door.

"I can't walk out . . ." Ba-ba-ba-ba-ba-ba-ba . . . *"baby."*

She mentally went over procedure for field collection. Her team hadn't answered a call since that big wreck the week of Christmas. She reviewed policy. Then reviewed it again.

Anything to keep her from thinking about what she'd say to Nick when she saw him again.

CHAPTER THREE

"It's human nature to gripe, but I'm going
ahead and doing the best I can."
ELVIS PRESLEY

About time. The sun would be setting soon, and
then gathering evidence would be more complicated.

An unmarked cruiser with flashing lights
whipped behind Nick. The medical examiner's
van pulled up alongside the white TBI field truck,
parking behind the cruiser. Three other vehicles
turned onto the street and parked behind them.
Nick closed the dossier on Tiddle and turned up
his jacket collar, then stepped into the cool air.

The man who unfolded himself from behind
the steering wheel of the cruiser spoke with two
men in TBI vests and caps, then approached the
scene with a determined step. The man had to
stand an inch or two taller than Nick's six one, but
his build was more gangly than muscular. He
narrowed his eyes at Nick. "You SAC Hagar?"

Nick nodded.

"Peter Helm. TBI. Crime Scene." He turned and
nodded at the truck where several people in
blue pants rolled open doors. "Our best forensics
team is here, per your request."

"Thanks. This one could be dicey." Nick nodded at Cullen McMichael as the Shelby County medical examiner passed, his investigator in tow. "Possible political connection, so we need to take every possible precaution."

"We normally do." Helm's tone left no question of his resentment.

Nick understood—he wouldn't like someone to go over his head on a case before he even got to the crime scene, but in this particular situation, time was of the essence. No mistakes could be afforded. Not a single one. He'd already taken a call from the deputy director. The senator hadn't waited long to call in favors. A powerful man could be just as dangerous as a criminal.

Doors slammed as the five-man team headed their way. Make that five-*person* team—two were definitely women. First one stood about five six, had a pair of long legs, and shoulder-length blond hair hanging out from under the blue cap. Carrying a case, she let one of the men on the team hold her elbow as they made their approach. The way she moved, how she carried herself— Nick could feel the confidence oozing from her. This woman was sure of her abilities and her appearance. His mouth automatically went dry. She reminded him so much of Joy.

Two news vans skidded to a stop behind the TBI field truck. Great. The vultures had arrived. Nick motioned to Officer Layton. "Get your men

44

to keep the reporters at the street. None of them are to get past my car, understood?"

The uniform nodded and sprinted, cutting off the cameraman heading toward them.

Nick turned back to Helm and nodded toward Gina's car. "Door was left open, so it's possible you'll find prints there."

"My team is the best. If there are prints there, we'll find them." Helm motioned for the team to join them.

Helm introduced the two men who reached them first. "This is Kurt Jackson and Neal Olson, our forensic technicians."

Nick nodded at the two men who closely resembled a pair of black-and-tan Doberman pinschers. Both had little eyes, lithe builds, and looked to be at attention the entire time.

Helm continued as the others joined them. "This is Ivan Goins, the best latent specialist in the state." At least Goins stood with a bit of girth with his almost six-foot frame. But the shockingly bleached ends of his long, black hair sticking out from under the navy cap made Nick raise his brows. How many tattoos did the guy have? And he didn't even want to start counting the visible piercings.

Nick slowly turned toward the lighter footsteps.

"And these two lovely, gun-toting ladies are our DNA/serology scientists Eva Langston and—"

Nick locked gazes with her. "Maddie Baxter." His gut tightened.

"Nick Hagar." Her big brown eyes blinked at him from behind her glasses.

He knew she worked in the crime lab. Knew she was a forensic scientist. Knew she was a specialist in her field.

He just hadn't expected to see her. Out here. Like this. In *his* world.

"You two know each other?" Helm's tone held a hint of proprietorship.

Maddie licked her lips. "Yes. My brother's an FBI agent, remember?"

"Oh, that's right." Helm turned his back to Nick and addressed his unit. "Okay, team, what we have is a female in her car. The door was found open, so Ivan, dust until you can find a print. There's little blood to the naked eye for retrieval, so Maddie and Eva, let me know if you need anything."

He shifted. "Kurt, I need photos from every angle, and I do mean every. Even from above and below. And Neal, make sure you measure every little distance and collect samples from every particle of foliage in the area."

Helm paused and turned to Nick. "Anything else you care to share with us?" The unspoken challenge hung between them.

Nick mentally shook off the shock at seeing Maddie again and focused on the task at hand. "There are two aspects here. First, the car is registered to the daughter of a very prominent politician who has reported her missing. Second, initial observation of the scene is that this is similar to that of the college girl's body found last week. A possible serial."

Helm cleared his throat. "Nothing gets missed, got that? We bag anything, test everything, and let the results speak for themselves. Any questions?"

No one said a word.

"Then let's do it."

The group moved to the car. One of the techs handed Nick a pair of shoe covers. He pushed them over his boots as he hobbled. He hurried to fall into step beside Maddie. "How are you?"

"Fine." She paused for a moment. "How've you been?"

"Good. Busy. With work." Something about her tied his tongue into knots. He steadied his footing as they crossed the yellow crime-scene tape fluttering in the wind. "Your sister okay?"

"Yeah. She's healing well. Thank you for asking." She motioned to one of the techs to set the stand for her case.

Could she be any more polite? Like they were strangers. He'd thought their date had gone well. They'd made a second date, but her little sister had gotten shot, and Maddie had hurried to Louisiana to check on her. She had told him she'd call when she got back into town.

His phone had never rung.

She set her case on the stand and opened it.

Maddie made it clear that the conversation was over. But Nick couldn't stop himself. "I heard Rafe got engaged."

She nodded as she slipped on greenish-blue gloves. "He did. Remington's great. They're good together."

"I'm glad. He deserves the happiness." Nick chuckled. "Even though I miss him in the office."

She smiled, then blushed. So cute. "I'm sorry I haven't called you. I've been swamped catching up after I got back and then—"

"No worries. I understand."

The other lady, who upon closer inspection looked nothing like Joy, thank goodness, approached. "You ready, Maddie?"

Maddie jerked her head, her long, auburn hair falling over her shoulder. The cap did nothing to hide the shine of her locks. "Well, I better get to it." She lifted the extraction tools.

"Yeah. Nice seeing you again."

She blushed again, then followed her associate to the car.

The medical examiner joined him. "Saw the press."

Nick glanced over his shoulder at the vehicles lining the road, their bright lights already blazing in the distance. "Yeah. Like cockroaches, they come out at the first scent of something." He spied

Timmons pulling along the line of media vans. Turning back to McMichael, he jerked his head toward Gina's car. "What's the story?"

"Three stab wounds to the chest. Neck appears to be broken. Ligature marks around the neck. I'll know more once I do the autopsy."

Nick stared at the car. "Same MO as the girl from last week?"

Cullen McMichael shrugged. "Hard to tell. The stab wounds are consistent with Hailey Carter's, but her neck hadn't been broken. We'll see once I do my complete exam."

"Estimated time of death?"

"Based on what I can tell now, I'd say this morning between eight and ten."

Nick made a mental note. "Any ID on the body?"

McMichael sighed. "Yep. Driver's license in her shirt pocket. TBI pulled her cell phone from the console as well. And before you ask, it's her. Gina Ford."

"He is hot, girl." Eva withdrew a blood sample from a drop no bigger than a dime from the car's floorboard and tilted her head toward Nick. "If you aren't interested, give me his number. I'll for sure call him."

"I never said I wasn't interested." Maddie glanced over her shoulder. Scowling at them, Nick still stood with the medical examiner.

"Ah, so you *are* interested?" Eva grinned as she labeled the sample.

Kurt stared at them through the front windshield, his digital camera clicking quietly, but didn't say a word.

"Give it a rest, Eva. Stay focused. We can't afford any mistakes on this one." She should take her own advice but could feel Nick's stare on her. Heat spread from her spine as she concentrated on swabbing under the girl's fingernails.

"I can concentrate and admire a fine specimen of the male species at the same time. Easy-peasy." She bagged and labeled the cell phone sitting in the console. The latest model of the popular smartphone was turned off.

Maddie pressed her lips together. The more she protested, the more Eva would tease. "Did you take samples from the jeans?"

"Yep. Labeled and stored."

"If this wind doesn't die down, we're going to have to set up a block. I think I have a print." Ivan's brows knitted into a scowl.

The sky streaked orange as the sun dipped toward the horizon. They had maybe ten more minutes of daylight.

Eva stored the samples and turned to Maddie. "Ready to check out the front?"

Maddie did a final inspection of the body's hands, trailing up her arms, to her shoulder . . .

"Hang on." She pushed her glasses back up to the

bridge of her nose. What was that? "Is that a blood spot on the shoulder blade?"

Eva leaned forward. "Looks like it. Not a splatter though. Not that far back."

"Hand me another swab. I'm taking a sample." She swabbed, secured, and labeled the sample and set it in the case. She stood, careful not to disturb Ivan's work, and glanced over the hood at Kurt. "You got all the shots you need before we move her?"

He nodded. "Ready when you are."

Maddie bent back alongside the driver's seat. She nodded to Eva, hovering through the passenger's seat. "Okay, now let's check out the front."

They eased the girl's body back against the car seat. Maddie shook her head as she peered into the girl's lifeless eyes opened wide in fear. Senseless. Loss of life was always startling and wasteful to her, but for someone so young, so on the cusp of life, so beautiful—her death was truly senseless. Much like her own parents' death, but justice had been served on the drunk driver who'd killed them. Maddie and her brother and sister had the benefit of closure. But not the loved ones of this girl . . . not unless the team flawlessly executed their jobs.

Maddie did an initial observation of the body. "Looks like her neck is bruising. And it's at an odd angle. Could be broken, I guess." She leaned back on her heels and stared up at Ivan. "You about done with the door?"

He nodded. "I think I got two fulls and three partials."

"Can you dust her neck before we touch her? I think she might have had someone's hands in that area."

"Sure."

She stood and moved back, letting Ivan have full access. Her gaze traveled over the area. Car was left close enough to the campus buildings to be detected soon enough, so the killer wasn't exactly trying to hide the body. And the open door was a definite calling card. Had the other victim's car door been left open? Maddie couldn't remember all the details of the news report.

The sun slipped another step closer to setting. Maddie shivered and slowly turned, scanning the area. Why here? Was it some sort of statement?

Her stare stopped on Nick, his focus on her. The epitome of tall, dark, and handsome. Not to mention the strong line of his jaw, the appeal of the stubble covering his cheeks and chin, and the pull of his single brow raised in question. Heat suffused her face, chasing away the cold from seconds ago.

"I'm not getting anything. I see impressions but no prints." Ivan stood. "I'm going to dust the steering wheel and dash as soon as the ME moves the body."

Maddie broke her eye contact with Nick. "Okay. We'll finish up here so they can get in."

"I'm going to get the lights and stands. It's almost dark." Neal rushed off toward the truck.

He was right—the sun was barely an orange glow on the horizon.

She moved with precision, careful not to disturb any possible evidence. She and Eva took samples from the girl's eyes, nose, mouth, even her ears. They didn't pause, even when Kurt and Neal turned on the lights, flooding the scene with stark brightness and shadows.

The darker it became, the lower the temperature dropped. They worked in silence, gathering samples, securing, labeling, and storing. Over and over. Under her tongue. From her lap. From her shoes. Off the steering wheel. Gather, secure, label, and store. They'd be busy once they got it all back to the lab.

Finally, Maddie stood. Rotated her head slowly, letting her neck pop. She stretched. "I think we're done."

Eva stood and met her gaze over the hood. "Me too."

Maddie turned to the ME team waiting. "You can remove the body now."

"Thanks."

As she carried her case back to the truck, she noticed Nick had already left. Funny how the disappointment settled in her chest. Especially since she'd been the one who hadn't called. She barely got near the truck when reporters began hollering.

"Can you confirm this is another young woman stabbed three times in the chest?"

She ignored them and concentrated on one of her favorite songs. *"Well, since my baby left me . . ." Da-da-da-da-da-da-daa . . .*

"Who is the victim?"

She kept her face down so no one would recognize her from this recent trial, stored her case and samples, then climbed into the passenger's seat of the truck and checked her watch—six o'clock. She laid her head against the headrest and pulled her cap over her face. It'd been a long, long day, and all she wanted was to crawl into a very hot, very steamy shower, then pour herself into bed.

". . . end of lonely street . . ."

She never could eat after working a scene. Just seemed wrong to do something as mundane as eating when someone else's life had been cut short. But she couldn't leave until Ivan, Kurt, and Neal had finished their part. The team didn't leave until they were all completed.

"At Heartbreak Hotel."

Whoever the first person was who hacked into a police scanner ought to have been tarred and feathered. Maddie closed her eyes against the line of reporters. Her little sister, Riley, was a reporter, but she didn't hound people. Not like this.

"You gonna call him?" Eva broke the silence as she slammed the driver's door.

Too late to pretend to be dozing. "I don't know."

"You should. He's interested in you."

Maddie lifted the cap and rolled her head to face Eva. "And you know this how?"

Eva smiled and shrugged. "I just know these things."

"Ah, I see." But he had made a special point to try to carry on a conversation with her. And he'd accepted her lame excuse for not calling him. Did that mean he blew it off because he didn't care?

"I'm serious, Maddie. The man's got eyes for you. Don't make light of it."

Her heart skipped a beat. "We'll see."

Eva clucked her tongue and shook her head.

"What?"

"You."

"What about me?"

Eva tapped her nails against the steering wheel. "Every time a man shows real interest in you, you find an excuse not to get involved with him. Works too many hours. Doesn't have ambition. Isn't a Christian. Doesn't like Elvis."

"Come on, some of that's bogus." But some of it, okay, a lot of it, was pretty accurate. Maddie drew in a slow, deliberate breath.

She stopped tapping and pivoted to stare at

Maddie through the dim light reflecting off the hood of the truck from the stands of portable lights. "It's always something. And I have to wonder. If you aren't interested in a relationship, why even go through the motions of dating?"

And like the elephant in the room, there sat the big question.

Problem was, Maddie had no answer.

CHAPTER FOUR

"More than anything else, I want the folks back at home to think right of me."
ELVIS PRESLEY

This part of the job truly was the absolute worst.

The night stole over Memphis, wrapping her in a cloak of temperatures below freezing. The wind rattled dry leaves across the well-manicured lawn.

Nick dared a glance at the road while he waited for Timmons to step out of his car, making sure telltale headlights didn't split the darkness. An eager reporter or two had followed him from the scene, but he'd lost them when he'd gone the roundabout way here.

Nick sucked in air as he and Timmons made their way past the uniform officer posted outside the front of the Ford home and up the stairs.

Senator Ford opened the door before he could even knock.

"Senator."

"What have you found out?" The man ushered them inside. "You have to have found something to come out here again so soon. What is it?" Ford's eyes were red and lined, but wide and focused.

"May we sit down?" He had a feeling Ford would need something under him when he heard the news.

With a sigh, the senator led Nick and Timmons into the study and plopped on the same chair as before. "Forgive my manners, Agents, but I'm quite anxious."

This was always the hardest. "Senator Ford, I'm sorry."

The man's face went blank. "Gina?"

Nick nodded. "We found her car just behind the campus."

"And Gina?"

"There was a body of a young woman inside. Identification on the body indicates it's Gina."

"But you aren't sure? It could be someone else?"

Every parent was the same: No matter their power or position, they needed to grasp at the last strand of hope dangling. Nick understood that all too well. "We need you to come and identify the body in the morning."

Ford shot to his feet. "Now. I'll come now. If it's not her, you need to keep looking. Keep searching."

Nick and Darren remained seated. Darren cleared his throat. "Sir, they are still processing the scene and collecting forensic evidence. Tomorrow morning would be best."

Nick paused as the senator slumped back to his seat. "I just didn't want you to hear about this from anyone but us."

"T-thank you." Ford stared at the photos on the mantel, then locked gazes with Nick. "Did you see her?"

"Not completely."

"So you don't know?"

"One hundred percent? No, sir. But I don't want you to get your hopes up that it isn't her and then it is. Let's wait until tomorrow."

Ford shot to his feet again and paced. "How did she die? This girl? Possibly my Gina?"

"The medical examiner will put that information into his autopsy report," Darren said.

The senator stopped pacing and glared solely at Nick. "Agent Hagar, I want an answer, and I want it now. How did she die? Like that other girl? Stabbed?" The man's political power returned.

Nick stood, absorbing the man's fury. "The victim was stabbed, sir."

Ford's Adam's apple bobbed once. Twice. He returned to his pacing. "Was she . . . was she . . . had she been raped?"

"It's too early to say, sir, but the victim was found fully clothed." Nick couldn't even imagine a father's pain of not only losing his only daughter —his only child, in fact—but to know she'd been so violated . . . No, he couldn't imagine.

"This other girl. From last week." Ford stopped moving and met Nick's gaze. "Had she been raped?"

"I don't know, sir. I wasn't involved in that case."

Ford nodded, the muscles in his jaw flexing. "Are there any suspects in her murder—this other girl? The news says there isn't, but we both know what's reported isn't always the truth." He took another turn in his pacing path.

"I can't say, sir. The investigation is under the TBI, not the FBI, because it's a homicide and will be prosecuted in state court."

"But if this one—possibly G-G-Gina—are connected . . ."

"Then the FBI will assist the TBI and provide all of our resources needed to solve the case and bring the responsible party to justice." Nick would do his best to see that happen, and soon.

"What kind of forensic evidence have they found?"

"Too early to say, sir. They're dusting for prints, taking fluid samples, examining the crime scene," offered Darren.

"And it'll come to the FBI lab for processing?"

The man was making Nick dizzy with his pacing. "The TBI's regional crime lab is here, sir.

Their response team collects the evidence and processes it. The FBI will assist only if needed."

"But isn't the FBI's lab the best?"

The image of Maddie rushed across Nick's mind. "I saw the team, sir. They're good. I'd say they're probably the best people to have on this case."

"If it were your daughter . . ."

He saw the way Maddie crouched to pull blood samples, the way she hunched in an awkward position to not disturb evidence as she got what she could from the victim. "If it were one of my loved ones, I'd want the exact same team working the case as was there tonight."

Ford stopped pacing and locked stares with Nick, who didn't blink.

"Okay." Ford hung his head. "What time tomorrow?"

"Nine. Would you like me to come get you?"

"No, I have my driver." He lifted his head. "I'm not bringing my wife. I won't subject her to this unless I know for certain it's Gina."

Nick nodded. "I understand." He moved toward the door.

Ford followed them. "Thank you, Agents. For coming here tonight and telling me in person. I do appreciate it."

"Yes, sir. We're doing everything we can to keep this out of the media as long as we can. At least until we get positive identification. But I have to warn you: there were news vans at the scene."

"Thank you for your efforts, Agent Hagar. I'll have my staff handle any inquiries. Once we know for certain."

"Good night, sir." Nick let out a long breath as he made his way back to the car.

Darren stood alongside the car and ran a hand through his short blond hair. "I need to run home and make arrangements for my daughter tonight."

Poor Timmons . . . a widower left with a young daughter who had a heart condition that required surgeries, medications, and specialized care. "Just go on home. I'll handle the rest."

"No, sir. I just need to make sure Savannah takes her medications and gets into bed without giving the sitter fits. It should only take me an hour or so."

Nick nodded. "Meet me at Gina Ford's."

Darren rushed to his car.

Nick got behind the wheel, started the engine, and stared into the darkness, knowing how the senator felt. Nick's own memories from the past were entirely too vivid . . .

The decorated Marine stood at the door, another just behind him. Nick stood in the hallway, watching as Dad's spine went taut and straight as a rod.

"Sir, may we come in?" The Marine's voice boomed over the television from the living room.

Dad stepped aside, his face paler than the cream paint Mom used throughout the house. The two men moved to the living room. Mom fumbled for the remote to mute her daytime story.

"Please, have a seat." Dad's voice came out a higher pitch than Nick had ever heard.

Nick ducked into the shadows of the hall. Dad would send him to his room if he saw him and Nick would never learn what his brother had done.

The two officers sat. Dad stood behind the couch, his hands on Mom's shoulders.

"I'm sorry, Mr. and Mrs. Hagar—"

"No! No! Nooooooo!" Mom shook her head as tears flew down her cheeks.

"Your son, Roger Hagar Jr. was killed in the line of duty."

Roger . . . dead? Nick's stomach tightened into a knotted wad.

Mom collapsed into a ball on the couch. Dad's shoulders slumped.

No, this couldn't be. Roger couldn't be dead! This had to be some sick joke. Bile burned the back of Nick's throat.

"I'm sorry, sir. Ma'am."

Dad swallowed hard. Nick could hear it over Mom's sobs. He moved around from the back of the couch, and then, it was like his knees gave out. He pitched forward.

One of the Marines was on his feet in a flash and caught Dad. Holding him up until he reached the couch. "My boy. My boy. Not my boy." The grief rolled off of Dad and filled the house with misery. Darkness.

Nick thought he might be ill.

"Mr. and Mrs. Hagar, I'm the chaplain of your son's unit. I knew Roger. Knew him to be an amazing young man."

Mom lifted her tear-soaked face and nodded. "Thank you," she whispered.

"Why *my* boy?" Dad's words chilled Nick.

"I can only imagine your grief, Mr. and Mrs. Hagar. I'm so sorry for your loss." The chaplain inched to the edge of his seat. "Would you like me to pray with you?"

"Yes—"

"Pray with us?" Dad interrupted Mom. "Are you serious? Pray? God just let our son die! Defending his country. What kind of God would do such a thing?"

"Sir, you're hurting and—"

Dad stood, his voice storming over the living room. "Of course I'm hurting. You've just told me that God stole my son from me."

"Roge . . . it's not their fault." Mom reached for Dad's hand.

He shrugged her off. "I think you should leave now."

The chaplain and other man both stood, but the chaplain had to try again. "I'm terribly sorry for—"

Dad led the way to the front door. "Yes, I know, you're terribly sorry for my loss. But you can't bring Roger back. God took him. Took the one perfect thing in my life."

"Sir—"

"Please leave." Dad opened the door.

The other Marine handed Dad a folder. "We'll deliver your son's personal belongings as soon as we can."

With that, the men left. Dad shut the door, then leaned against it. He slid to the floor, sobbing so hard Nick's heart pounded over his own tears.

From that moment on, life would never be the same.

"That's it. Last sample logged in. All ready to begin the extractions in the morning." Nothing like working on a weekend. Maddie couldn't hold back the yawn. Or the next one.

"Girl, it's still early yet. You're acting like an old woman who goes to bed as soon as the sun goes down." Eva hung her lab coat on the hook. "Glad Lance said meeting later would work excellent for him. I have time to freshen my makeup."

Maddie reached for her purse. "Well, you have fun. I'm going home, taking a long, hot shower, then crawling into bed."

"It's official: you've turned into a senior citizen when I wasn't looking."

Maddie chuckled and looped her arm through her friend's. "If that gives me permission to be snug in my bed before midnight, then call AARP and get me signed up." She turned off the lights, pulled the door closed behind her, and checked to make sure it was locked.

The security lights were dimmer than usual, or perhaps the moonless night added to the shadows as Maddie and Eva crossed the parking lot to their cars. Or maybe the wind whistling reminded Maddie a little too much of the crime scene they'd left not long ago. She shivered and hugged Eva as images of the girl's lifeless eyes invaded her mind. The cases she worked always stayed with her. And stayed with her. Until the case was closed and, hopefully, justice served. "You be careful tonight."

Eva flashed her high-wattage grin. "Always. Go home. Get some rest. I'm going to grill you about Agent Hagar in the morning."

Maddie shook her head and pushed the button on the remote to unlock her car. Without intent, she checked the backseat as she opened the door and the interior was flooded with light, making sure no intruder lurked there, ready to stick a gun to her head and kidnap her. She laughed at herself later as she steered toward home.

Having a brother who was an FBI agent made her more than a little cautious. Rafe had installed a state-of-the-art security system in her home as soon as she'd bought it seven years ago. Five turns and ten minutes later, she pulled up to the gate of her subdivision. Moments later, she whipped into her driveway and parked in the garage. She waited until the garage door had closed before getting out of the car and dragging herself into the house.

She tossed her purse onto the entry table as she sang.

She glanced at her home phone LCD display: Twenty-two missed calls.

Twenty-two? Too many for telemarketers. The voice mail indicator wasn't lit up. Someone would call twenty-two times and not leave a message? She pressed the button to reveal the caller ID. Unknown number.

Maddie dug into her pocket and pulled out her phone. No missed calls registered.

Strange.

"Wise men say, only fools rush in . . ."

She headed down the hall to her bedroom, stored her gun on the bedside table, kicked off her shoes, and entered the bathroom.

"But I, can't, help, falling in love, with you."

Humming, Maddie flipped the shower on hot, got undressed, and stepped under the steamy spray. If only the goat's milk and oatmeal soap could wash away the memory of that poor girl's lifeless eyes. The fear hanging in the cloudy orbs, frozen forever.

Who could do such a thing? Why?

As usual when she asked the question, no answer came. She'd asked it many times over the years, rarely ever getting a strong resolution in response. She just knew she had to help families of victims get closure. Had the driver who'd killed her parents not been convicted and imprisoned, Maddie didn't think she'd have been able to go on in life. It was hard enough to deal with their loss without having unanswered questions as well.

Brring!

Was that the phone? Maddie turned off the shower and reached for a towel.

Brring!

Scrambling and nearly slipping, Maddie stepped out of the shower.

Brring!

She ran into the bedroom, her hair dripping cold onto her shoulders. The phone wasn't on her bedside table. Where had she left it?

Brri—

Her office. She tightened the towel around her and strode down the hall. There sat the phone, on her desk, right where she'd left it this morning after she'd talked with Riley. She yanked it up and read: 1 missed call. She checked the caller ID. Unknown number. Big surprise. She almost broke her neck for the unknown caller.

Back in her bedroom, she placed the receiver on the base.

Brring!

She jumped, then jerked the receiver to her ear. "Hello."

Heavy breathing reverberated against her ear. "Hello?"

Just breathing.

Chilled that had nothing to do with standing in nothing but a towel with water dripping from her hair, Maddie shivered. "Hello? I can hear you breathing."

A woman's sobs filled the silence. Heart-wrenching sobs.

Maddie swallowed. "Hello?"

The connection broke, leaving only a faint electronic buzz on the line.

She pressed the button to turn off the phone, then let it drop to the bed. Probably a wrong number and she should just shake it off. But those sobs . . .

Maddie hummed as she stood.

Brring!

She snatched up the phone again. "Hello?"

"How would you feel if you were attacked?" The masculine voice, gravelly and coarse, boomed.

He laughed, deep and evil.

Then, the man hung up.

She sank to the bed, a death grip on the phone. Maddie ignored the cold settling into her bones.

Brring!

She threw the phone to the floor. The battery

cover shot across the room and the battery slid under the bed. The ringing stopped.

Maddie covered her mouth with a shaking hand. In her line of work, she'd been exposed to more crime data than the average person, but never had she been threatened before. She hated to call anyone—after all, she *was* a gun-carrying TBI officer who could handle herself—but she had to report this.

She put the phone back together, got a dial tone, dialed 911, then asked to speak to the non-emergency dispatcher. She reported the threat and was told an officer would come take her report soon. Maddie hung up, then rushed to get dressed. So much for her plans of an early night. *"You ain't nothin' but a hound dog . . ."*

After shoving her feet into her worn Uggs, she shuffled to the kitchen to make some hot chocolate.

She opened the refrigerator door and pulled out the skim milk. *"Cryin' all the time."*

Brring!

The gallon slipped from her hand and crashed to the floor. Milk splashed on the legs of her yoga pants and oozed over the ceramic tile.

Maddie froze.

Brring!

CHAPTER FIVE

"The image is one thing and the
human being is another. It's very hard
to live up to an image, put it that way."
ELVIS PRESLEY

Seven forty-five. Not late by anyone's measure.

Sitting in a car in the senator's driveway probably wasn't the best place to be at the moment, considering the news he'd just delivered. Timmons wouldn't meet him at Gina Ford's for at least thirty or so minutes.

Nick glanced at the dossier sitting in the seat beside him. He'd meant to return it to the senator, but he didn't have the heart to go back and disturb the grieving man now. Not to mention the deputy director was now putting on pressure for the case to be solved. Pronto.

After slipping the car in Reverse, Nick left the Ford residence and headed toward US Highway 72. It was time he met Gina's boyfriend.

He drove toward the address listed as David Tiddle's current residence. The drive to Farmington Gates Apartments only took Nick fifteen minutes, but he'd used the time in the car to organize his interrogation tactic. He parked next to Tiddle's apartment building, double-checked the number, then moved toward the stairs.

It took two hard knocks before the door swung open. Nick took a quick appraisal of the man. Six feet tall with brown, wavy hair. Green eyes that were almost too close together and eyebrows with a natural arch. "David Tiddle?"

"Yes?" The man's voice was a hair right of nasally.

Nick flashed his badge. "Agent Hagar, FBI. May I come in and ask you a few questions?"

The man hesitated.

"Just a few minutes of your time. It's important."

"Sure." Tiddle opened the door and stepped aside. "I'm just getting back into town, so I'm a little tired. Please excuse the mess."

Nick surveyed the room as Tiddle shut the door behind him. Couch and love seat faced a flat-screen television. A coffee table stood crooked in front of the scratched brown leather couch. Ugly and dated table lamps matched the cheap miniblinds covering the front windows. An open suitcase lay in the middle of the floor, wadded-up socks in the corner.

"Uh, have a seat." Tiddle motioned to the couch. He kicked the suitcase under the coffee table and dropped to the love seat. "What can I help you with?"

Nick nodded to the suitcase. "Where have you been?"

"Clarksville. Scouting out the area for my boss."

"Scouting?"

Tiddle smiled. "My boss is a photographer. He's working on a book of graffiti art from the state."

"Interesting." Now to move in for the kill. "When did you leave on this trip?"

Tiddle's smile slipped off his face and his beady eyes narrowed. "Yesterday. My boss had called me the previous night and requested the trip."

"Where did you stay?"

"The Holiday Inn on Sango Road. Why?"

Nick pulled out a notebook and jotted the information. "What time did you leave yesterday?"

"Around nine or so. Why?"

"When did you return?"

"About an hour ago." Tiddle shifted his weight from one side of his body to the other. "What's this about?"

His alibi would be easy enough to check out. "Do you know Gina Ford?"

"Yes. She's my girlfriend." Tiddle's face tightened. "Has something happened to her?"

"Why would you ask if something happened to her?"

"Maybe because I tried to call her several times today, and she didn't answer. Her phone went straight to voice mail. Gina never turns off her phone and never forgets to charge it. She stays in constant contact with her father." Tiddle's shoulders squared. "And maybe because an FBI agent shows up at my door, asking where I've been, when I came home, and if I know her."

Touché. "Gina's father reported her missing this morning." Nick never took his eyes off Tiddle.

The man's eyes widened to almost normal. "She's missing?"

"Her car was found."

"But she's missing?"

Nick couldn't quite get a read on Tiddle, which was highly unusual for him. Normally, Nick's training and experience kicked in instinctively and he could read most anyone. Maybe he could use shock value as an instigator for a reading.

"Actually, Mr. Tiddle, a body of a young woman was found in Gina's car. We have reason to believe that person is Gina."

"Gina? Dead?" The pastiness of Tiddle's skin paled further. "No, that can't be. Gina can't be dead."

Even with the shock value, Nick still couldn't tell if Tiddle faked his reaction or not, or if he was just a really good actor. They'd check his alibi and see if a follow-up interview was needed.

But not being able to read him . . . it bothered Nick. Had he lost his touch? "We're waiting for positive identification now."

Tiddle shook his head and ran his fingers through his hair. "She can't be dead." The young man's voice shook.

"One of Gina's friends reported she was upset yesterday. Do you know anything about that?"

"No. She didn't say anything about being upset about anything to me. Who said that?"

"Cynthia Mantle. She was with Gina last night at study group."

Tiddle scowled. "Yeah, well, I wouldn't hold up anything Cyn says as the gospel. She and Gina weren't exactly the bestest of buds recently."

Interesting. "How's that? Her father says Cynthia's been Gina's best friend for years."

"They were, but over the past couple of years, they've not been as close. Gina had finally gotten enough of Cynthia's jealousy."

"Jealousy?" Mantle hadn't mentioned any falling out.

"Yeah. Gina made better grades. Had more friends. Had a stable relationship. Definitely had more money. Everything Cyn wanted, Gina had."

"I see." Nick made a note. "When was the last time you spoke with Gina?"

Tiddle stroked the stubble on his chin. "Yesterday morning, before I left town."

"So, that would be before nine?"

"I guess."

"She didn't sound upset to you?"

Tiddle shook his head. "She was a little stressed about something to do with her dad, and she had a big project coming up."

Nick chewed the inside of his lip. "What about her dad was stressing her?"

"Dunno. She didn't say. Just that she was worried about him."

Now that *was* interesting. "Did she mention her plans for the morning?"

"No. We got off the phone so I could leave. She said she was going to head to the gym to work out later."

"And call her dad?"

Tiddle smiled, although it came across more as a sneer. "Of course. Same time, every day of the week. Just like clockwork. Her dad would have it no other way." Only a hint of disapproval in his tone.

"You don't agree?"

"Not for me to agree or disagree. It's just the way it is."

Nick pushed. "But you don't like it?"

Tiddle shrugged. "I think it silly that a man feels such compulsion to have twenty-four-hour tabs on his twenty-five-year-old daughter. A little odd, wouldn't you say, Agent?"

"Considering who her father is, it's a security precaution."

"Just like it was for security reasons he had her sit out three years before enrolling in college?" Tiddle gave a dry laugh. "Sounds like you're drinking the Kool-Aid, man. Security? Not hardly. Senator Ford just liked having his little girl under his thumb."

Now the real emotion flew out. "Your opinion, or Gina's?" Nick recalled Cynthia Mantle's remarks about Ford's overbearing ways toward his daughter.

"Gina adored her father, don't get me wrong, but lately, she'd grown tired of his constant attempts to control her life."

"What did she say?"

"It wasn't so much what she said, but the way she acted."

"What do you mean?"

Tiddle lifted a casual shoulder. "Like when he'd call when we were out. She'd tell me to be quiet so he wouldn't know we were together. She'd tell him she was studying or something and cut the call short."

Nick tapped his pen against the little leather notebook. "Did the senator disapprove of you?"

"He didn't disapprove of me, per se, but of any man Gina had more than a passing interest in." Tiddle snorted. "And as I'm sure you know, the senator has been quite outspoken with his views regarding different races."

All of Tennessee had heard Senator Ford's speeches regarding the divisions in life based upon race. "Did you know Gina kept her relationship with you from her father until recently?"

"Of course. She told me that as soon as she told him about me, he'd be all up in our business. And she was right." Tiddle grinned and shook his head. "He continuously called and asked us out to eat, telling Gina he wanted to get to know *'your young man better,'* but really, he just wanted to see for himself how serious we were. His daughter, fraternizing with a white man."

"And how serious are you?"

Tiddle's eyes widened. "I love Gina and want to marry her. We plan on doing just that as soon as she graduates in June."

Mantle had it right. They were practically engaged. "Did Gina tell her father that?"

"Are you kidding? So he could start causing us problems?" Tiddle crossed his legs at the ankles. "Gina didn't want a big to-do, even if her father accepted our relationship. She wouldn't even let me buy her an engagement ring."

"How was she planning on telling her father?"

"We'd discussed just eloping. Make it easier."

"Really?" Nick couldn't imagine the senator not making a huge affair out of his daughter's wedding, interracial relationship aside. It would pack quite the political punch.

"We went back and forth on the idea. Gina wanted to for my sake with her father, but didn't because she knew how much a big wedding would mean to her mother." He stood. "Is there anything else?"

Nick stood too and passed his business card to Tiddle. "If you think of anything that might be helpful or if you hear from Gina, please call me immediately."

Tiddle accepted the card. "So you aren't positive the woman you found is Gina?"

"No, sir."

"So there's still hope she's alive and well somewhere?"

Funny, Tiddle's face didn't reflect any optimism. "Nothing is confirmed yet." Nick opened the front door.

"Will you call me?" His voice hitched. "When you know for sure, I mean." He leaned against the door frame. "I doubt her father will call me."

"I'm sure you'll hear." Nick headed to his car. His cell vibrated. He took it from his hip. "Hagar."

"It's Darren, sir. I'm on my way to Gina Ford's."

"I'll meet you there." Nick cranked the engine.

If only he could be sure one way or the other if Tiddle had just played him or not. He remembered what it felt like to believe you were in love. He'd thought he felt that way about Joy. What a revelation it'd been when he'd found out the truth. But now, he had a job to do: get to the truth. And there was no better time than the present.

Nick eased his car onto Poplar Avenue. What was it about David Tiddle that he didn't trust? The guy's alibi would be checked out thoroughly, so he'd have to be an idiot to lie to Nick. He called the office and put in the order to have the alibi verified, then drove the twenty or so minutes to Gina Ford's condo in the Woodlands.

Timmons's car waited at the guard shack. He and Nick had to show their credentials to gain entry into the town-house community. Once done, they pulled up in the driveway on the left and parked. No light blazed over the door in welcome. No soft glow flickered behind the front window.

Nick used the senator's key to unlock the door and stepped over the threshold. He felt along the wall until he found a light switch and flipped it. Light bathed the room in a warm glimmer. He blinked to focus on the iron staircase to the right, with its slight curve to the left opening into the second story.

"Wow, nice digs for a college kid, huh?" Timmons pushed the door closed.

"Dad probably pays the note. Did you find out anything important from your interviews with the other study-group members?"

"Just confirmed what the senator had told us. Was there, didn't go for pizza, said she was going home instead. Last any of them heard from her."

"Did any of them mention Gina acting strange or upset?"

Timmons shook his head. "Nothing. Most of them said they only knew her through the study group, but that she didn't socialize with them much outside of schoolwork."

Nick glanced around. Nothing appeared out of place—throw pillows propped neatly against the back of the sofa facing the fireplace, blinds on the back window drawn, shielding the deck from view, and no drag marks across the white carpet. No sign of forced entry. No sign of a struggle.

"I'll check out the upstairs." Timmons bounded up the stairs.

Nick checked out the master bedroom on the main floor. Nothing of interest. By all appearances, Gina Ford was a neat person. She didn't have piles of clothes on her bedroom or bathroom floor . . . her closet didn't hide mounds of discarded shoes. The only thing of interest Nick ran across was her date book.

He swallowed hard as he hovered over the leather-bound book. It was one of these that had first led Nick to learn Joy was cheating on him. That she had someone she saw at least twice a week, only staying with Nick because of the security he provided. He knew better than to get involved with a former victim. Knew better, but hadn't been able to refuse Joy's big, green eyes begging him to protect her from her sister's kidnapper. How was he supposed to know how badly the relationship would end once her sister's kidnapper was finally found?

Nick shook off the bitter memories and concentrated on Gina's date book. Flipping through it using a pen to turn pages, he noticed she listed each of her classes, study groups, and dates methodically. Consistent to Tiddle's and Mantle's statements, Gina and Tiddle were an exclusive and serious couple. They'd gone out practically every night of the past two weeks with the excep-tion of study-group nights. Movie-ticket stubs, concert tickets, even fortune-cookie fortunes were taped on the day with notes. Nothing was listed for today except her class schedule.

Timmons met him in the hallway. "Nothing upstairs. Just got the call that her cell records are in."

"Good. I want to know who she talked to after eleven last night."

Together, they concluded the inspection of the home, finding nothing else of interest. They checked the backyard, looking around both decks, then secured the property and returned to their cars. Nick waited until Timmons had pulled out, heading back to the office to write up the reports for the briefing in the morning and get the phone records on Nick's desk.

Darkness engulfed Nick as he sat in the car, the moon not even high enough in the sky to cast any light down on him.

Obviously Gina hadn't been murdered at home—there was nothing amiss that Nick could tell. If her identity was confirmed, TBI would send a unit by tomorrow for a more thorough inspection. But for now, nothing at her home indicated she had met with foul play.

A glimmer of hope, faint as his reality

conscience could allow, that the victim wasn't Gina sparked. The medical examiner could've been wrong. There were plenty of young women with similar enough features that an identity could be mistaken.

Who was he fooling?

It was Gina Ford. So young, with her whole life ahead of her, now gone.

Senseless.

She'd been murdered, and Nick hadn't a single working clue on the case.

A film of sweat glistened on her hands. Maddie stood paralyzed in the kitchen, milk drying on her Uggs and pants, her eyes glued to the phone sitting on the kitchen counter.

Brring!

Maybe the police needed to talk with her about her report. She grabbed the receiver. "Hello?"

The woman's sobs grew in pitch and intensity. Maddie made her way into the bedroom and pulled her handgun to her. "Who is this?"

"You should have left things alone." The man's voice . . . unlike anything Maddie had ever heard, was as chilling as a Hollywood version of a demonic voice.

She dropped the phone. It clattered to the floor. The woman's sobs spilled from the earpiece.

"What do you want?" Despite her grip on the gun, Maddie's body trembled.

The doorbell rang.

She pivoted, stubbing her toe on the edge of the stove. "Ouch!"

"Memphis police, open up!"

Maddie exhaled as she limped to the front door, splashing in the puddle of milk and leaving behind a trail of white footprints until she flung open the door.

Two uniformed officers stood on the doorstep. Both men had their hands on the butts of their handguns. They spied the gun in her hand and drew their weapons. "Drop the gun, ma'am."

"Whoa, I'm a TBI agent. Let me get my badge. I'm going to set my gun down." She slowly squatted and set her gun on the entryway floor.

The police holstered their guns and stepped into the house while Maddie grabbed her badge out of her purse sitting on the entry table. She showed them. "I'm sorry."

"No problem." The tall, older officer sat on the couch. "I understand you've had a threatening phone call?"

Maddie perched on the arm of the love seat opposite the couch and recounted the two calls. The younger officer with flaming red hair filled out the report form. Inside of thirty minutes, they'd concluded the report, given her the report number so she could acquire a copy next week, and informed her they'd send a cruiser through her neighborhood as they could spare patrols.

"I understand. Thank you, Officers." She led the way to the door.

"If you get any more calls, I'd suggest you consider changing to a private number. You have a safe night, ma'am."

After shutting the door behind them, she secured the locks, then grabbed her gun before heading to the kitchen. Every limb weighted her down as she set her gun on the counter and reached for the dish towel. Tears blurred her vision as she bent to wipe up the floor.

No use crying over spilt milk.

That thought made her laugh. And laugh. And laugh so hard she lost her balance and landed on her bottom. Which made it all the funnier.

Maddie laughed until tears ran down her face. She really needed to go to bed. Exhaustion tugged at her from all directions. As she mopped up the mess, she began humming "Amazing Grace," the first Elvis song she ever remembered hearing. Her mother sang it to her whenever she was hurt or scared or heartbroken. Mom had been the one who'd bought Maddie all those Elvis albums back in the day.

On days like this, she missed Mom more than ever.

CHAPTER SIX

"The truth is like the sun. You can shut it
out for a time, but it ain't goin' away."
ELVIS PRESLEY

Nick leaned against the cold wall outside the morgue while Senator Ford paced the hallway. The February morning delivered below-freezing temperatures, or was it just where he was that had the hair on the back of his neck standing at full attention? Either way, he hated being here.

"How much longer?" Ford made another lap, his soft-soled shoes barely squeaking on the waxed linoleum.

Nick glanced at his watch—8:58—but he knew Ford didn't really expect an answer. In a few minutes, the senator's entire life would change forever, so Nick would indulge his impatience for a few more minutes. No matter how many times he'd been in this place with the same or similar situation, nothing made this part of his job easier.

After the team briefing this morning, Nick had time to review Gina's phone records. Only two calls were made between 11:00 on Thursday night and 10:00 on Friday morning: One at 11:14 Thursday night, to her father, as he'd stated. The second to David Tiddle at 7:50 Friday morning.

Duration of call lasted only four minutes.

The registered incoming calls were all on Friday morning. Only one was logged before the time of death, from Cynthia Mantle. They spoke from 8:04 until 8:06. All the other calls were less than a minute, indicative of a call going to voice mail. Most of the calls were from the senator after Gina failed to call him on schedule and from David Tiddle. According to the phone records, Cynthia was the last person to speak to Gina.

Cynthia hadn't mentioned talking with Gina on the morning she went missing when Nick had questioned her. Then again, she hadn't mentioned being on the outs with Gina either. Perhaps it was time to visit with Ms. Mantle again.

The door of the morgue creaked open and McMichael stepped into the claustrophobic space. He nodded at Nick, then addressed the senator. "Sir, she's ready."

Chills spread out from Nick's spine and pressed against his lungs as he pushed off the wall and stood beside Ford. The medical examiner held open the door for them as they passed into the room.

The brushed finish glistened under the harsh light over the table holding the sheet-draped body. The very tip of the woman's head peeked out from under the white cotton. As always, Nick's mouth went drier than the Mojave Desert. He stood on the wall farthest from the body.

"Sir." McMichael situated the senator beside

the table while he moved to the opposite side. He folded down the sheet once. Twice.

The senator sucked in air, hissing over his teeth.

McMichael tucked the sheet around the body at the top of the shoulders so only the young woman's face and neck were exposed, her smooth mocha skin almost translucent against the unyielding stainless steel.

Ford hunched over as if someone had jabbed him in the gut. He exhaled in a resounding *whoosh*.

Nick's chest tightened as his own memories flooded him . . .

"I don't want to see him," Dad boomed in the quiet funeral home. "And I don't want everyone else gawking at him either."

"But Roge, I need to say good-bye." Mom hadn't stopped sobbing for two solid days.

"Then you go say good-bye the way you have to, but I refuse to have an open viewing. It's morbid."

Nick sat on the overstuffed love seat in the funeral home's reception area. He gripped his hands together in his lap, watching his parents like he watched a tennis match on television. Not ever see Roger again? That his brother was gone still hadn't sunk in. He kept waiting for Roger to jump out from behind a door, laughing that he'd worried everyone so.

"What about you, Nick? Do you want to

say good-bye to your brother?" Mom asked.

"Yes." To have just five more minutes with Roger . . . to tell him that he loved him. That he was sorry for all the times he resented him being Dad's favorite. That none of that mattered.

"Then come along." Mom moved across the carpet.

Wait. He didn't mean he wanted to say good-bye to him like this. To see him? Dead? On second thought, maybe he should stay here with Dad.

Mom grabbed his hand and squeezed. Fresh tears dampened her cheeks. No, he couldn't let her do this alone. Dad should be here, being strong for his wife. Nick glanced over his shoulder to stare at his father's back. Dad wouldn't even look down the hall to where Mom led Nick.

The lady at the door opened it, letting him and Mom in. The room was cold . . . so, so cold. And the lights? So dimly lit Nick had to squint. In the center of the room, a table waited. A table holding a body. It was Roger. Nick even recognized the Marine uniform he wore that Mom had picked up from the cleaners and given to the lady yesterday, but his brother was so still. And so . . . white.

The paleness of his face made him look almost like he glimmered . . . but Roger never glimmered. Roger was always in motion, always on the move, always laughing or smiling.

The body on the table didn't laugh or smile as Nick and his mother approached.

He stood over Roger's body, staring into his face. Eyes closed, no hint of expression. Lifeless . . . dull . . . like a wax figure.

Mom wailed and slumped to the floor. Transfixed by Roger's appearance, Nick couldn't even move to help her. Dad should be here for Mom.

But Nick wished he'd never seen Roger like this. He still hadn't forgiven God for taking his brother . . .

"It's her. It's Gina." Senator Ford's wavering voice yanked Nick from his memory.

"Are you sure?" The question was stupid, as always, but had to be asked every time.

Ford turned his tear-filled eyes to Nick. "I'm positive."

McMichael reached for the sheet.

Ford jerked his hands over the medical examiner's. "Don't. Please." He licked his lips and turned to include Nick. "May I have just a moment alone with my daughter?"

Nick cocked his brow at McMichael, who nodded. "Sure. Take all the time you need. We'll be in the hall." He motioned for the ME to follow him.

"That's hard. No parent should outlive their child." Cullen McMichael and his wife had four children, all under the age of thirteen.

"Agreed. It's too hard on the families." Like

how Mom and Dad had to move to Florida to get away from the memories, even though Nick still needed Mom in his life. Nick shook off the sentiments and leaned against the wall. "I know you haven't performed the autopsy yet, but can you give me anything other than the time of death?"

"While I can't be a hundred percent, I'm pretty certain Gina Ford wasn't murdered by the same person as the other girl." Cullen was a good man, a brilliant doctor, and an honest government employee. Nick had never had a reason to doubt any of Cullen's findings.

"Hailey Carter." She was a victim and had a name. Nick rested his head against the wall. "Both women had three stab wounds to the chest, right?"

"Yep. Most serials are very methodical about their MO. These wounds aren't in the same locations. They aren't even at the same angle, which indicates Gina's murderer was taller than Hailey Carter's." McMichael rubbed under his glasses. "I'd estimate Gina's murderer was at least six feet tall. Hailey's murderer is about five eight or nine."

"Hmm." Nick shifted his weight from one leg to the other. "What about boot heels? Could that make up the difference?"

The ME shook his head. "Too much of a variance. And Hailey's wounds were made with an assailant attacking from behind. With Gina, I believe she was stabbed with her killer facing her."

"What else besides the height and location of the wounds?"

"Again, I can't say for sure until after the autopsy, but I'm fairly certain Gina's cause of death wasn't any of the stab wounds."

What? "I'm not following."

"Unlike Hailey's wounds that were deep enough to reach her heart, Gina's stabs were shorter and without much penetration. Even from the front, they weren't as deep as they should've been. They were almost like an afterthought. I suspect they were delivered postmortem."

"You mean someone stabbed Gina Ford after she was already dead?" That was crazy.

McMichael nodded. "I'll know for sure once I conclude the autopsy, but I think her neck was broken prior to the stabs."

Why bother stabbing her if she had a broken neck? Nick shoved off the wall. "Then Gina was stabbed to make it look like Hailey Carter's murder."

A cover-up.

Out of all the furniture in the Jungle Room, Maddie's favorite was the table made from a tree stump. The intricately carved wooden arms of the couch were beautiful, but she would bet her bottom dollar that the leather couch was beyond uncomfortable. What was it about the furnishings from the seventies that just looked stiff and . . . well, ugly? And the floor-to-ceiling carpet? Uh, no.

She'd loved Graceland since the first time Mom snuck her out of school and took her. It was one of their special moments, just Maddie and Mom.

She left the mansion and headed to her car, singing under her breath. *"Little things, I should have said and done."*

Her shoes crunched on the asphalt.

"I just never took the time."

She unlocked the door and slid behind the steering wheel. *"You were always on my mind."*

Her nerves were no longer bunched into tight knots. She continued to hum as she steered onto US 51. Now she was in the right frame of mind to go into the lab and finish processing the samples from last night. Last night . . . what a nightmare. After the police had left, she received two more calls before she gave up and unplugged her phone. If work needed the team, they would've called her cell.

She merged onto I-240, picking up speed. As she had for the better part of the night, Maddie racked her brain for people she knew—not a single person she could think of would make such calls. Well, unless it had to do with her court appearance a couple of weeks ago. If the calls started again tonight, she'd just have her number changed like the police had suggested.

Her cell phone vibrated. She secured her earpiece, then pushed the button. "Hello?"

"Morning, sunshine. Ready for a little DNA extraction?" Eva's voice almost sounded lyrical.

"Well, aren't you the bright little sunbeam this morning? Guess your picnic last night with Lance was fun?"

"Oh, it was the best. I'll tell you all about it when you get here."

"I'm on my way. Should be there soon." Quicker if the traffic would move out of her way.

"Where exactly are you?"

Maddie swallowed a groan. "On my way."

Eva chuckled. "You went to Graceland again this morning, didn't you?"

"Just for a few minutes. I had a rough night." And just visiting Graceland made Maddie feel better, almost as if Mom were still with her.

"Oh?"

Now it was Maddie's turn to say, "I'll tell you all about it when I get there."

"Okay. Listen, the reason I called is to give you a heads-up."

"For?" She eased onto Walnut Grove Road.

"Peter came down a few minutes ago to check if we needed anything. Ivan got a decent print to run. He didn't get a match through AFIS, so he's called Nick Hagar to have it run through the federal fingerprint database. Nick will be here soon, and I'm sure he'll want a status update on the lab work. Just thought I'd warn you."

Lovely. Just hunky-dory. They so didn't need any complications right now when they were fighting for their jobs. "Thanks. Any problems with any of our samples?"

"Nope. All good. Right on schedule with no hiccups. Already finished the reference samples."

"I'll start on the quantitation when I get there. Almost there." Maddie veered onto Farm Road.

"I'll pour you a cup of coffee. See you in a second."

Maddie tossed the earpiece into the console. A print was excellent. If it wasn't the victim's, chances were very good it might lead them to the girl's killer. The thought of playing a role in bringing the person responsible to justice for murder . . . well, it always made Maddie feel better. And if they solved this one quickly, with all its political overtones, maybe the money for their lab expansion would free up, courtesy of the hidden powers-that-be.

She turned into TBI's parking lot and slipped into her space. She grabbed her cell, then locked her car. Her jacket provided mediocre protection against the strong wind gusting over the open space and shoving against her. She shivered against the cold as she headed in the back door.

"Coffee's on your desk." Eva greeted her at the door to the lab. "And Peter's on his way down."

She put her cell and purse in her drawer, then traded her leather jacket for her blue lab coat. "Is something wrong?"

"Nope, but your hunk-a-hunk-of-burning-love is on his way, so Peter wants us to be on our toes."

What a way to spend their Saturday. So much for a day off. "Joy and rapture." She reached for her coffee.

Eva chuckled and led the way into the actual lab area. Maddie slipped disposable covers over her shoes and followed, slipping on latex gloves. She took a seat at the lab table and began preparing the samples by adding the necessary chemicals, in the exact required amount, to each of the sample tubes.

Working through the samples, Maddie and Eva finished the preparations within thirty minutes. Maddie took the trays of tubes to the real-time PCR sequence detection system, then set the samples to run for two hours.

"I'm guessing the coffee's past cold now." Maddie tossed her gloves and shoe covers in the trash after she passed the divider separating the laboratory from the office portion of the lab.

The door opened with its customary creak.

"Good morning, Maddie."

She smiled at her supervisor. Peter Helm could be considered a handsome man, if a woman liked the studious look. Maybe a little too slim because of his height, but there was no denying the sincerity glimmering in his green eyes hiding behind his dark-framed glasses. His sandy blond hair was a bit of a shock, the way it was so curly and full on top, but only because of the pallor of his skin.

Over the years, he'd made no secret that he found Maddie attractive and would love to ask her out, but she'd made it just as plain that she didn't date people in her daily environment. She'd learned that lesson the hard way back in college. With a teacher's assistant, of all things.

It didn't matter that was a decade ago. Memories of Adam's betrayal still caused her heart to clutch when she thought of him.

"That FBI agent is on his way." Peter sat on the edge of her desk. "I got the impression you two knew each other?"

Despite making it clear she wouldn't go out with him, she didn't want to hurt Peter. "He was my brother's supervisor when Rafe was here."

"Ah." Peter nodded.

Eva shot her a pointed look. "And she went out on a date with him before she went to Louisiana."

Peter's face tightened. "I see." He stood. "Will it be a problem for you to work this case with him?"

"No." Maddie swallowed. "Not at all."

"Good. I don't have to tell you we can't afford any mistakes or problems." He marched to the door. "I'll go see if he's here yet."

"Why would you tell him that?" Maddie glared at Eva.

"Hey, he needs to accept you aren't going to suddenly change your mind about going out with him. He needs to get over it."

"There's no reason to hurt him unnecessarily, though."

"Whatever." Eva rolled her eyes. "Now, tell me what you and Mr. Super Agent did on y'all's date."

"Nothing much. Went out to eat."

Eva leaned against the divider wall. "Tell me all the juicy details."

Maddie laughed. "There aren't any juicy details to tell. We had dinner, he took me home, and that was that."

"There's always something more than that with someone as handsome as him."

Oh, he was handsome all right. Deadly handsome. So handsome he should carry a license for those smoldering ebony eyes.

Eva tapped her red-tipped nails against the side of the divider and stared at her. "You really like him. I can tell."

Heat barely tinged Maddie's face. "Of course I like him. What's not to like? He's an honest man, according to Rafe. A good agent."

Creeeeak.

"And Lord knows he looks like Adonis—"

Eva cleared her throat.

"But Nick Hagar makes me go stupid whenever

97

I'm around him, and I hate that a man has such an effect on me."

"Good morning, Maddie." No mistaking that voice, especially when memories of it were what had haunted her dreams last night more than the dead young woman or the anonymous caller.

The room shifted. No, the entire earth shifted under her feet. Heat flooded her whole body as she slowly turned toward the voice.

She stiffened her back. "Good morning, Nick."

CHAPTER SEVEN

"I never expected to be anybody important."
ELVIS PRESLEY

So he made her *go stupid,* did he?

Nick bit back a smile as Maddie faced him. She had turned the deepest shade of red he'd ever seen in a blush. Not just her face, but her entire neck to her collarbone until her flesh met with the collar of her shirt.

"The DNA results won't be concluded until tomorrow afternoon." Peter Helm's face had turned red as well. Not as much as Maddie's, though.

Nick raised a brow at Helm. "I understand that. I want to get the technicians' impressions of the crime scene. Anything unusual."

"Everything will be in the reports." Helm had

taken a step back toward the door out of the lab.

"I'm sure it will, but a few questions now won't hurt, right?"

"Of course not." The other woman approached him, hand outstretched. "I'm Eva Langston, in case you didn't remember. Come on in and ask your questions." She smiled wide. "We're happy to help, right, Maddie?"

The auburn-haired woman he made *go stupid* looked anything but happy at the moment. "What do you want to know?"

He sat on the edge of her desk, deliberately leaning in her personal space. "Was there anything in your initial analysis of the crime scene that was odd?"

Maddie sat in her chair and rolled it back from the desk. "Every aspect of our job is odd. Every crime scene is unnatural."

"What I mean is, specifically, something that struck you as, I don't know, *off* about this particular crime scene?" He leaned a little further over her desk and stared into her big, brown eyes outlined by her glasses. If he made her go stupid, why hadn't she called him when she got back in town?

Maddie shrugged. "You'd probably do better to talk with the ME's office. They actually removed the body and have it."

"I have. He's performing the autopsy right now and is rushing his report. We have positive identification that the victim is Gina Ford."

Maddie's eyes widened. "Senator Ford's daughter?"

He nodded. "That's why we're pushing hard." He twisted and faced Helm. "I'm sure the senator's office will be contacting you soon with an official statement." Goodness knew his office lit up the lines to the deputy director fast enough.

Helm jerked his head, almost like a twitch. "We'll handle it."

Nick was sure Helm would. "I'm sure you agree we should withhold her name to the press as long as we can, but Ford will soon be chomping at the bit to demand justice. I can't imagine a scenario where he doesn't go public with that demand." Like Dad had celebrated each successful report of the ground Marines in Desert Storm.

"Da-da, da-da-da."

He glanced back at Maddie. She'd opened a notebook filled with her scribbles and held a pen against her lips as she read. Humming.

Nick smiled as he watched her, Maddie totally unaware of the audience.

"Baby, let me be . . . your lovin' Teddy Bear." She dropped her pen, seemed to realize no one was talking anymore, and looked up. The pretty blush returned. "I do remember something."

"What?"

"The drop of blood on her back." Eva moved beside Maddie but locked gazes with him.

"Maddie keeps detailed notes of her impressions at scenes."

"Last night, I found a drop of blood on her shoulder. Not in a place consistent with where any blood splatters should be, considering the crime scene."

"And you think it might be . . . ?"

"It's possible it's not the victim's blood. Not back there." Maddie lifted her pen and tapped it against her notebook. "Or I could be wrong and it could be an old stain."

"You know it didn't look old," Eva interjected.

"No, it looked fresh."

"And you took a sample of it?" If a match came back from the fingerprint database and then they could match it with DNA to a stain on the back of her shirt . . .

Maddie frowned at him. "Of course I took a sample. That *is* my job."

He raised his hands level with his shoulders. "I didn't mean to offend. We just have nothing but forensics to go on at this point." And his supervisor sitting on his shoulder.

Her expression softened. "We'll have all the results tomorrow late afternoon. After this step that's running now, we have to set up the PCR and run that for about three and half hours. Then, we'll be able to type. That's the longest part of the process."

"How long?"

"System has to run twelve and a half hours for the typing, then it'll take us three or four hours to review the data and interpret for the report. After that, our lab supervisor and Peter review everything for technical and administrative verification of our scientific analysis and conclusion."

"I'll let Ivan know you're on your way to get that print. I'm sure you're anxious to get it into IAFIS." Helm waited on a response.

Nick stood. "In a minute."

Helm nodded and left.

Nick turned back to Maddie. "In your professional opinion and experience, what were your observations of the crime-scene staging?"

She leaned back in the chair. "Obviously she wasn't killed in the vehicle as there were no blood patterns or anything to indicate that's where she died. Not enough blood."

He sat back on the edge of her desk. "Go on."

"And if that's accurate, there's no explanation for a blood drop where I found it on her back, so that would logically lead me to believe it might be someone else's." She cocked her head. "With stabbings, it's not unusual for the assailant to accidentally cut himself and leave a blood trace on the knife or the victim."

True.

"So if he cut himself, then put her in the car, it's possible he transferred his own blood to her back."

She tapped her finger against her chin. "I'm also wondering about the cause of death."

He crossed his arms over his chest. "The stab wounds?"

She wrinkled her nose and shook her head. "That's just it—there's something off about them."

"Why do you say that?"

"Her eyes."

Huh? McMichael hadn't mentioned anything about Gina's eyes. "What about them?"

Maddie shook her head slightly again. "They were open. Fear and shock were preserved at the time of her death."

"Getting stabbed wouldn't surprise and scare you?"

She stood and shoved her hands into her coat pockets. "Usually I see shock, but fear indicates dying after processing what's happening to you."

"I'm not following you." But she intrigued him that she thought more like a detective than a scientist.

"Okay, let's say that Eva is going to stab me."

Eva grabbed Maddie's pen. "Oh, goodie. I don't have to be the one who dies this time."

Maddie grinned and shook her head. "Now, I'm unaware she's coming up behind me."

The pretty blonde moved behind her. She threw an arm around Maddie's throat, then made stabbing motions with the pen toward Maddie's heart.

"See, I'm shocked. I'm being attacked. But because of the stabs, I die before fear has a chance to set in." Maddie turned to face Eva. "But now, Eva comes at me head-on."

Eva advanced on Maddie, making stabbing motions toward her.

"So I'm shocked, yes, that I'm being attacked, but, because I'm seeing my killer, I'm also scared."

Had to respect a lady using logic and science. In his line of work, the combination was rare. Sure hadn't been in Joy. "I see."

Eva tossed the pen on Maddie's desk.

"But that doesn't make sense either because I didn't see any defensive wounds on her hands." She shook her head. "I can't figure out why she didn't raise her hands to stop the assault. I don't get it."

Nick would normally never discuss unconfirmed details, but in this particular case . . . "Would it make more sense if I told you the stab wounds were delivered postmortem?"

Maddie closed her eyes. She hummed very softly for a moment, then blinked to look at him. "Yeah, yeah it would. It would explain the lack of defensive wounds, the staging . . . we can't know for sure until the ME finishes the autopsy, though."

"Right. That's just his impression before the autopsy. What about the blood drops in the car?"

"Minor, confirming the stabs were postmortem. If I had to guess, and again, I'm not the ME, but I'd say she was stabbed soon after death, then set inside the car for staging." Her eyes narrowed. "Then we don't have a serial killer on our hands."

"Doesn't look like it."

Eva ran a hand over her golden curls. "So whoever killed the senator's daughter wanted it to look like a serial killing."

"Seems that way."

Maddie shook her head as she dropped back into her chair. "There are some true monsters in the world today. The things people do to each other . . ." She shivered. "It's just horrible."

For the first time in a long, long time, Nick had the urge to hold a woman. To pull her against his chest and loan her his strength. He managed to stop his arms from reaching for her.

Why hadn't she called him?

It was too much to hope for that the ground would open up and swallow her whole.

The door opened and Peter glared from the doorway. "Agent Hagar, Ivan's got the print ready for you."

Nick stood. "Thank you, ladies, for sharing your insights. I look forward to your full reports." He smiled the smile of his that was a threat to her pulse, then joined Peter. "I'll also need to get Gina

Ford's cell. I believe it was recovered at the scene."

The door had barely closed before Eva plopped onto Maddie's desk. "Oh. My. Gosh. That man's swagger is like watching the smoothest tango."

"Eva."

"I tried to warn you that he was in the doorway. I cleared my throat as loud as I could."

"I know." Maddie pinched the bridge of her nose under her glasses. "I am beyond embarrassed and mortified." Another reason she shouldn't discuss her feelings in public. It wasn't like she hadn't already lived through a very public humiliation. She should've learned her lesson.

Then again, they didn't often have guests show up in the lab on a Saturday. But she should've known better. She knew he'd been on his way. Knew he'd come in the lab.

"If you could have seen his face . . ."

Maddie snapped her attention to Eva. "Why?"

"He smiled pretty big before you knew he was there."

Was there no end to her humiliation? "Good thing he wasn't smiling when I turned around."

Eva chuckled. "Further proof the man is wise."

Maddie groaned and laid her head on the desk. "I won't be able to face him again."

"Yes, you will."

"Maybe he'll get a hit on the print and I won't have to interact with him anymore."

"You jerk." Eva jumped to her feet and snatched foot covers and placed them over her boots. She practically stomped around the divider and into the actual lab.

"What?" Maddie followed after she'd covered her shoes and gloved up. "Why am I a jerk?" She checked the gauges on the genetic analyzer. "I didn't do anything."

"Except not call a very handsome, very eligible man who is clearly interested in you."

Maddie opened her mouth to argue.

Eva shook her head. "And who you are obviously interested in as well. So that makes you a jerk."

Maddie transferred the utensils from the bleach wash to the ethanol bath, anything to keep her hands busy. "Because I'm being cautious?"

Eva spun on her three-inch heels. "Seriously, Maddie? If a woman goes out on a date with a man and the date goes well, and he is supposed to call her after he gets back in town, and then doesn't for no good reason, we women call him a jerk." Eva glared at her. "You know I'm telling the truth."

Yeah, but that didn't mean she wanted to admit it.

Eva sighed as she monitored the temperatures of the refrigerators housing the reagents. "You told me how much you've been hurt in the past, but take it from me, all men are not like the two

107

who hurt you. How can you get your happily-ever-after if you don't let yourself take a chance on falling in love?"

"It's not that." But she didn't know any way to defend herself other than the truth, and she certainly didn't want to admit that. Maddie irradiated the utensils with ultraviolet light.

"Then tell me. I want to understand. Want to help you."

"I don't need help."

"Uh, yeah . . . you do." Eva began the decontamination of the hoods with ultraviolet light. "Might as well go ahead and spit it out—you know I'm not going to drop it."

Wasn't that the truth? Maddie headed back to the office part of the lab. She tossed her gloves into the trash and sank into her chair.

Eva followed, sitting atop her own desk, swinging her legs.

"Fine." Maddie made a point to sigh loudly. "Apparently I can't make good choices when it comes to men."

"What?" Eva's eyes widened and her legs stopped swinging.

"Well, look at my track history. One man cheated on me and the other was a liar and married." Maddie swallowed against the dulled pain. "Just call me the cheater magnet."

Eva laughed. "You're kidding me, right?"

"No. And stop laughing. It's not funny."

"You're what, thirty-four?"

Maddie nodded.

"In your life, you've only been serious about two men." Eva wagged two fingers at her. "Two. In thirty-four years, you've been in love twice."

"So?" Maddie's mother and father had met each other in high school, fallen in love, gotten married, had children, and lived happily ever after until they were both killed when a drunk driver hit their vehicle. They'd found their true love first time out of the chute.

"You don't have enough experience to claim yourself a cheater magnet." Eva chuckled. "You haven't even gotten three strikes."

"That's not funny."

"No, it's not, but it isn't funny that you've only had two relationships and you're basing your dating standards on those two losers." Eva pointed at her before hopping off the top of her desk and moving to her chair. She smiled across the lab. "Haven't you ever heard the saying that third time's the charm?"

So she heard. Didn't mean it applied to her. Maddie had thought she'd found the perfect man in Adam. That turned out to be a disaster, but she'd moved on. Chocked it up to experience and licked her wounds. Then she'd met Kevin in book club. She'd taken the relationship slower because of her past mistake but eventually allowed herself to fall in love again. She'd been so sure her happily-ever-after was just around the corner. Let herself believe in the fairy tale ending like her parents.

Then she'd found out Kevin had a wife.

She couldn't risk a third time. What would be left of her heart if it broke again?

CHAPTER EIGHT

"When I was a boy, I always saw myself
as a hero in comic books and in movies.
I grew up believing this dream."
ELVIS PRESLEY

"She's waiting in the conference room." Timmons ducked his head into Nick's office. "Looks quite uncomfortable there to me."

"Thanks. I'll let her stew for a minute."

"Yes, sir. I'm going to watch the crime-scene unit go over Gina Ford's place."

Nick nodded at Timmons, then stared back at the most-recent update on the case.

The print Helm's expert had gotten was a full and clean, but AFIS didn't have it in the system. Timmons ran it through the FBI's maintained IAFIS database. Match came back to David Tiddle. While that would be encouraging, Tiddle was her boyfriend, apparently a serious one, whose defense would be that he'd touched that dash numerous times over the course of normal and expected contact.

He stood and stretched, then ambled toward the conference room. He grabbed a cup of coffee on his way.

Cynthia paced, hugging her arms as he entered. "Agent Hagar."

"Have a seat, please." Nick sat on one side of the table and gestured to the seat across from him. He opened a file, perusing his handwritten notes, then looked over the table to address her. "I don't like being played, Ms. Mantle."

Her young eyes were wide. "W-What do you mean?"

"You weren't exactly forthcoming with me about the state of your current relationship with Gina." He slammed the folder closed, then glared at her. "Were you?"

"I-I don't understand."

"Why didn't you mention you and Gina hadn't been very close lately? That there was some serious animosity brewing between you two?"

She blinked three times rapidly. He'd scored. "All friendships go through rocky patches. This certainly isn't our first."

Good, he had her on the defensive. "What rocky patch is that?"

Mantle sighed. "David. Her boyfriend."

This could be more interesting than he'd thought. Nick leaned back in the chair and took a slurping sip of his coffee. "Go on."

"Ever since she and David got serious, she's been different. With all the sneaking around to keep it hush-hush from her father, she never has time to hang out with me or her other friends. When she isn't in class, she only wants to be with David. And everything out of her mouth is 'David this' and 'David that.' It's tiresome."

"You sound jealous."

Mantle shrugged. "Maybe I am a little. I saw him first. He probably would've asked me out if Gina hadn't come along." Her lips went into almost a perfectly straight line. "But as usual, the golden girl showed up, flaunting her father's money and power, and she got whatever she wanted."

Jealous and bitter. Nick shifted in his seat. Many a time he'd felt almost the exact same way about Roger and the way Dad would give him anything he wanted.

"But he started to poison her against me."

"Who?"

"David. He would tell her how much better she was than me, encourage her to cut ties to those of us clinging to her, using her." She swallowed and set her hands on the table. "I told Gina if she really wanted to stand on her own two feet like she proclaimed, then she needed to start taking care of herself and stop relying on Daddy or David." Mantle shivered. "She didn't like that too much. Called me some ugly names, said some mean things, and we just left it at that."

"When was this?"

"A couple of weeks ago."

"But y'all stayed in the same study group?"

"Of course." She tapped her fingers on the table. "Like I said, we'd been friends for too long and knew this was just a spat. We'd had them many times over the years. Both of us knew we'd work through this once we both cooled down."

"Yet you didn't?"

"Actually, Thursday night she was acting more like herself, but upset. I asked her what was wrong, like I told you, and she just told me that she had to confront someone about something she'd found. I knew it had to be someone close to her because of how upset she was."

Interesting she'd left all this information out of her previous statement. "Did she tell you any more than that?"

"No, but she asked if she could call me in the morning if she needed someone to talk to after she was done with her confrontation. I told her of course."

"Even though you two hadn't worked through your latest . . . spat?" Did she really expect him to believe her?

She smiled. "You aren't a woman, Agent Hagar. We go through these cycles with our best friends. Ask any woman and she'll tell you that. But no matter what, when the chips are down, your best friend is there for you."

If that was true, he really didn't understand women at all. Not that he ever thought he did.

"Ms. Mantle, why didn't you mention earlier that you spoke with her on Friday morning?"

Her cheeks pinked. "I forgot about that. I just called to check on her, because she'd been so upset the night before. I wanted to make sure she was okay."

"And was she?" Nick held his pencil so tight, it was a wonder it didn't snap in two and splinter across the conference room.

"She said she was on her way to have one of the most serious discussions in her life. I asked her was this about the confrontation she'd mentioned the night before and she said yes. She realized she had to confront two people, and both would leave her scarred."

Nick finished scribbling and looked back at Cynthia. "And what else?"

"Nothing. She said she had to go and that she'd call me later." Tears pooled in her eyes, but she blinked them away. "I never heard from her again."

He could respect her not using the tears ploy. So many young women he questioned used them for sympathy. Never worked on him. "I have to ask, Ms. Mantle, where were you when you spoke to Gina?"

"In my apartment, about to head to class."

"Do you know where Gina was?"

"She was in her car. I could hear the wind noise. No matter how cold it was, Gina always cracked her car window. She had to have fresh air."

"What did you do after you got off the phone with her?"

"I hit the shower, then went to class."

"What class and what time did it start?"

"You think I'm not telling you the truth?"

"Just answer the question, Ms. Mantle."

"Fine." She sat straight in the hard, metal chair. "It's my creative writing class, and it starts at eight thirty. I was there until the end of class at ten fifteen, you can ask Professor Emmel because I helped collect papers for him and set them on his desk at the end of class."

"That's cutting it a bit close, isn't it?"

"What?"

"You got off the phone with Gina at 8:10, took a shower, then made it all the way across campus for an 8:30 class." Her type usually took two hours to get ready to go check the mail, much less go to class.

She narrowed her eyes. "I might've been a minute or two late. It's no big deal."

Ah. So she could've been even later than she let on. "Exactly what time did you get to class on Friday, Ms. Mantle?"

She hesitated. "Should I have a lawyer?"

Thank goodness she hadn't asked that question earlier. "Do you need a lawyer?"

"I think I should probably talk to one." She stood. "Can I leave?"

"Sure. Just don't leave town." He stood and grabbed his coffee and folder. "And let me know who you retain as an attorney. Just in case I have any other questions."

She hustled out of the room like a hound of hell nipped at her heels.

Nick returned to his office. He retrieved four messages from the senator's office, not to mention two from the head of the University of Memphis and a call from the mayor's office. That wasn't counting the stack of messages from the press he'd thrown into the trash. Everyone needed him to have a lead and wanted an arrest forthcoming. Quickly.

He read his notes. So David Tiddle had been causing problems? Maybe.

Nick accessed the Internet on his computer, looked up the number for the Holiday Inn on Sango Road, then dialed the number.

"Thank you for calling Holiday Inn. This is Marge, how may I assist you?"

"Marge, I'm Nick Hagar with the FBI. I'm verifying a person of interest's statement. Can you help me?"

"I can try."

"I need to verify the room you had for a David Tiddle."

Typing clicks sounded over the phone. "Mr. Tiddle checked in on Thursday. His checkout date was yesterday."

"What time did he check out?"

"Sir, that information isn't available as Mr. Tiddle utilized our express checkout option."

It'd been a while since Nick had stayed at a Holiday Inn. "What, exactly, is your express checkout?"

"If the bill slipped under your door is correct and you want the bill to be paid with the credit card on file, then you don't have to come into the office to check out. You can simply leave the room key in the room."

"So you have no way to know when someone actually checked out."

"No, sir. Checkout time is eleven. If they are out by the time housekeeping comes to clean before our three p.m. check-in, then we have no issues."

"Was there any such issue with David Tiddle's reservation?"

More typing clicks. "There's no record of any, sir."

Technically, Tiddle could've checked in on Thursday, left the key in the room, then turned right back around, getting back to Memphis in ample time to kill Gina on Friday morning. "Can you tell me if David Tiddle's bill was still on the floor where it'd been slipped under the door?"

"You'd have to ask whoever was working housekeeping that day."

"Can you tell me who that was?"

"We can't give out that information over the phone, sir."

He almost laughed. "Thank you, Marge." Nick hung up the phone and concluded his notes. If needed, he could send an agent to speak with housekeeping about the bill under the door.

His intercom buzzed.

"Hagar."

"Agent Hagar, this is Cullen."

"You finish the autopsy?" Nick grabbed a pen and flipped to a clean page on his notebook.

"Official cause of death is a broken neck. Stab wounds are superficial, nonfatal, and were delivered postmortem."

"Time of death?"

"Still between eight and ten yesterday morning. I'd say closer to eight than ten."

"Anything else?" He needed something. Anything. "Come on, Cullen, give me some good news."

"Well, there is something . . ."

"What?" He'd take any sort of lead. No matter how minor, just so he had something to buy a little space from the people breathing down his neck.

"I detected a few areas of bruising delivered around the time of death."

"Cause?"

"They were located right below the collarbone area. Pattern is consistent with someone shoving her there. Pretty hard."

"Definite?"

"No, I tried to see if I could pull conclusively that they were handprints, but I can't."

Would've been nice. "How close to time of death?"

"With the bruising and rigor, I'd estimate within half an hour."

"You think she was arguing with someone and he or she shoved her?"

"No way to prove that."

"But that's your professional opinion?"

"Yes. And that's what I'm putting in the autopsy report."

Good. At least that was something. "Thanks, Cullen." Nick hung up the phone just as Timmons entered.

"They swept the house, but don't expect them to have anything."

"I wasn't." Nick filled him in on the new information. "You get anything on the list the senator gave you?"

"Actually, one went hot on my way in."

"Really?"

"Yeah. Senator Ford sponsored a bill on policies and procedures regarding stem-cell research. Some of the pro-lifers got up in arms about it. One

in particular acts as a leader of the lynch mob."
Timmons glanced at his notebook. "Leo Ward."

Name didn't ring a bell with Nick.

"Ward seems to instigate trouble, at least according to reports."

"What kind of trouble?"

"Organizing protests that end up anything but peaceful. Threats made from his office to those who support ideas opposed to his group's stance. He's never been formally charged as there has never been enough physical evidence, but the police and government security definitely watch him."

"Big difference from organizing protests and murder."

"Not as much as you might think. His group has hung carcasses of dead family pets on the porch of bill supporters. They've slashed tires and made threatening phone calls. They have stalked family members of bill supporters, brandishing knives in some instances. All reportedly on Ward's instructions."

"But no charges have been filed?"

Timmons shook his head. "Everyone is terrified of retaliation, so no one will come forward and implicate him."

Sounded like true scum. "Has he made any threats lately directed against the senator?"

"According to the head of the senator's security team, indirectly, yes." Timmons set papers on Nick's desk. "That's a report from the security detail in which they've intercepted several packages meant for the senator. Containing dead rodents with cutout messages like 'Next time it could be your wife' or other such threats. The most recent and related to this case was the package of a decapitated African American doll with the cutout message of 'What if the stem-cell research came at the cost of *your* child.' "

"And Ford hasn't had this man's head delivered on a platter?"

Timmons let out a slow breath. "He doesn't know."

"What?" There was no way Ford couldn't know.

"His chief of staff thought it would distract him at, and I quote, 'a delicate time in his political maneuvering.' "

If it turned out Ward was responsible for his daughter's death, Ford would have the man's head. For him to have received a warning and everyone kept it from him . . . the possibility that he could have prevented his daughter's murder . . .

Nick snatched up the paper and scanned. "They can link this to Ward?"

"Not directly. The number of the bill the senator sponsored is on the cutout threat, but it's vague enough that a defense attorney could have a field day with it in court." Timmons sat in the chair in front of Nick's desk and ran a hand over his blond hair. "There's plenty of circumstantial evidence to point to Ward and his group, but not anything incriminating enough to charge Ward and make it stick."

"See what you can find out on Leo Ward." Nick studied the photograph of the doll and the message. "Find who has this evidence—get it and run it through TBI's lab and see if we can get a match on any forensics to the crime scene." He set the report down as Timmons left.

This might be the break he needed.

"How'd it go on your picnic last night?" Maddie finished her soft drink, sucking the straw until it made slurping sounds.

Eva glanced at her from across the table. All during their lunch of sandwiches and chips, she'd been reserved, very unlike Eva. Giving Maddie the silent treatment. Or maybe just being quiet and letting Maddie think. Either way, Maddie was ready for conversation as she stood and threw her sub wrap and napkins into the break room trash.

Eva sighed and did the same before following Maddie down the hall to their lab. "The picnic itself was amazing."

"Just the picnic?" Maddie unlocked the lab and headed to the sink where she washed her hands.

"Unfortunately, Lance is more of the clingy type than I'd believed." Eva joined her at the sink. "The picnic was lovely, but I was tired and went home early. He called three times last night before I turned off the phone, and he's already called me four times this morning, wanting to set a date for tonight."

"I thought you wanted men to want to see you all the time." Maddie slipped on her lab coat and shoe coverings before leading the way into the lab area.

"I do, but . . . well, I don't want them to be desperate. I can't stand a man who becomes so obsessive. Been there, done that. Men like that are control freaks, and you know how I do around control freaks."

Maddie laughed as she pulled the tubes and sat down to review the determination of amount of human DNA in each of the samples. "Are you referring to me?"

Chuckling, Eva sat at her own lab station to run the same procedures as Maddie, for assurance of accuracy. "No comment."

"Look, about earlier—"

"I'm sorry. It's none of my business and I shouldn't have butted in." Eva stared over her monitor. "I just want you to be happy."

Same thing Rafe and Riley kept telling her. Ever since they'd fallen in love with Remington and Hayden respectively, they were bound and determined that she find a man to share her life. "And I love you for caring." If only love came with a guarantee.

"What about at your church?"

Maddie looked over the top of her glasses.

"What about my church?" She'd invited Eva so many times over the years but always received a turndown. It wasn't as if Eva didn't believe in God, she did, but she refused to be beat over the head with a Bible. So she stayed on Maddie's prayer list.

"Isn't there a guy who goes to your church you could be interested in? That'd be one of your requirements met right off the bat."

Maddie concluded her calculations and passed them to Eva, who handed Maddie her results. Too many times to count, Eva had made fun of the list Maddie had for prospective men in her life. It wasn't as if she had like a gazillion items. She had less than a handful. "I don't go to church to scout for men."

She scanned Eva's calculations, which were the same as her conclusions. "Great. Same results. I'll do the dilutions and you take the concentrations."

"Okay."

They worked in silence for the next hour and a half, then Maddie began the preparation of the samples for PCR.

"Hey, you never told me about your rough night last night." Eva worked on the sterilization of the utensils they'd used.

As briefly as possible, Maddie told Eva all about the calls. "So, if I have a lot of missed calls registered on my caller ID today, I'm changing my number."

Eva's eyes were wide. "That's scary, Maddie. You should call your brother."

Maddie snorted. Sounded just like what he'd tell her if he were here. "Why on earth would I call Rafe? I carry a gun, just like he does."

"Or maybe you should tell *him*."

"Him who?"

Eva groaned. "Nick Hagar, who else? The guy who's crushing on you pretty seriously. Are you keeping up with the conversation?"

"Hey, the last thing you mentioned in regards to my love life was about finding a guy at church." Maddie put the samples in the PCR instrument and set it for the necessary three and a half hours. "Besides, I thought you said it was none of your business."

"It isn't."

Maddie laughed. She discarded the contamination-protection items in the trash as she crossed back to their office part of the lab. "And you just can't help yourself, can you? You simply have to voice your opinion and offer advice." She gave Eva a mock bump with her hip. "But I love you."

"Even when I annoy you?"

"Yes, even then."

"I still think you should tell him. Or your brother. Or someone."

"Drop it, Eva." The phone on Maddie's desk rang. She reached for it. "Forensics lab."

"Maddie?"

Her heart skipped a beat. "Hello, Nick." She turned her back on the wild grin Eva plastered across her face. "We just completed the next step in the process. Everything is right on schedule."

"Good, but that isn't why I called."

"Oh. What's up?" She sat in her chair, keeping her back turned so she couldn't see Eva or her antics.

"I was wondering . . . well, I thought maybe we could have dinner. Together. Tonight." The insecurity in his voice was such a contradiction to the way he carried himself as an FBI agent.

Something about that made her heart race even more. "Uh, sure."

"Is six good?"

Maddie glanced at her watch. "Let's make it seven thirty. I'll need to transfer the samples at five."

"Great. I'll pick you up at seven thirty."

"The gate code is pound-one-nine-eight-nine. See you then." She hung up the phone.

"You have a date with him?" Eva almost danced around her desk.

"Don't get excited. We're just going to discuss the case." He hadn't said that, but they probably would discuss it.

"Uh-huh. If you say so." Eva grinned. "Maybe you can get Darren to be willing to *discuss the case* with me."

Heat raced to Maddie's cheeks. Oh. Goodness. She was going on a date with Nick Hagar. A second date. Panic seized her. She jumped to her feet and grabbed Eva's arm. "You've got to help me."

"With what?"

"I have nothing to wear."

CHAPTER NINE

"Every time I think that I'm getting old,
and gradually going to the grave,
something else happens."
ELVIS PRESLEY

The wind pushed the leafless tree limbs as Nick made his way into the house. February had stormed into Tennessee like the blues. He'd wear his coat tonight as the news on the radio had stated the temps would drop into the twenties later.

After checking his phone's voice mail, he flipped through the snail mail. Most everything was trash. Aside from work and going to the gym, he didn't do much else. Nick dropped the mail into the trash and stopped. Where had that line of thinking come from?

His phone rang. He checked the caller ID before answering. "Hi, Mom. How are things in sunny Florida?"

"Good. Just wondering when you're going to come visit." As always, Mom's voice lifted with hope.

"I'm really swamped right now, Mom. A big case. Political." This time, he wasn't even exaggerating to avoid going.

"Oh. We just haven't seen you since Christmas. We miss you, honey."

The weekend of Christmas was enough to remind him that Dad still considered him the second-best son. Every time Nick was around his father for more than an hour, guilt over his living and Roger not nearly choked him. Not that his father ever came right out and said that, of course, but the implication was pretty clear.

"Do you think you'll make it down before Easter?"

"I don't know. This case has me pretty tied up." He'd better change the subject or his mom would start sniffling and the next thing he knew, he'd be shoving clothes in a duffel for a weekend trip to Hades. "So how is your bridge club shaping up this year?"

His mother began telling him all the details of her latest venture. His mind wandered as it did so often, to how his life might be different today if Roger hadn't been killed. His parents would probably still live here. His brother would have married Ashley and they'd probably have a kid by now. He and Dad would get along. And Nick wouldn't be furious with God.

"Nick, your dad . . . he misses you. I can tell."

He stiffened at his mother's words. "I miss you

both too, Mom. I'm just really busy with work."

"Well, if you're okay . . ."

"I'm fine." He didn't mean to sound so sharp.

"Try to come down before Easter, won't you?"

"I'll try." He glanced at his watch. "Mom, I'm sorry to cut this short, but I have someplace I need to be."

"Oh, of course, honey. I love you."

"Love you too. Tell Dad I said hello." Nick hung up the phone and ambled to the kitchen for a glass of tea. He shrugged off his unease. He had plenty of time to shower and shave before picking up Maddie for their date.

Date.

Nick hadn't realized how much he'd enjoyed their first date until she hadn't called and then he saw her at the crime scene. Especially since he hadn't been amused when he discovered she was the blind date Timmons had set him up on. Rafe's sister. Inappropriate and unacceptable. Yet highly pleasurable.

He could beat around the bush as much as he wanted, but he enjoyed being around Maddie Baxter.

His cell rang. "Hagar."

"It's Timmons, sir. The doll and message are on their way to Peter Helm."

"Excellent work. Did you get my note about Mantle's alibi?"

"I did. I'll hunt up the good professor and

try to pin down an exact time she was in class."

"Thanks." Nick glanced at his watch: almost six thirty. "Go home, Darren. Spend some time with your daughter."

"I was just about to leave but wanted you to know about the doll."

Nick waited. "Is there anything else?"

"Well, sir, it's not really related to the case. At least, I don't think so. But maybe it could be. I don't know if it's something—"

"What is it?" It wasn't like Timmons to rattle on.

"It's about Maddie, sir."

Nick set his glass of tea on the counter. "What about her?"

"Well, it seems she filed a report with Memphis police last night. Threatening phone calls. Repeatedly."

"What kind of threats?"

"The implication of her being attacked was clear."

Nick fisted and unfisted his hand. "What did Memphis PD do?"

"Took the report and advised her to change her number if the calls persisted. Wrote up the request for drive-bys to her neighborhood, if patrols could be spared."

"She only got involved in the case yesterday."

"Yes, sir."

Not likely the calls had anything to do with

Ford's murder, but . . . "What about Eva Langston? She report any threatening calls?"

"I checked. No record of it."

"Any media on the TBI team who responded?" Maybe the killer had seen her on television and targeted her.

"I haven't reviewed all the locals, but the shots I've seen weren't definitive of the people."

So it probably had nothing to do with their case, but just the thought of her receiving threats made Nick's pulse race. "How did you find out about it?"

"Well, sir . . . um. I have a friend in the police department. When Rafe left, I asked her to flag Maddie's address in the event anything came up and to make me aware."

Nick grinned. "Rafe asked you to look after his sister, did he?"

Timmons gave a nervous chuckle. "Yes, sir."

"Smart move." Then something else dawned on him. "Was I part of the looking after her? The date you set us up on?"

"Uh . . . well . . . um . . . sir . . . uh—"

"Never mind. I get it." Nick shook his head. "Does Rafe know you set us up?"

"No way." Timmons whooshed air. "I don't mean it like that. I just meant that I didn't tell him because he's so protective of his sisters."

Nick laughed. "I understand. Don't worry about it."

"Thank you, sir."

"But Timmons?"

"Yes, sir?"

"I'd sure like to see a copy of that report. And let me know if your friend passes you any additional reports about Maddie, would you?"

"I'll get that copy and keep you in the loop."

"Just to make sure the threats aren't related to the Ford case."

"Of course, sir."

Nick grinned. He wasn't fooling the man. "Good night, Timmons." He hung up and headed to the shower.

As the hot water splashed down on him, he mulled over the details. His mind could come up with a number of scenarios, but the two biggest questions were: Who would threaten to attack Maddie? Why? As Nick dressed, he determined to figure that out.

Nerves hit him during the fifteen-minute drive to Maddie's, and he couldn't explain why. Maybe it was knowing she'd been threatened. He punched in the code at the neighborhood gate and waited for the wrought-iron bars to swing open. Perhaps it was being reminded she was Rafe's sister. Or could it be he had accepted he was intrigued and attracted to her? He rolled into her driveway. No matter, he needed to get his cool on.

He sank deeper into his leather coat as he bounded up to the front entrance of her house and stepped under the two-story, bricked arch. He rang the doorbell, then glanced around the area. While her neighborhood was gated, there were numerous places outside her home for someone to hide in wait. Like in the dark space of the small flower bed between the garage and the entry. Or someone could crouch in the flower bed to the right of the front door. And he hadn't noticed a security light on the front-right corner of the house. Anybody could lurk undetected by the wooden fence surrounding the backyard if there weren't any motion-detector lights.

Why hadn't Rafe ensured his sister's property was better lit? Nick would figure out a way to make minor suggestions. Just a couple of non-offensive tips, like how she could—

The door opened and Maddie stood there, bathed in the light from behind her. Every sane thought left his head.

It was as if time froze as he took in every detail. She wore black slacks, form-fitting, that tucked into knee-high black boots. Her black sweater hugged every curve from her shoulders to mid-thigh. She had a deep red scarf around her neck that hung to her knees. A shiny band held her auburn waves off her face. She'd switched her black-rimmed glasses for metal-framed ones. But it was the smile she wore that made him forget his name.

"Hello, Nick." Her voice even sounded huskier.

"Maddie. You look beautiful." His tongue

was suddenly three times too thick for his mouth.

She smiled wider and her telltale blush flushed her cheeks. "Thank you. And you look very dashing yourself."

"Are you ready? Our reservations are for eight."

"Sure. Let me grab my coat."

He helped her slip on the long, red coat, then watched as she set her security system. At least he could feel somewhat better about that. "Have you ever thought about getting a dog? A big guard dog?" The question slipped out.

She chuckled as he led her to his car. "I hadn't thought much about it before, but Rafe's fiancée, Remington, has a beautiful dog."

Nick secured her in the front seat, then rushed around to his own. He started the car quickly, keeping the interior warm. "I didn't know what you liked to eat, so I made reservations at Folk's Folly. I hope that's okay."

Maddie grinned and fastened her seat belt. "I've never met a steak I didn't like."

And he'd never met a woman who fascinated him quite so completely.

Nick Hagar's smoldering stare should be outlawed.

Or at least registered. Women needed to be warned.

Maddie focused on his small talk about dogs

134

while her heart thumped wildly against her ribs. She'd nearly fainted when she opened the door and saw him. It was as if he'd stepped off the cover of *GQ* and onto her doorstep. The man certainly knew how to make an entrance.

"Do you have a dog?" She didn't really want to know, just wanted to hear him talk. With his voice, he'd missed his calling to be a deejay.

"With the hours I work, I can't. I'd love to have one, though."

"Yeah, I work a lot myself. Like this weekend."

"Does that happen a lot?"

She gripped the armrest as he made a sharp right turn. "We have two teams and rotate being on call as the response team. If we gather the evidence, we stay with it until completion. Less chance of contamination that way."

"Makes sense. Do you get called out a lot?"

"Depends. We had three calls in December, none in January, and this one is our first in February."

"Do you like it? Your job, I mean?"

"I do. I love it, actually."

He shot that intense stare of his at her for a moment. "What about it do you love the most?"

"I like seeing justice prevail." She pinched her lips together. Maybe she'd said that a little too glibly. "I mean, there's so much unexplained violence in the world that causes so much pain, that I like being able to help bring justice." The image of Simon Lancaster's face stamped against her memory. "That doesn't undo the horrible things, but sometimes, just sometimes, it provides a measure of comfort to know justice has been served."

He was quiet for a moment. She'd said too much. Gone too serious on a date.

"You're referring to the man who killed your parents?"

"Kind of."

"We don't have to talk about it if it's too painful for you."

"No, it's okay." She stared out the windshield into the dark. "He killed my parents because he was drunk. No amount of jail time would ever bring them back. The pain my siblings and I went through can never fully go away. But in prison, I understood he became a Christian. He apologized for his actions. Took responsibility. That's why I didn't testify at his parole hearing, even though Riley was livid."

"You didn't testify?"

"No. In my heart, I felt like he had been punished enough. His staying behind bars any longer wouldn't bring Mom and Dad back. Simon had changed."

"Because he claimed to become a Christian?"

She cut her eyes at him. "I believe he found Jesus in jail and gave his heart to Him, yes."

Rafe had said many, many times that Nick was

a good, honest man. Yet she couldn't recall him ever mentioning if Nick was a Christian or not.

"So you believe people can change?"

"I have to believe that. I don't know if I could accept living in a world where everything was set—good or bad, black or white, guilty or innocent." She watched the headlights of oncoming vehicles starburst against the windshield. "Don't you believe people can change?"

"In my experience, very rarely do I see someone change. I mean, really change." Nick pulled the car into the restaurant's lot and made a first pass, looking for a space. "I'd like to believe people can, but I just don't see it. Not enough anyway."

She clicked loose her seat belt. "But even if it's just one person who truly changes, doesn't that mean we should keep trying to let those who do change start over?"

"Is it worth it if we think someone's changed and they aren't, and they hurt someone else? I can't live with that."

"But on the flip side, look at the man who killed my parents. He changed, was released, and ended up dying taking a bullet for my sister. That saved her life." She pushed back against the seat as he whipped into a vacant parking space. "To me, yeah, it's worth it."

Nick killed the engine and shifted to face her. "I see your point, but you have to understand that situations like that are few and far between."

She nodded. "I do. But I'm willing to at least consider the possibility that people can and do change. Not every time. Not even most of the time. But sometimes. And I'm okay with that."

"Me too." He unlatched his seat belt. "You ready?"

Well, at least he could sense when they needed to agree to disagree. She smiled, letting him lighten the mood. "I'm starving. Eva and I had sandwiches at the lab."

"Then let's go. Have you eaten here before?" He slipped out of the driver's seat and was at her door to open it for her before she could reply.

"It's one of Rafe's favorite restaurants. Right behind B.B. King's on Beale Street."

"Ah. The best ribs in Memphis. Love 'em, but usually get them to go." He held her elbow as he led her to the restaurant's door. The heat transferred through the wool of her coat.

She chuckled. "They do make a mess, don't they?"

"But they are the best." He smiled at her, and Maddie's heart pounded.

This man could make her take the third chance with her heart.

Maddie Baxter confused the tar outta him.

She'd forgiven Lancaster, even when Rafe and Riley had spoken to prevent Lancaster's parole. Rafe was a Christian too, but Maddie forgave when Rafe didn't. How did that make sense? Was Maddie a more devoted Christian than her brother?

The maître d' sat them quickly, a nice table in the corner. The soft music coming from the pianist in the lounge drifted into the restaurant, providing a perfect ambiance. The enticing aroma of steaks and onions grilling made Nick's mouth water.

"What are you going to have?" He knew what he wanted . . . could almost taste it already: the Filet a la Duxelles, a petite filet piped with seasoned mushroom puree, wrapped in Applewood smoked bacon, and smothered with sliced garlic mushrooms. Medium well, of course. Nobody made prime cuts of steak quite like Folk's Folly. It'd been a tradition in Memphis since 1977.

Maddie scrunched her nose as she perused the menu. "There's so much to choose from. Can I just say yes to everything?" She chuckled.

As if. The woman was slight, probably weighed no more than a buck ten, soaking wet.

The waitress appeared table side with their iced teas and waited for their orders.

"I'll have Maker's Mark Medallions. With extra peppercorn sauce, please."

Nick gave his order, then the waitress took the menus and whisked away.

Maddie propped her chin in her hands and peered at him with those knockout chocolate eyes of hers. "So, tell me something I don't know about Special Agent in Charge Nick Hagar."

They hadn't really gotten into much on their first date. It'd been cut short when she'd gotten the call that her sister had been shot. "Well, there's not much to tell. You already know what I do."

"What are your hobbies?"

"Working out. I've run a couple of marathons and enjoyed them."

There was that cute nose wrinkle again. "What kind of music do you like?"

"Country. What about you?"

She gave a little shrug and took a sip of her tea, after she squeezed her lemon into the glass. "I actually like most all music, but I absolutely adore Elvis Presley."

That's right, he remembered hearing her singing that under her breath. "Everybody loves the King, right?"

She grinned. "What about books? Do you like to read?"

Heat teased his face. "I do. I'm an avid reader."

"Let me guess: true crime?" She chuckled.

"Ah, but you'd be wrong. I love science fiction."

She frowned. "Like outer space stuff?"

Now it was his turn to laugh. "Yeah. Like *Dune. 2001: A Space Odyssey*. All those kinds of works. Let me guess, not your thing?"

"I like to read inspirational romantic suspense. Where something bad happens but everything goes on in the end. And that there's hope. Always hope."

Her strong religious ideals were coming out to play again. "You like hope, huh?" He grinned, hoping to disarm her.

"I do." She narrowed her eyes at him. "What about you? Are you a Christian, Nick?"

He hated this question. Didn't know how to answer it honestly, really. "I believe in God, Maddie. I believe in His son, Jesus. But I'm having a hard time just accepting what happens. Too many times, I think, God sleeps on the job."

Her eyes widened. "How can you say that?"

"Because I can." His tone hardened, even though he really had no intent of doing that. "I mean, let's just say I'm having a hard time dealing with some of the things God lets happen. Can we leave it at that?"

"Okay." She took another sip of tea and nodded. "What about your family? You already know mine."

"Dad's retired Marines. Mom always the homemaker. They live in Florida now. Moved there when I was just out of college." They'd needed to get away from the memories, at least that's what Mom said. He'd always figured Dad was the one who needed to get away.

From Nick. From the reminder that Roger was taken but Nick was left behind.

"Do you have any brothers or sisters?" Maddie's

chin was back in her hands with her elbows propped on the linen tablecloth. "Terrible pests that they can be."

His throat clogged. He took a sip of tea. "I had a brother. Older. Roger, Junior." He took another sip. "He was a Marine. Died in Iraq, Desert Storm."

"Oh, I'm so sorry." Maddie reached across the table and laid her hand over his, squeezing.

"It's okay." He sure liked the feel of her hand on his. Made him almost forget the ache that he was always second to Roger in every way imaginable. And Dad had never let him forget it.

"No, it's not. I'm really sorry, Nick. I know how it hurts." The empathy in her eyes nearly had his heart and stomach swapping places. She did know. She could understand.

Yet another thing they had in common—grief.

CHAPTER TEN

"After a hard day of basic training,
you could eat a rattlesnake."
ELVIS PRESLEY

"That was perfect." Maddie set her utensils on the plate. While she'd indicated the food, she also meant the company.

She and Nick had laughed at movies they both found silly, debated political policies without either getting riled, and talked about the sad state of the nation's economy.

"Mine was excellent as well." Nick pushed aside his plate too. "Now, how about the crème brûlée for dessert?"

"I don't think I can eat any more."

"Split it?" His expression was like a child on Christmas morning and she couldn't deny him.

"Fine, but you have to eat most of it. I don't need the fifteen hundred calories."

He smoldered her with his stare. "As if you have to worry about your figure."

Her mouth went dry at the compliment. She shot down the rest of her tea. Mercy, but the man twisted her up at times.

"I have a strange question for you."

"Okay."

"You and Eva . . . you're pretty close friends, right?"

She nodded. Where was he going with this? If he asked for Eva's number, she'd smack him.

"And do y'all ever have . . . spats?"

"Spats?" Where on earth had he come up with that?

"You know, times where you get into arguments and go for weeks without really speaking?"

She recalled the silent lunch. "All the time."

"Seriously?" His eyes popped open wide.

She chuckled. "Yes. Close friends will argue and then go for weeks, sometimes even months, without speaking, then fall right back into the same friendship." She shrugged. "It's the way women's friendships work. Rafe never understood it."

"Me either."

"Why do you ask?"

"Oh, someone I interviewed said that and I just didn't understand."

"It's because you're a guy." And was she ever thankful he was.

He grinned back. "I guess."

Maddie leaned forward, dusting crumbs off the table. "So, tell me why you chose the FBI."

"You know, I've been asked that many times over the course of my career, usually when under consideration for a promotion."

She waited. "That's not really an answer, you know."

"I know." He shot her a sheepish half smile. "I guess I wanted to do something that mattered with my life."

"You didn't consider going into the Marines, like your father and brother?"

Nick stiffened. Ah, she'd hit a sore spot. "No, much to my father's disappointment. He thought there was no question I'd join right behind him and Roger. I just never felt the strong pull to the military. I always wanted to be working for the right side in the civilian realm, so to speak. Then, after Roger died . . . well, it was better I'd gone into a different field."

"I see." She smiled across at him. "I bet your parents are so proud of you." It hurt that her parents hadn't lived to see her reach the level of success in her career that balanced her. Or met Remington and Hayden.

"Yeah. Sure."

But he didn't sound so sure. Before she could ask anything further, the waitress came and took their dessert and coffee order, then disappeared again. The staff at Folk's Folly was well trained and extremely professional. Unobtrusive. It was one of the reasons so many business deals were set upstairs in the private dining rooms.

"What about you? Forensic science. Proving people's guilt or innocence."

"I love science. Like figuring out the pieces of the puzzle. Not so wild about testifying in court, but it's part of the job."

"But you help bring criminals to justice."

"And help stop infractions of injustice."

"What do you mean?" He cocked his head.

"For instance, the hearing I testified at a few weeks ago. A convicted sex offender. His defense attorney resubmitted fluid samples from the crime scene. We ran the DNA and it didn't match. The man, while creepy, was innocent of the crime he was incarcerated for. He was released based on my testimony."

Nick leaned forward, pinning her to the chair with the intensity of his stare. "But you think he's guilty?"

"No. I think he's a creep. And he's probably guilty of something, but not this particular one."

"But if he's guilty of something . . ."

She shook her head, voicing the battle she had with herself all the time. "It's not my job to find a crime he is guilty of. My job is to run the tests, evaluate and analyze the results, and base my testimony on science." She swallowed. "Science doesn't lie." Even when she desperately wished the results were different.

"What hearing?"

She nodded. "The one that set Mark Hubble free. It was all over the news."

His face twisted into a grimace. "I normally avoid the media, and that means the news by extension, but I remember this highlight. That guy is scum of the earth."

"I agree."

"But you helped set him free? On a technicality?"

She shook her head, defiance threatening to rear its ugly head. "No, on science. Because I ran those results a half-dozen times. So did Eva. Peter went over every spec and technical data line by line, looking to see if we'd made any mistake. Then our scientist supervisor ran the tests yet again. All to the same conclusion: Mark Hubble's DNA was not at the scene of the crime."

His face wore an expression of horror.

Nick waited to reply until the waitress had

delivered their coffees and crème brûlée. "Does it bother you?"

She set down the cup, a little hard so the whipped cream of her latte splashed to the saucer. "Of course it bothers me. I hate seeing men like that go free. I detest looking into their smirking faces and know they'll be on the street again to terrorize other women." She tented her hands over the steaming mug. "But it's my job. Evaluating data and reporting the conclusions, good or bad. My personal preference in how the results turn out doesn't factor into the considerations."

He shook his head as he scooped a spoonful of the French vanilla custard, flavored with hazelnut liqueur. "I guess I'm so on the case-building end that what you're telling me sounds counter-productive."

The coolness in his voice straightened her spine. She took another sip of coffee. "I suppose it sounds that way, but I'm sure the prosecution's best friend when the results help convict."

He held up his hands in mock surrender. "Sorry, I meant no offense. It's just hard for me to grasp."

She lifted her spoon. "Sometimes it's hard for me as well. Especially when everyone makes out like it's all my fault. Like I choose to let monsters out." She remembered the iciness in the caller's voice. The sobs of that woman. "I don't have a choice at all."

"I never considered it from your angle. That's

got to be hard." He slipped a spoonful into his mouth, swallowed, then swiped a napkin over his lips. "Speaking of things from your angle, why don't you tell me about the threatening phone calls you reported to Memphis PD?"

She set her spoon on the edge of her saucer. "How did you know about that?" Had he been checking up on her? Looking into her for some reason? Did it have anything to do with all these questions and nonimplications/implications?

He smiled, almost seductively. "I *am* an FBI agent, remember? I get paid to know things."

"I don't think anyone's paying you to keep up with me." His assertion that he was an agent as if that made everything okay rubbed against her. It was the same with Rafe—just because he was FBI, he thought he was the big, bad protector. It didn't seem to matter that she was a commissioned law enforcement officer who carried a gun. Or was it that he was a man and she a woman?

"Whoa. Didn't mean to hit a nerve or offend." He looked innocent enough. "I just keep my ears open about everyone involved in any case I'm working. Especially one with such political overtones as this one. I expect all the crazies to come out to play."

Oh. Now she felt like a jerk, just like Eva had called her. "I'm sorry. Just a little sensitive about the perception I can't take care of myself."

He chuckled. "Oh, I know Rafe, so I can only imagine. I didn't mean to imply you can't take care of yourself. I just wanted to know what was going on."

"Sorry I overreacted." She took a sip of her coffee that had cooled quite a bit. "It's just some crank. Called first with a woman sobbing, then again with a man asking me how I'd feel if I was attacked." She would never forget his voice. Gun on nightstand or not, his threatening tone had kept her tossing until the wee hours of the morning.

But no more than the memory of Nick's voice had.

Maddie scared off every preconceived notion he ever thought of women. While beautiful and nothing but feminine, she wasn't squeamish like some women, nor was she so determined to be *one of the guys* like some of the female agents in the bureau.

Just when he thought he had a grasp on her, she showed another side to her personality. The woman had to have a zillion facets. Funny thing was, he enjoyed learning about each and every one. Except maybe when she had to testify to release criminals.

"Do you think it has anything to do with the Hubble hearing?"

She nodded. "More than likely. That's the first

thing I thought. Either someone who feels like he has to stand up for the victim, or a member of society who believes in public outcry."

"What did the police say about that?"

She smiled as she set her napkin on the table. "What do you think? Same spiel as usual—we'll file the report, try to get a unit to drive by and monitor your neighborhood even though we're so short staffed, blah, blah, blah."

Wasn't that always the way with local police? "Yep, same old runaround." He motioned for the waitress to bring the check. "I noticed you used your security system tonight. Do you use it all the time?"

Her eyes narrowed a fraction.

"Just asking because I'm concerned, not because I don't think you can handle yourself. I'd ask the same question of any of my agents in the same situation."

"Yes, I use it religiously."

"Can I get you anything else?" The waitress appeared at his elbow.

He shook his head. "No, thank you."

She slipped the leather padfolio on the table at his right hand. He pushed his American Express card inside, then set it back on the edge of the table. He stared into Maddie's eyes, quite certain he could get lost in their darkness if he let himself. "I see so many people who have them and never use them. Some people act like the sign of the security service on the door is enough of a deterrent."

The waitress rushed past, grabbing the padfolio in a fluid movement.

"Seems like a terrible waste of money to do that." Maddie flipped her hair over her shoulder, wafting the clean scent of her shampoo over the table. "You don't have to worry about me, though. I follow all safety measures and I carry a gun." Her scent tickled his senses.

He shifted in his seat. She made him want to fidget. "So, what's on your agenda for tomorrow?"

She glanced at her watch. "Actually, I'm due back in the lab at four thirty."

"In the morning?" Was she serious?

"Yes." Maddie chuckled. "Did you think the samples prepped themselves and walked from one instrument to the other?"

"No, but I thought you put them on at five and it would take at least twelve hours."

The waitress returned and handed him the padfolio. "Y'all come back and see us again. Have a good evening."

"Thank you." He added a tip, signed his name, stuck the credit card back into his wallet, then stood. He took Maddie's elbow as she stood as well.

"It takes twelve and a half hours, actually. But we need to be there at least an hour before the cycle is finished to sterilize, clean, and prepare for the data review and interpretation."

The wind whistled as they crossed the parking lot with ducked heads. Bitter cold crept through their coats. The faint hint of rain carried on the gusts. A thunderstorm was scheduled for later tonight.

Nick sat Maddie in the front seat of his car, then got behind the steering wheel. He started the engine and blew on his hands. "Wish they'd invent a car with instant heat."

"That'd be nice." She fastened her seat belt and stuck her hands under her thighs.

"It'll warm up soon—"

His cell phone chimed. He jerked it off his hip. "Hagar."

"Have you seen the news promo?" Timmons's excitement wasn't necessarily an indication of a good thing.

"What?"

"I caught it on commercial from one of Savannah's shows. It's Senator Ford. Talking about his daughter's murder."

Nick sighed. "Just great. I'm sure it'll hit all the locals at ten."

"Thought you'd want a heads-up."

"Thanks, Darren. Now, go put your daughter to bed."

"Night, Boss."

How much damage would the senator do to the case?

"Bad news?" Maddie asked.

He shoved the phone back on his hip and put the car in reverse. "Promo of Senator Ford addressing the public. News at ten."

"Oh." She paused as he pulled out of the restaurant's parking lot. "That's bad?"

"Yeah. Until we get a break in the case, we prefer controlling what information is put out to the public."

"Ah. I see."

He chanced a glance at her before turning in front of oncoming traffic. "You disagree?"

"Not at all. Especially if you have reason for withholding specific information. But in this case, when you really don't have much this early, what could he tell the public that could harm the case?"

The senator didn't know his daughter's murderer and Hailey's weren't the same. He didn't know about the doll and the threat.

"Well, actually, not as much as I'd initially thought, now that you asked me." He let out a breath as he steered toward Maddie's subdivision. "But still, I wish he'd clear his statements through our office." Nick could see her grin by the dashboard light. "What?"

She shook her head. "Are all you FBI guys control freaks?"

"Me, a control freak? Surely you jest." But he couldn't help grinning himself. He'd been called a control freak more than once. And stubborn. Muleheaded. Pigheaded.

"Ah, it *is* something taught at the academy. For years I've suspected this, now I know it to be true." Her laughter caused a tightening reaction in his gut.

And that perfume she wore? Vanilla and spice, yet earthy too—whatever it was, he'd never be able to smell it again and not think of Maddie Baxter.

He pulled up to her subdivision's gate, punched in the code, then slowly headed to her house. He parked the car in the driveway, then rushed to open the door for her. The wind nearly knocked him over as he helped her from the car.

Thunder rumbled overhead. Flickers flashed in the distance. The promised storm would arrive right on time.

Nick hurried to her front door.

She pulled out her keys from her purse, then unlocked the door. Was she trembling from the cold or from being so close to him? He hoped it was the latter because all of a sudden, he felt like a teenager out on his first date with the prom queen.

The beeps echoed in the foyer as she turned off the alarm system. She let out a slow breath. "Would you like a cup of coffee?" Her voice was even throatier than usual.

His gut reacted but his head prevailed. This was one woman he didn't want to scare off. "I would, but I know you have an early morning."

But man, did he ever want to stay for a cup of coffee, a glass of water, anything.

"And you need to do damage control over whatever the senator puts in his statement."

"I do. But I'll call you tomorrow, okay?"

She nodded. "And I'll have the results for you in the afternoon."

He knew he should just tell her good night and head home to watch the newscast, but his feet refused to budge.

Maddie turned to him. Light spilled from another room, washing her in light akin to candlelight. "I had a really lovely time tonight. Thank you."

He leaned forward . . . slowly . . . taking a single step toward her. He put his arms around her waist and drew her closer. The scent that was all Maddie and nothing else wrapped around him, smothering him like a security blanket.

Nick leaned down and placed a kiss on her cheek. "I had a wonderful time too." It took every command to force his muscles to release her. "I'll talk to you tomorrow."

"Good night." Maddie's voice was barely a whisper.

He turned and jogged back to his car and slammed the door before he forgot himself.

Now the score was even between them. Maddie Baxter had just schooled him about what *go stupid* meant.

CHAPTER ELEVEN

"From the time I was a kid, I always knew
something was going to happen to me.
Didn't know exactly what."
ELVIS PRESLEY

"I think you might be right."

Eva looked up from her desk and met Maddie's stare. "I usually am, but what am I right about, specifically, this time?"

Maddie chuckled. "About me being scared of risking my heart again. That all men aren't like Adam and Kevin." She'd lain awake for hours last night and come to the brilliant conclusion that neither jerk could even come close to comparison with Nick Hagar.

"Hallelujah. It's about time you saw the light of day." Eva reached for her coffee. "So, I'm taking it the date went well last night?"

"I had a wonderful time." As she'd replayed Nick's and her discussion over and over last night, she realized how much she truly enjoyed being in his company. And she knew for a fact he was honest and single. Two of her requirements met. She just needed to find out if he met the rest of them.

"Well, good." Eva slurped her coffee. "I

wondered why you were all smiley and cheery at four in the morning."

Thunder roared outside, trembling the walls inside the crime unit. The storm had blown in around eleven, just as forecasted. It hadn't let up all morning. The drive in had not only been dark, but gloomy as well.

She *had* woken up in a great mood, despite the few hours of sleep she'd had. *"Is your heart filled with pain, shall I come back again?"* she sang softly.

"Please don't." Eva shook her head. "I can't handle Elvis this early in the morning."

"Tell me, dear, are you lonesome tonight?" she sang a bit louder.

"Stop!" Eva covered her ears and groaned. "Hey, all kidding aside, did you get any more threatening phone calls?"

Maddie took a sip of her own coffee. "There were ten missed calls, so I just didn't turn the phone on. I figured if anyone needed me, they'd call my cell. I'll call the phone company tomorrow and get my number changed."

"You seem awfully blasé about it."

She shrugged. "What can I do? I utilize my security system, live in a gated community, and I sleep with my gun on my bedside table. There's not much more I can do." She smiled. "Except maybe get a dog."

"Get a dog? What kind of nonsense is that? Why would you want a dog?"

Maddie laughed. "I don't, really."

"Then why bring it up? Have you lost your mind? A dog? Why in tarnation would you even think about that?"

Maddie couldn't help herself—she laughed harder. "My soon-to-be sister-in-law has a really cool dog." She snorted.

Eva narrowed her eyes. "I don't know what you find so amusing. Dogs. You have to feed them, walk them, clean up after them."

Swallowing the laughter, Maddie ducked her head. It'd been some time since she was in such a good mood so early in the morning on a day she'd missed church, when she had less sleep than she required and had outside stress smacking her from all sides. Taking all that into consideration, she'd come to the conclusion that Nick Hagar could be quite good for her mental health.

When he'd leaned in to her last night and planted that feathery kiss on her cheek—mercy, her knees almost went weak. The man smelled almost as good as he looked.

"So, are you seeing Nick again?"

Maddie couldn't stop the smile from stretching across her face again. "He's going to call me later this morning."

"Told you so. I do love being right." Eva stood and stretched, then checked the clock on the wall. "It's about that time. Run's almost complete."

Maddie opened the software program on her

computer. "Hey, will you turn on the radio? I want to hear the news."

"Seriously?"

"Yeah. Just the news, then you can turn it off."

"Who are you and what have you done with my best friend?"

"Or we could listen to the Elvis station. *A little less conversation, a little more action please.*"

"Oh, please stop."

"*All this aggravation ain't satisfactioning me.*"

"Okay, I'll turn on the news. Just please, stop singing Elvis songs. You're gonna make me hurl my coffee at you." Eva moved toward the radio in the office. "And you know how much I hate to waste good coffee."

Maddie giggled as Eva flipped on the radio, then set it to the local all-news station before heading into the lab area to wait for the run to complete. The station's commercial ended and the newscaster returned on air.

"Is this the work of a serial killer? Should our young women be warned?" Mary Peters, area investigative reporter, asked over the airwaves.

"Young women should always be vigilant, Mary." Senator Ford's voice sounded as it usually did. "I haven't been told this is the work of a serial killer. All I can say for certain is my daughter was murdered—stabbed three times in the chest. If those wounds are similar to Hailey

Carter's, I can't say. I'm not in law enforcement nor am I a medical examiner."

"What are the police saying?"

"I haven't spoken with the local police. I've dealt only with the FBI. Special Agent in Charge Nicholas Hagar."

Oh no. Maddie cringed, imagining how Nick would hit the roof if he hadn't already.

"I've been told forensic evidence is being processed—fingerprints, DNA . . . stuff like that. My staff inquiries reveal results should be forthcoming this week."

Nick was really going to have a cow. So would Peter.

"They have concluded their evidence gathering at my daughter's home already, as well as her car, which is where her body was found." A heavy pause. "I'm sure everyone can understand that passing bills for harsher sentences for those who commit violent crimes is my primary focus during this most difficult time."

Was this man really using his daughter's death as a political move?

Eva handed Maddie a large stack of papers, each containing data she would review to determine the DNA profiles from all samples taken at the crime scene. "Can we turn off the radio now?"

"Yeah." She grabbed the papers and pulled her hair back into a ponytail. Eva would independently run the same. They would then perform a statistical analysis using their special computer program to determine how frequently these specific DNA profiles appear in the human population. Finally, they would each generate a report that effectively summarized all of the scientific findings of the case.

Eva flipped off the radio, then sat at her station. They worked in silence, full concentration on their work for two and a half hours before Maddie stood. "About to generate my report. How about you?"

"Give me ten more minutes."

Maddie stretched. "I'm going to the ladies' room. Want me to bring you back a fresh cup of coffee?"

"Please!"

She left the lab, walking down the dim hallway. The unit was eerily silent, save the storm rumbling outside.

"Maddie."

She turned back to the door to the lab. Eva's head stuck out. "Hurry up. Peter just called. The director's on his way to talk with us. The whole team's been assembled."

The director? Something serious must be coming down the pike because the director had only made an appearance in the lab a handful of times in the ten years Maddie had worked for TBI. And on a Sunday . . . before eight?

Dear Lord, please don't let there have been another murder.

• • •

He could strangle the senator.

Nick had spent the better part of last night on the phone with the bureau's public relations officer and the senator's staff. No matter what he or the state's district attorney said, the man seemed bound and determined to continue spouting off at the mouth regarding his daughter's murder. And he didn't seem to care that it could jeopardize the case.

Matter-of-fact, he seemed more determined to go even further public once the bureau had requested he stop. What kind of father did that?

A political one.

Nick had heard Ford's multiple interviews and replays of them. They were getting more airtime in one six-hour segment than Hailey Carter's murder had entirely.

"Hey, Boss." Timmons hovered in the doorway to Nick's office.

"What are you doing here, Darren? It's your day off."

"I know. I'm out picking up Krispy Kreme donuts for Savannah and her sitter, Kimi, per Madam Savannah's instructions, but forgot to put this report on your desk and figured you might want to see it today." He handed Nick a folder.

Nick opened it and glanced at the name on the top sheet. "Leo Ward."

"Basically, he's clean. Several issues with

authority, but he's never been charged with so much as a speeding ticket. Almost too clean."

Those usually indicated they either had someone doing their dirty work for them, or they had someone who cleaned up after them. "I think I might pay Mr. Ward a visit later this afternoon."

"I'm going with you."

"No, you're spending time with your daughter. I can handle Ward by myself."

"Sir, with all due respect, I'd really like to come with you." Timmons had been busting at the seams to prove himself since Rafe left. Rafe Baxter had voluntarily moved to the Arkansas location and thereby postponed any possible promotion so Timmons could stay in Memphis where his daughter's doctors were.

"Okay. Meet me here at four. Maybe we can hit Ward when he's having dinner."

"Thanks." Timmons ducked out of the office.

His cell phone buzzed. "Hagar."

"Where are you?" The FBI's head PR officer growled in Nick's ear.

"At my desk, of course. Where else would I be?"

"That might not be the best place for you. Did you hear the latest? Senator Ford's set to appear on the morning show in less than fifteen. Channel three."

"He'll probably just repeat everything he said at ten. And eleven." But Nick reached for his remote anyway. He flipped the television to channel three, then muted it.

"According to my source at the television station, he's going to announce that his daughter was not murdered by the same person who murdered Hailey Carter."

Nick dropped his pen to the desk. "How does he know that?"

"We don't know, Hagar. Is it true? Can we demand the station hold it as it's false information?"

"No."

"Then how in all that's holy does he know?"

"I don't know, but I'll find out."

"You'd better hurry or the public's gonna be knocking on your door. In case you missed it, he's naming you as his contact person. Naturally, everyone is going to assume you're the one who is giving him information on the case."

"I know."

"I'll do what I can to defuse him. I have a couple of personal security people lined up to be interviewed to discuss common safety protocols."

"That won't distract what Ford tells the general public."

"No, and my source informs me that he's already called the mayor this morning."

As if Nick's day wasn't bad enough already?

"Oh, and one more thing?"

"Yeah?"

"There are media vans outside the office already. Being held outside the fence, of course, but you know how the vultures are."

Nick expelled a breath. "Great."

"I'll call you when I learn anything else. Until then, turn your television on. He's about to go live."

"I'm watching it." Nick shut his cell and unmuted the television. He leaned forward, focusing as the camera pulled in close on Senator Ford's ebony face.

"While my wife and I are deeply grieving the violent loss of our beloved daughter, we are relieved that forensics reveal there isn't a serial killer in our midst."

"All of us here at the station are deeply sorry for your loss, Senator." The female interviewer managed to work an angle where she looked as if she might cry.

"Thank you. I can't even begin to describe the enormous pain my wife and I have had to endure over the past twenty-four hours."

"I'm sure."

"But as I said, the entire university campus is breathing easier now that it's confirmed there isn't a serial killer on the loose, preying on our young college ladies."

"What evidence is that, Senator?"

"It's been proven that my daughter was not killed by the same man who took poor Hailey Carter's life."

"How is that, exactly?"

"Forensics, of course. The stab wounds weren't the cause of death in the case of my dear Gina."

Nick balled his hands into fists.

"They weren't?"

"No, Gina's cause of death was a broken neck."

Nick leapt to his feet. There was no way he could know that. Someone had to have leaked the information to him, but who?

"We were told she'd been stabbed." The interviewer looked confused.

"She *was* stabbed. Three times, just like Hailey."

"But if her neck was broken?"

Senator Ford stared directly into the camera. "Someone killed my daughter, then stabbed her as he'd heard reported on the news about Ms. Carter, we can only assume to make the police think it was the same murderer."

Nick paced, stomping his feet harder and harder with each pass on the worn carpet. His eyes never left the television monitor.

"Rest assured, Nick Hagar at the FBI is working with the forensic lab at the Tennessee Bureau of Investigation, and they are processing the forensic evidence as we speak. They will find the person who did this. I've been assured by the district attorney that they will bring this person to justice and will seek the harshest sentence possible."

"The death penalty?" The interviewer interrupted Ford's tirade.

He stared at her, then looked directly back into the camera. It panned closer, just so you could see Ford's eyes, nose, and mouth. "I won't rest until I see this monster sentenced to death. I'm also sponsoring a bill to decrease the time inmates are on death row. Why should citizens' tax dollars be spent providing necessities to those criminals who have robbed upstanding citizens of their loved ones?" He slammed his fist on the counter. "They shouldn't."

The camera focused on the interviewer. "There you have it, ladies and gentlemen, a father in the throes of grief, but a senator determined to take the tough stands for his constituents."

Nick flipped off the television, then tossed the remote onto his desk. His day had barely started and already had gone from bad to worse.

CHAPTER TWELVE

"I don't think I'm bad for people. If I did think I was bad for people, I would go back to driving a truck, and I really mean this."
ELVIS PRESLEY

"Here he is." Peter straightened as the director waltzed into the lab. Peter hadn't had three seconds to warn Maddie, Eva, Ivan, Kurt, and Neal what bee had climbed in the director's bonnet this early on a Sunday morning. For him to come out in the raging storm and bring in the entire team, it had to be of the utmost importance. And since money was always an issue . . .

"Ladies and gentlemen." The director shucked off his coat and passed it to his assistant who looked an awful lot like the fictionalized Oliver Twist. "I appreciate you all coming in so quickly." He stood a little under six feet but was stocky. Portly, even. "We have a situation both the mayor and the governor have so generously brought to my immediate attention."

Kurt and Neal shifted from their seats on the edge of Maddie's desk, the only place left to sit. Maddie and Eva sat at their desks while Ivan and Peter perched on the edge of Eva's desk which was closest to the door. The rest of the building sat as silent as a tomb.

"It seems someone has released confidential information regarding a crime scene to an unauthorized person." The director's thinning gray hair sparkled under the stark fluorescent overhead lights.

The senator, of course. Maddie swallowed.

"I'm not accusing anyone here, of course, but I'm reiterating policy that you are not at liberty to discuss any evidence on any case except to properly authorized persons."

"Sir, most of us have heard about Senator Ford's public statements from last night and this morning." Peter stood, addressing his boss. "I can assure you, none of my team has spoken with the senator, even in passing."

The director flashed a condescending smile—er, expression. "Mr. Helm, I appreciate you standing up for your team, but it is unnecessary at this point. What I am stressing is the reminder for everyone affiliated with the case to remember not to speak to unauthorized persons."

Peter slumped back to the edge of Eva's desk.

The director ran his gaze over the team before continuing. "It's been released that forensic evidence has proven the two girls' murders are not related. Since we hold the forensic evidence, it is implied the information was released from this office." He held up his hands as Ivan groaned and Peter stood again. "I'd like to know where we stand on the forensic testing. Perhaps that will enable me to find where confidential information has seeped past our safeguards."

"We were able to secure a clean, complete fingerprint from the car door at the crime scene. We ran it through AFIS. No match was found. We turned it over to the FBI agent overseeing the case, Agent Nick Hagar, and he was to run it through the bureau's IAFIS."

"Did he get a match?" the director asked.

Ivan shrugged. "He doesn't report back to us, sir."

"Hagar, you say?"

He was going to blame the leak on Nick? Maddie shot to her feet. "Agent Hagar wouldn't release information. He was furious the senator was addressing the public. He fought to have the senator's press officer get in contact with Peter for approved statements."

The director glanced at Peter.

Nodding, Peter stood again. "He did, sir. We've stressed to the senator's press team how vital it is to keep details of the investigation out of the public, but the senator is adamant about using the media."

"You should have stressed it more strenuously." The director turned back to Maddie, who hadn't yet sat back down. "Madeline Baxter, isn't it?"

She nodded.

"So this FBI agent was furious?"

"Yes, sir."

"Interesting." He ran a finger over his bottom lip. "Where are you and Ms. Langston in the process of DNA analysis?"

Maddie straightened her back. "We've almost concluded our analysis and conclusion report. We should have it to Peter within the hour. Once he and our science supervisor, Dr. Sebrowski, verify and attest the reports, we'll run any unknown samples through our local system and see if we get a match."

The director nodded. "Very good. But if we don't get a match?" He knew all this. Was he testing her?

She took a deep breath. "Then Dr. Sebrowski will contact the Nashville office for the CODIS administrator to upload the samples into the national database, and we'll pray we get a hit."

"Have you been in discussion with this Agent Hagar regarding the case, Ms. Baxter?"

Maddie licked her lips. "Yes, sir. I believe it was your directive that we coordinate with Agent Hagar and the FBI." *"With the rain in my shoes . . ."*

One of the director's eyebrows shot up. "I believe the word I used, Ms. Baxter, was *liaise*. I instructed the team to liaise with the FBI at the crime scene." He narrowed his eyes at her.

"Searching for you . . ." His statement didn't require a response, so she stood her ground. She wouldn't flinch under his scathing stare. She'd endured much worse.

"Oh. Yes. Isn't your brother with the FBI, Ms. Baxter?"

"In the cold Kentucky rain." "Yes, sir. He's an agent based in the Little Rock, Arkansas field office."

"I see." His tone left little mystery as to what he saw.

A heavy pause filled the lab.

Peter cleared his throat. "Sir, it's very unfortunate there has been a breach of security regarding the information, but I can assure you, our team members follow set policy and protocol regarding safeguarding of evidence and information regarding that evidence."

"It doesn't appear so in this case, does it, Mr. Helm?" The director crossed his arms over his chest, his stance as wide as his shoulder width.

"Sir, again, I assure you the information was not released by any of our team members."

The director glared at Maddie. "Not even to the FBI?"

The lab grew as threatening as the raging storm outside.

Eva stood and flashed her highest-wattage smile at the director. "Sir, our physical tests weren't even concluded until after five this morning. Maddie and I have been in the lab alone since then, reviewing the data, analyzing, and generating our reports. This early, there's nothing to tell the FBI, or anyone else for that matter." She blinked her eyes, her lashes fluttering.

"I heard on the news this morning that the senator commented on the cause of death not being the same in his daughter's case as that other girl's. Wouldn't that information come from the medical examiner's office, not us?" Peter pivoted slightly, addressing the director face-to-face.

"As I said, Mr. Helm, I'm not accusing anyone."

Maddie crossed her arms and refused to sit down again. Sure . . . he wasn't accusing anyone. Just implying someone in the room had leaked the information.

"I'm merely ensuring proper procedure regarding the release of information is followed."

Right. Like any of the team believed that.

Peter nodded. "And I assure you, sir, that we have been and will continue to follow such procedure to a T."

The two men stared at one another. Maddie's admiration for Peter grew as the men each held their ground. She'd never seen Peter so assertive. It was impressive.

Finally, the director nodded. "See that it stays that way." He let his glare settle on Maddie. "I'll look forward to hearing the results of your reports."

"They'll be sent to Peter and Dr. Sebrowski for verification within an hour."

"Then I'll let you get back to work." He snapped at his assistant and held out his hand for his coat. "All of you back to work." He stuffed himself into his coat and marched from the room without another word, his assistant trailing two steps to one of the director's.

No one said a word for a long moment.

"Well, *that* was fun." Leave it to Eva to break the uncomfortable silence. She clapped her hands. "Y'all get out of our lab—Maddie and I have to finish those reports and get them out within an hour, or I'm afraid the director will order us beheaded." She laughed, but the tension lingered like the stench of formaldehyde.

"Man, I didn't say anything to anyone besides

Agent Hagar, and it's policy to ask the FBI to run fingerprints through IAFIS if we don't get a hit through AFIS." Ivan ran a hand over his jagged-cut black hair.

"Don't worry about it. We know the leak isn't here. The director's just got the mayor and governor chewing his case, so he's got to chew someone else's. That's us." Peter clapped Ivan's shoulder. "Go home and get some rest. Forget about this morning."

Ivan nodded and ambled out of the lab. Kurt followed behind, leaving only Neal.

"What is it, Neal?" Peter asked.

"That doll and letter you asked me to run tests on?"

Peter nodded.

"Is it connected to this case?"

"It doesn't matter. Have you gotten the results yet?"

Neal nodded. "Sir, the items are forensically clean. Not a fiber, not a print, not anything. I've checked and rechecked. Used ALS. It's as if both haven't had contact with any human at all. I've never seen anything like it."

"Just put the report on my desk, please, and secure the items. Thank you."

Smiling shyly at Eva, Neal backed out of the lab.

Peter turned back to Eva and Maddie. "Looks like that's a dead end."

"We'll bring you the DNA report as soon as it's

done, Peter. You might want to go ahead and get Dr. Sebrowski on her way in. It might take her longer because of the weather." Eva moved, blocking his access to Maddie.

He hesitated, then headed to the door. "I'll wait in my office."

Eva paused until he'd shut the door behind him before she spun and faced Maddie. "What's going on?"

Maddie sat at her desk and stared at her screen. "Everyone's furious with the senator because he's talking to the press, but nobody can come down heavy on him, so everyone else is getting read the riot act."

"What about Nick?"

Maddie hit the print sequence before leaning back and staring at Eva. "What about Nick? He's livid too, but not much he can do about it."

"No, I mean, he was telling us basically the same information that was leaked."

Heat burned in Maddie's gut. "Are you saying you think Nick leaked the information to the senator?" She shook her head. "No way. He wanted to throttle Senator Ford. I saw his face when he found out."

"Maybe, and just hear me out before you react, but maybe he told the senator the information in confidence and got mad when he learned the senator was going public with it."

Eva couldn't be accusing Nick of this. Maddie

175

pressed her lips together, struggling to keep her unfiltered comments trapped inside her. No way would Nick ever put his case in such a situation. He hated the press getting involved. They'd just discussed this last night.

Maddie shook her head. "I hear what you're saying, Eva, but no, it's not possible. Nick guards the case facts too closely to tell the senator, knowing how the man likes to preen in front of a camera so much."

"If you're sure . . . you know him better than I do." Eva returned to her desk. "I've got two more lines to finish, then I'm done."

"I'm grabbing mine off the printer." Maddie moved to take the stack of papers, but her mind reeled as she did.

Had Nick's empathy for a grieving father caused him to share too much with the senator?

Nick smiled at the caller ID screen on his cell. "Hi, Maddie." He'd called earlier today but had been routed to leave a message on voice mail. He'd been too disappointed—something he didn't want to think about, couldn't think about—to leave a message.

"Sorry I missed you earlier." He leaned back in his chair.

"I was in a meeting with the director here." Something about her voice seemed . . . distant . . . off.

"Yeah. Helm called me and told me there wasn't anything on some evidence I'd sent over. We just can't seem to get a break in this case."

"I'm sorry." Her tone sounded reserved.

He sat up, plopping his feet onto the floor. "Is everything okay? You sound different."

"I'm fine. Peter and Dr. Sebrowski have verified the DNA results."

"And?" He lifted his pen.

"Most of the samples are a match with Gina Ford." All professional, as if she didn't know him.

As in most cases, the vast majority were matches to the victim. "Any that weren't?" He held his breath. He needed this break.

"There is one unknown sample confirmed."

Yes! "From the blood you found on her back?"

"Yes. We've run it through our local database as well as NIBIN. Neither resulted in hits." Her tone was almost monotone as she gave the results from the National Integrated Ballistics Information Network.

Thunder rattled the windows in his office.

"Are you sure you're okay, Maddie? Have you gotten any more threatening calls?"

"I'm fine." She let out a breath. "We've sent the sample to our Nashville office to run them through the state and national CODIS system." Hopefully, Nashville would get results from the Combined DNA Index System sooner rather than later.

Lightning lit up the cloud-darkened Tennessee sky with its jagged finger splitting the atmosphere.

"Great. I'll call the Knoxville FBI office and see if I can get an agent to Nashville to speed things up."

"It normally takes a few days up to a week for results."

"We don't have that long. Not as long as the senator keeps making his press appearances."

Her breathing hitched over the connection. Almost as if she held it, then released. Not at all natural.

"Maddie, what's wrong? What aren't you telling me?" If there was any chance something was wrong with the evidence on this case . . .

"There's no way you mentioned any specifics about the case to the senator, is there? I mean, inadvertently, of course."

He tightened his grip on his cell. Had she just accused him of . . . ? "Excuse me? Are you actually asking if I jeopardized my case by feeding the media confidential information via the senator?"

"I'm sorry, Nick. I didn't think so, I just—"

"Why would you ask?" How could she even consider he'd do such a thing? Didn't she know him better?

The storm outside reached a fever pitch. A siren wailed in the distance from the street below.

"The TBI director had a meeting with the team, reaming us because of the senator's announcement. Since Senator Ford said forensic evidence had proven the murders weren't committed by the same person, and we're the ones who processed all the forensic evidence . . ."

"He accused your team of leaking the information." He'd heard the director was a real piece of work. A puppet for politicians. "The mayor and governor contacted him when they did me, asking us to work together on the case. I'm sure he's getting the firestorm like the rest of us since the senator pulled his little press-conference stunt."

"So you can see why I had to ask. You understand since we just discussed this yesterday, right?"

He swallowed.

"Nick?" Her throaty voice abated his disappointment and anger.

"I can see the logic, but I thought you knew me better. That you wouldn't even have to ask."

"I'm sorry, Nick. So sorry." Her voice cracked, then the connection broke.

He shut the cell and tossed it on his desk. He'd hurt her feelings, but she should have known him better.

It hurt that she'd had to ask.

"You ready?" Timmons waited outside Nick's office.

He snatched his keys and cell, then joined

Timmons. As they drove to Leo Ward's address, Nick brought Timmons up-to-date with all the lab results.

"Man, we needed something. I'd hoped for a break of some kind."

Nick turned the car into Ward's driveway and parked. "Me too. Me too."

Lights blazed inside the home. The roar from a television greeted them as they knocked on the front door of the comfortable split-level house. Timmons had been thorough in his report. Leo Ward, fifty-eight, had been married to Miranda for twenty-two years. Together, they had one daughter, Virgo, nineteen, and one son, Aries, seventeen. Middle-classers right down to the Labrador family pet. Modest home. American-made cars in the garage. All blondes with blue eyes, they were the poster family for the all-American image.

A woman in her fifties answered the door. "Yes?" She wore a pleasant smile, a dress that covered her knees, and her hair pulled back in a becoming bun.

"Mrs. Ward?"

"Yes?"

"Honey, who is it?" A voice rose over the television.

Nick flashed his badge. "I'm Agent Nick Hagar and this is Agent Timmons. We'd like to speak to Leo for a moment, please."

The lipstick smile slipped as she turned her head toward the home behind her. "Leo."

A man wearing slacks and a sweater appeared, looking nothing like Nick had expected. He had to stand six ten if he was a foot, was cut like he competed in the Mr. Universe contest, and boasted what could only be a spray tan. His look was nothing short of intimidating.

"Can I help you?" His appearance was not near as shocking as his voice. High-pitched, it didn't match the man's physique. Reminded Nick of the boxer Mike Tyson—bulky man with a kid's prepubescent voice.

"Are you Leo Ward?"

"I am."

Nick held up his badge and introduced himself and Timmons again. "We'd like to speak to you for a moment, please."

"What's this about?"

"We just need a moment of your time, sir."

"It's okay, honey. I'll just be a minute." He kissed his wife's temple, stepped outside, and pulled the door closed behind him. "Follow me," he instructed Nick and Timmons.

They followed him to the side of the house. "Now, what's this all about?"

"Sir, can you tell us where you were between eight and ten, Friday morning?" Timmons asked.

Ward crossed his roped arms over his defined chest. "What's this about?"

"We're investigating a murder, sir. Can you tell us where you were during that time on Friday?"

"A murder investigation—wait a minute. This is about Senator Ford's daughter, isn't it?"

Timmons looked at Nick, who shifted to face the hulk of a man. "Yes, sir, it is."

"She was murdered between eight and ten Friday morning, so you need me to alibi up, is that it?"

"Yes, sir."

The man hesitated, then threw back his head and laughed. "That's rich. Did Ford turn you on to me as a suspect?"

"Sir, can you please just answer the question?" Nick refused to be baited.

Ward shook his head. "I'm a man who is interested in preserving life, gentlemen. I protest abortion and killing of the unborn for research. Unlike the senator, who proposes stem-cell research on human fetuses. Are you asking him about those murders? The murders of innocent children?"

"Sir, we'd rather not to have to ask you to come to our office to answer our questions, but if you'd prefer—"

"I was here, in my home office."

"Can anyone verify that?" Timmons asked.

"My wife, who is also my secretary."

"Anyone not related to you?" Nick asked.

"No."

"Were you on the phone with anyone during those times?" Timmons asked.

"Not that I can think of right off the top of my head."

Nick shook his head. "Anyone who can establish you were here? A repairman? A neighbor? A deliveryman?"

"Wait . . . Friday?" Ward slowly smiled. Wide. "That's the day we had our new big-screen set up with our new satellites. Serviceman was here from about eight thirty until almost noon putting up the dish and wiring the two receivers and four televisions."

Well, they'd asked for an alibi. "We'll need the name of your satellite provider, sir."

"Sure." Ward nodded. "You tell Ford that I'd never stoop to harming a child, no matter how sorry the parent was."

CHAPTER THIRTEEN

"I learned how important it is
to entertain people and give them
a reason to come and watch you play."
ELVIS PRESLEY

An unknown source of blood on the victim and David Tiddle's fingerprint on the dash of his girlfriend's car. That's all the physical evidence they had. Everything else was circumstantial. Weak. Certainly not enough to take to the DA. The district attorney wouldn't touch this one yet.

Nick propped his feet on the open bottom drawer of his desk and stared out the window. He mindlessly noticed the dried leaves floating on the puddles on the side of the road. Winds pushing the leaves like boats afloat on the ocean. At least it'd quit raining. Monday morning had dawned dry but gloomy.

He'd called Knoxville and an agent should reach the CODIS administrator in Nashville by noon. If he got lucky, which he doubted, the agent would push to give the unknown blood sample top priority.

"Boss?" Timmons stuck his head in the office.

Nick waved him in. "Whatcha got?"

"Got in contact with Ward's satellite company

this morning. We've requested the time logs for installations on Friday morning. We should get the records this afternoon."

Probably another dead end.

"We have an appointment this afternoon with Professor Emmel to verify Cynthia Mantle's arrival time on Friday."

"Good." He had to figure out something. The mayor and governor were tag teaming him with calls, wanting updates. What they wanted was an arrest and conviction. Anything to shut up the senator.

Timmons hovered at the door.

"Anything else?" Please.

"Maybe nothing . . ." Timmons stepped inside, holding a file. "You asked me to look into everyone close to Gina, especially their whereabouts during the window for time of death, see if they had an alibi."

Nick nodded.

"Well, Senator Ford's alibi can't be confirmed."

Nick dropped his feet to the floor with a plunk and jerked upright. "What?"

"The senator said he'd been on a business call from eight until nine, then he changed into his workout clothes in his bedroom before going downstairs to his home gym where he waited for Gina to call."

"Yeah?"

"Well, we've pulled the phone records from the

house and his cell phone. There are no calls on either during eight to nine that morning." Timmons shrugged. "I'm sure it's probably nothing, I mean, it's his daughter, but you asked me to let you know of anything I couldn't confirm."

Nick stood. "Not much else I can do at the moment anyway. Let's go talk with the senator." He grabbed his coat from the rack in the corner. "Besides, let's make sure he sees how *thorough* we're handling this investigation. How we leave no stone unturned."

Maybe he could explain to the public why his alibi couldn't be verified. He sure liked to talk smack about how the wheels of justice moved slowly. Let's see how he felt about that wheel when it was running over him.

He and Timmons braved the cold as they crossed the lot to Nick's car. Unverified alibis usually meant secrets that had some bearing on the case.

"You don't really think he had anything to do with his daughter's murder, do you?" Timmons asked.

"No. But I've been wrong before." Nick steered in the direction of the senator's manor. "Remember several years ago that congressman who hired someone to beat up his own homosexual son so he could claim it was a hate crime and gain the gay votes in his upcoming election?"

"I do. That's sick to hurt your own kid."

Darren's daughter had a heart condition that had already caused at least four operations with a couple more scheduled.

"Yep, but there are some seriously warped people in the world today. I never thought political motivation would cause someone to hurt his own kid, but the congressman did. Oh, and remember that senator from some state up north a couple of years ago? He hired someone to attack his wife so he could push for more stringent sexual-assault laws, only his wife had fought back and ended up being killed." Nick shook his head. "I've learned not to let people's motivations surprise me."

"I think you've been at the job too long, Boss." Timmons cut his gaze to Nick. "If you don't mind my saying."

"How's that?"

"You've become quite cynical the last few years. At least that I've seen."

Had he? "I don't think so, Timmons. I think you're just the target of my brilliant commentary and slapstick humor since Rafe moved."

Timmons laughed. "Slapstick humor? You are the most humorless man I know."

"I'm real funny."

"No you aren't."

"Really?" Nick thought he could be quite amusing at times.

"No, you're actually too serious. Scares the ladies off."

Nick exited off the highway. "Now I know you're crazy. I have no problems with keeping the ladies around."

"What about Maddie?"

Nick tightened his grip on the steering wheel.

"I'm sorry. It's none of my business." Timmons stared out the passenger window.

"You're right. It's not." He hadn't tried to call her back after she'd hung up on him yesterday. It stung that she'd questioned his work ethics. More than he imagined it would, not that he'd ever considered she'd question him like that.

The rest of the ride to the senator's was made in silence. Maybe Timmons was right and he had become cynical. Then again, maybe the whole world had just gone crazy and he was the only sane one left.

Nick and Timmons had barely reached the stairs when Senator Ford threw open the door. "Do you have news? Has an arrest been made?"

Nick hesitated. The man hadn't asked who was responsible for his daughter's death, had instead focused on an arrest. "May we speak to you in private, Senator?"

Ford showed them inside, back into the study. Mrs. Ford sat in the hard, high-back chair. Normally a beautiful woman, her eyes were puffy and red.

Nick ached for the pain that was obvious in every smooth curve of her face. "Mrs. Ford." He nodded as he sat across from her on the sofa. "I'm so sorry for your loss."

"Thank you." Her voice came out louder and much stronger than he'd expected.

The senator moved to stand behind her, placing a hand on each of her shoulders. "What news do you have for us?"

Well, he had asked to speak privately. The senator had brought them to the room with his wife, so Nick could only assume it was permissible to speak openly in front of her. "As we continue to confirm every aspect of the case, we've come across an alibi for the time of death we can't verify."

The senator spread his hands out at his sides. "How may I help you, Agents? Whose alibi can't you substantiate?"

"Yours. Sir."

Ford's expression slipped—just for a fraction of a minute, but it slipped. Nick had watched for it. Saw it. Recognized it.

Senator Ford had a secret. One he wasn't prepared to share.

"I was in my home gym, waiting on Gina's call."

"I meant before then." Nick waited, watching the senator's face tighten.

Ford gripped the back of the chair. "As I told Agent Timmons here, I was on a business call from eight o'clock until almost nine."

"That's the problem, Senator." Nick leaned forward resting his elbows on his knees and letting his hands dangle in front of him. "We can't find a record of any call during that time. Not from your house phone or your cell."

Mrs. Ford blinked, the only indication she was even paying attention to the conversation.

"That's ridiculous. Of course I was on a call."

Nick sat back. "Then we'll just need the name and contact information of who you were talking with. When that person corroborates the day, time, and length of conversation, we can close this part of our investigation."

Ford stiffened, his shoulders pulling back. Nick recognized the changing of strategy, moving away from the defensive and pushing forward offensively. SEC football teams were famous for it. He patted his wife's shoulder. "Honey, why don't you go lie down? It's time for your medication."

With the elegance of a woman raised with social graces, Mrs. Ford stood. "Gentlemen, if you'll excuse me."

Nick stood as well, nodding at her before she moved past him and into the hall, shutting the door behind her.

Ford took the moment to pounce on the attack. "What kind of questions are these? This is my daughter's murder we're talking about. Why are you here asking unimportant questions instead of out there finding out who killed my daughter?" The transition was so smooth, like a well-practiced offensive play.

"Sir, to do our jobs effectively, we must treat every person in the case the same, no matter his relationship to the victim." Time to rough the kicker, just a bit. Nick sat back down on the sofa beside Timmons. "Do you realize how many people fall victim to members of their immediate family?"

Ford's eyes narrowed as he took the seat his wife had just vacated. "Are you accusing me of something, Agent Hagar?"

"Not at all. I'm just trying to verify your alibi so we can move on and concentrate on other leads in the case." Nick crossed his legs at the ankles, stretching his legs out in front of him. "So, who were you talking to between eight and nine on Friday morning, Senator?"

"Okay, what's wrong?" Eva wadded up her napkin and set it inside the cardboard carton bearing the logo of the closest Chinese takeout. "You've been moping around all morning like someone kicked your puppy." She pointed chopsticks at her. "And don't start in on getting a dog again either because that's just crazy."

"Just the weather getting me down." Maddie hadn't heard from Nick since her call yesterday. She'd hung up after apologizing, and he hadn't bothered to call her back. That hurt her more than she cared to admit. *"But don't you step on my blue suede shoes."*

Had he felt like that when she never called him after getting back from visiting with Riley? If so, she was triply sorry, if there was such a thing. *"You can do anything but lay off of my blue suede shoes."*

Eva leaned back in her chair in the break room and studied Maddie. "Don't try to con a con, sweetie. You've always said you love cuddling up with a good book when it's dark and gloomy out. You told me it's the perfect time to read a murder mystery."

She leaned forward, her hair curling around her face, and laid her palms-to-elbows flat against the lunch table. "So I have to ask again, number one, what's wrong with you? And number two, why are you lying to me about it?"

If Maddie didn't share, it'd bottle up inside her and drive her insane. It was already breaking her concentration. "He hasn't called me back."

"Nick?"

Maddie rolled her eyes and stabbed her chopsticks into the empty carton. "Of course, Nick. Who else?"

"I'm not following. You called him yesterday with the results of our report, right?"

"Yes."

"And . . ." Eva tossed her hands into the air.

"I'm guessing he was supposed to call you back last night and didn't?"

"No." She should've kept her mouth shut. Now she'd have to explain about hanging up on him. "When I called him with the results, I thought about what you said."

"Me? What'd I say?"

"About Nick inadvertently slipping a detail of the case in front of the senator."

"Oh. That." Eva had the decency to blush. "I was talking out of my head. Nick wouldn't do that. He's too much of the professional. Has too much experience to slip up like that."

"Yeah, I know. Only thing is, I should've known it yesterday before I mentioned it to him."

"You did not." Eva's eyes were wide.

"Oh, but I did."

"And he got offended?"

Maddie rolled her eyes again before shoving their cartons into the trash. "What do you think, Eva? Of course he took offense."

"Uh-oh. What'd he say?"

She leaned back against the table, her arms tightly crossed over her chest. "That he thought I knew him better. That I shouldn't have had to ask."

"Ouch." Eva reached out and squeezed Maddie's arm.

"I apologized. He didn't readily accept, so I apologized again and hung up."

"You hung up on him?"

"Yeah." Her chest hurt. "And he hasn't called back."

Eva stood and put her arm around Maddie's shoulders. "Oh, honey, he will. It's that male ego thing. You wounded his pride so he's punishing you by not calling. It'll be okay." She patted Maddie's back.

"I don't know, Eva. He sounded really hurt."

"Well, he shouldn't be. I mean, yeah, for a second, but then he should consider you're only protecting the case." Eva popped her fists onto her hips. "Matter-of-fact, he should really respect you for showing such integrity and profes-sionalism."

"Eva." Maddie shook her head.

"No, I'm serious. It's not like you two have been dating for months. Not even weeks. You just had your second date, for pity's sake. How could you *really* know what he would or wouldn't do?"

"You just said you were positive he wouldn't do such a thing, and you've never gone out with him. Now you're telling me that since we've only gone out twice, there's no way for me to know he wouldn't slip up." She knew her friend was only trying to make her feel better, but Maddie felt lousy and Eva telling her it was okay wasn't going to make her feel any better about it.

"Okay, so why was he so offended? Did you hit a nerve, perhaps?"

"No. He sounded hurt, then angry. Like I'd disappointed him." She felt like such a heel. Her wad of emotions urged her to call him and apologize yet again.

She just didn't think he'd listen. Again.

"I still think he'll get over it and call you." Eva smiled.

"And if he doesn't?"

"Well. Then I guess he isn't the man we thought he was."

Or she'd offended him so deeply that he didn't want anything more to do with her. Why had she let herself like him? She hadn't been able *not* to notice the care he took in his work. The way he treated people with respect. The way he didn't play games like other guys. Why had she noticed all the little things about him that made him cancel out every other man around?

CHAPTER FOURTEEN

"I don't know anything about music.
In my line you don't have to."
ELVIS PRESLEY

"Work schedule from Ward's satellite dish company for Friday came in." Timmons leaned against the open door of Nick's office, waving a paper.

They'd returned to the office after Ford had given them all the information he could for his alibi. Now they could only follow up, and the day seemed to drag on.

If only he could get a break on the case. "And?"

"Installer's time card reflects he arrived at the Ward residence at 8:11. He signed out on that job at 12:18."

"Did Ward sign the order?"

Timmons nodded. "But that's at the time of completion. I asked if the installer could verify who let him into the house, Mr. or Mrs. Ward." He shook his head before Nick could ask. "We have to ask the installer, who is out on calls until five. Guess what I'm doing on my way home today?"

"Thanks, Timmons. We really need some kind of break here."

"We still can't get in touch with Mr. Whitlow."

"Let me guess, the international investor is still unavailable?" As he had been since eight o'clock this morning.

"You guessed it. So, unfortunately, we can't verify or disprove Senator Ford's alibi at this time."

"Color me shocked." Nick leaned back in his chair and propped his feet up on the bottom desk drawer he kept open for this purpose. "Keep on it. Matter-of-fact, hand it off to Agent Martin to keep trying tonight. Since we're in a different zone, maybe he'll get in touch with Whitlow."

"Yes, sir. Have we heard anything from CODIS yet?"

Nick shook his head. "Agent Zanca from the Knoxville office is practically sitting on the Nashville's CODIS operator's shoulder to rush. I've been assured it's going as fast as humanly possible." He ran a hand over his hair. He needed a haircut. Like he had time?

"I hope it's fast enough for us."

"Me too." Nick took note of the time. "You ready to head to the university?"

"Waiting on you."

They arrived at the University of Memphis and parked near the building where Professor Emmel taught the creative writing class. The late afternoon, overcast and cold, seeped over the campus. Both Nick and Timmons huddled into their coats as they made their way to the professor's classroom.

"Good afternoon, gentlemen. I assume you're the FBI agents who made the appointment and requested to meet in my classroom?" Professor Emmel had a ready smile as he stood to greet them. "Come in, sit down." Two comfortable chairs sat facing the lectern at the front of the room. Emmel motioned Nick and Timmons to sit.

It was easy to understand why his classes were full each semester. Again, Timmons had turned in a very detailed report, so Nick knew about Professor Rick Emmel. Forty-nine, in a long-term relationship with one Dawn Salister, no children. They shared a home close to the university. Dawn was an artist, a painter. She'd had a couple of shows, not all that successful. Meanwhile, the professor was popular with his students because of his ease of teaching and making learning fun. He had a stellar reputation, both professionally and in his personal life.

"Now, how may I assist you?"

"It's about your Friday creative writing class."

"Yes?"

Nick leaned forward in his chair. "Cynthia Mantle."

"She's a student. One of the better ones, actually. Although I believe she has promise, I don't see her passionate about writing." The professor rubbed his shaved chin. "Pity, because if she applied herself, she has the talent to become published."

Interesting. Nick picked imaginary lint from his pants. "Professor, was Ms. Mantle in your class this past Friday?"

He nodded. "Yes, I recall she was here. At the close of class, she assisted me in collecting homework assignments."

Just like she'd said. "Your class is from eight thirty until ten fifteen, correct?"

Emmel nodded. "Every Friday."

"Do you know Gina Ford?" Nick asked.

"She's not in my class, but I know who she

is. I've seen her with Ms. Mantle in the hall."

"Recently?"

The professor shrugged. "I can't say." He shook his head. "I heard about her murder on the news. I'm terribly sorry for her parents. I can't imagine."

"It is a tragedy. About Friday, Ms. Mantle stated she was late to your class. Do you recall that?" Nick noticed the theater-style setup of the classroom. At least one hundred people could fit in the chairs with the small trays attached to them. Just big enough to hold a Netbook or tablet. Different from back in Nick's college days.

"I'm sorry, gentlemen, I don't recall when she came in. I don't take attendance at the start of class. I'm of the opinion that students pay to attend my class. It's up to them whether they actually show up or not. If they can turn in the work and pass the class without physically being here, that's their choice."

"You have no way of knowing what time Ms. Mantle arrived in your class then?"

"Oh, I can tell you exactly what time she came in." He pulled his laptop to him, clicked his mouse a few times, then typed. "Just a moment." A few more clicks of the mouse. He leaned forward toward the screen and pushed his glasses up to the bridge of his nose. "Ms. Mantle entered my class at exactly 8:59."

"Professor, if you don't mind my asking, how

do you know the exact time of her arrival, especially if you don't take attendance?"

Emmel turned his laptop to face them. On screen was what appeared to be a security camera feed, date and time stamped in the bottom right-hand corner, and an image of Cynthia Mantle stepping into the classroom. Her blond hair pulled back in a ponytail, with hairs sticking out all over at odd angles.

"Why? How—?" Timmons started.

The professor laughed softly. "This isn't my first rodeo, Agents. I've learned students will cheat, even the good ones, if they feel they can get away with it." He nodded at the laptop. "That's just my security to ensure those who do, get caught."

He pointed at the light fixture over the front of the class. Just on top of the front side, the security camera was barely visible. But you'd have to be looking for it to see it.

"Slick." Timmons looked rightly impressed.

Nick was too. Eight fifty-nine was more than a few minutes late. And plenty of time to kill Gina around eight, clean up, then rush into class almost an hour later.

"May we get a copy of that?" Nick asked.

"Sure. Let me screen shot it. Give me a minute."

As the professor clicked keys and a hum from the printer filled the silence of the room, Nick's pulse kicked up a notch.

Cynthia Mantle's alibi had just fallen apart.

● ● ●

Tuesday had brought clear, sunny skies to Memphis but kept her temperatures in the thirties. Beautiful, like an ice queen.

Maddie stared out the window over her kitchen sink. Eva had come over for an early dinner on their day off, and now Maddie watched the last vestiges of day fade away. Night settled like a welcoming cloak. The moon climbed high, shining bright in defiance of the last two nights.

Maddie smiled and lifted her oversized mug. Definitely a night for reading the latest in the series from her favorite inspirational mystery author.

All day, Nick had been on her mind. She'd resisted the urge several times to pick up the phone and call him. He most likely was still hurt by her questioning him. If she could turn back time and take back that one conversation, she would in a heartbeat.

She closed her eyes. *Dear Lord, please help Nick. Help him understand I didn't mean to be offensive. Guide him as he works this case. I pray You'll provide him protection. And God, I pray You'll draw him closer to You during these tough times. Amen.*

She settled on the couch with her book and hot chocolate, the kind made with milk and hazelnut creamer, topped with whipped cream. The taste was worth the eight hundred calories. The local

Elvis station played softly in her bedroom down the hall, the beat of the chorus tiptoeing down the hall. Just enough to make her tap her toe, but not clear enough to distract her from reading.

Maddie flipped the book open to the place held by her bookmark, then took a sip of the hot chocolate. She set the mug down—

Bam! Bam! Bam!

She knocked the mug to the floor. Chocolate shot across the wood planks while Maddie leapt to her feet. Was that someone at her back door? The fence's gate was locked. She was sure of that. Positive.

Brring!

She jumped, then dove for the phone. "Hello?"

"Are you alone? All alone?" The man's gutty voice raised the hair on the back of her neck. She pressed the Off button.

Bam! Bam! Bam!

Maddie ran for the bedroom, her socked feet slipping on the wood floor she'd recently had polished.

"Let's rock, everybody, let's rock," Elvis jammed from the radio.

She dialed 911 as she jerked open the night-stand drawer. It took her four times to get a grip through the sweat on her palms.

"Everybody in the whole cell block . . ."

"Nine-one-one dispatcher, what is the nature of your emergency?"

"Was dancin' to the Jailhouse Rock."

Maddie hit the button on the radio, pitching the house into silence. "I think someone's trying to break into my home." She grabbed her gun and unsheathed it from the holster with a pounding heart and trembling hands. "I'm a TBI agent and armed."

"Ma'am, how is someone trying to break into your home?"

"I've filed a report this past weekend of threatening phone calls. He just called again and asked if I was all alone." She checked the magazine to make sure it was full and chambered a bullet. "And now someone's at my back door."

"Ma'am, do you know who's at your back door?"

"I have a fenced-in backyard that no one should be able to get into. Send a unit and please notify them that I am armed."

"Ma'am, I need you to stay on the line with—"

Creak!

The loose second stair of the back steps leading to the kitchen!

Maddie dropped the phone onto the bed. Her heart lodged in the back of her throat. She'd been meaning to ask Darren to fix that loose stair for her.

She inched into the hall, keeping her back pressed against the wall. She flipped out the lights as she moved toward the back door.

Past the formal dining room. She hit the switch. The hall plummeted into darkness.

Slipping past the living room.

Another light out.

Into the kitchen. She stayed against the wall and eased herself to the floor.

The motion-detector lights blazed in the backyard.

Bam!

That was against the sliding glass door of the mudroom!

Screeeech! Bam!

Little pieces of glass tinned across the ceramic tile of the mudroom.

Why wasn't the alarm going off? Oh. She'd forgotten to turn it on after she'd seen Eva out.

Still crouched, Maddie pivoted on her toes, gun drawn.

A siren screamed against the silence of the night.

Crunch. Crunch. Crunch.

Maddie tightened her stance and secured her grip on her handgun.

The siren shrieked into her driveway.

The footsteps stopped, then quickened. Growing fainter.

Her doorbell rang. "Memphis police. Open the door!"

Maddie let out the breath she'd been holding and tried to stand. Wobbling, she used the wall to climb to standing.

"Memphis Police Department. Open the door!"

"I'm coming." Just as soon as her knees promised to support her.

The phone's insistent ringing pulled Nick from his shower. "Hagar." He dripped all over the rug Mom had sent him from their travels last year.

"Nick, it's Darren."

Was there a new development? Timmons had met up with the dish installer who set up Ward's satellite and could only verify he saw Mr. Ward first around ten on Friday morning. Had they heard from Whitlow on Ford's alibi? "What's up?"

"It's Maddie."

Nick's gut knotted. "What?"

"Someone broke into her house. She's pretty sure it was the guy who made the threatening calls."

"Is she okay?" He wrapped the robe around him tighter. If something had happened to her, after the way he'd left things . . .

"She's fine. Pretty shook up, but okay. The problem is, she doesn't really want to be alone, but Savannah isn't feeling well and I don't want to get her out in this cold. And, of course, Kimi's already gone home for the day and—"

"I'll go. I'll get dressed and head there now."

"Are you sure? I mean, I can go. I can ask my neighbor to come listen for Savannah. Maybe I should just do that."

Nick was already heading back into the bathroom to get dressed. "No, you take care of your daughter. I'll go take care of Maddie."

"Uh, Nick . . ."

"Yeah?"

"She called me, pretty unsteady and not wanting to be a bother. She won't expect you and might lash out at you when you show up. It won't be personal. It's a girl thing."

Nick grabbed a pair of jeans from the drawer. "No worries. I got this." He snatched a pullover as well. "And Timmons?"

"Yes, sir?"

"Thanks for letting me know."

"Yes, sir."

Nick had never dressed so fast and then rushed to his car. The entire drive, he mentally ordered himself to calm down. It would only upset her more for him to charge in and try to order her around. Especially since he'd left things so . . . so . . . awkwardly between them. She might even be furious at him and refuse to let him in.

Would she?

No, she wasn't like that. She wasn't into head games. He needed to kick off the memory of Joy and concentrate on Maddie. Man, he wished he'd called her back. She hadn't really accused him of anything. She was only being diligent.

His anxiety pressed his foot harder on the accelerator.

Timmons had said she was shaken up. He didn't say if they caught the guy. Probably not, or Darren would've mentioned it. Did he hurt her?

Nick's grip tightened on the steering wheel as he raced faster.

For the first time since he could remember, Nick whispered a plea for her safety. To who, he didn't want to think about, but at that moment, he just wanted someone to watch over Maddie until he could get to her.

CHAPTER FIFTEEN

"I have no use for bodyguards, but I
have very specific use for two highly trained
certified public accountants."
ELVIS PRESLEY

"Ms. Baxter?"

Sitting at her kitchen table, Maddie lifted her gaze to the young Memphis police officer. "Yes?"

"There's someone here—"

"Maddie!" Nick rushed into the room. He sighed visibly as he spied her. "Are you okay?" He moved toward her.

The fear and exhaustion she'd battled the last hour pushed her to him. His strong arms wrapped around her, giving her the strength she no longer had but so desperately needed. She buried her face in his shoulder. His breath was warm against her skin as he kissed her temple.

She had no idea how long they stood there, him holding her and her letting him. Comfort and safety rolled off of him and wrapped her in tenderness.

"Excuse me, Ms. Baxter?"

She just might have to shoot the cop. Maddie took a step back from Nick, enough to turn and face the officer. "Yes?"

"A TBI team is here."

"Thank you."

"Maddie, are you o—?" Peter burst into the room, his face pulled in concern. He looked at Nick, then back at her. "I guess you are."

Ivan and Neal crowded into the kitchen behind Peter.

She moved farther away from Nick. "Let's all sit at the table." She tugged on Nick's arm. "I only want to tell the story once."

Nick and Peter sat on opposite sides of the table, Ivan dropping in the chair beside Peter, and Neal sitting beside Nick. Maddie sat at the head of the table, between Nick and Peter. "I'm fine. Let me start at the beginning."

After she'd gone through the night, step-by-step, she could hardly hold her head up, the energy drained from her. Physically. Emotionally. Even spiritually.

"Dust the whole mudroom glass, Ivan. Neal,

search for any evidence in the yard." Peter barked orders and the team members rushed to obey. This was one of their own. If there was evidence to be found, they'd find it.

"As per your request, I didn't call Eva." Peter ignored Nick.

"I already checked. Nothing for her to get."

"She'll be furious when she finds out, you know."

Maddie grinned. "Yeah, but she's on a date with a new guy. Don't wanna mess that up for her."

Peter shook his head. "You women." He stood. "I'm going to talk to the officer in charge. Don't want to step on any toes."

"Thanks, Peter. I appreciate it."

He smiled at her, scowled at Nick, then entered the living room.

She focused on Nick. "Darren called you, didn't he?"

He hesitated. "How do you know I don't have ESP?"

Tired as she was, Maddie chuckled. "He called you. Outside of the police and my team, Darren's the only one I called. He shouldn't have called you."

"I asked him to." His voice was as soft as warm butter.

So that's how Nick knew about the phone calls to begin with. "Has he been telling you all my secrets?" She was flirting and she knew it. Didn't care.

Nick smiled his perfectly disarming grin. "Oh, you'll never get me to admit to anything, lady."

She arched a brow. "Oh, really?" It was almost a release to flirt and tease. Like an emotional outlet to the punch she'd taken tonight.

He leaned forward and planted a peck of a kiss on the end of her nose. "That's a fact, ma'am."

That he teased and flirted back and didn't push to talk about the break-in made her heart even lighter. "Thank you for coming, Nick."

"Don't mention it." He tucked a curl of her hair behind her ear. The barest of contact, yet heat infused her face. "I'm just glad you're okay. I was worried about you." His stare held her hostage in her chair in her own kitchen.

"Were you?" Why was her heart hiccupping?

He nodded. "Very."

"I'm sorry you were worried." She had a hard time forming words.

"Don't be." He shook his head, never breaking eye contact with her. "Not your fault. Not at all."

No words came to mind. Only his stare. His voice. His *presence*.

"Honey, you're done. Let me take you to your room and get you settled down."

"I'm okay."

"You're almost asleep on your feet. Please, let me help you."

She nodded.

He stood and moved to her. Slowly, he reached

for her. She stood . . . swayed. The room went to spinning.

Nick scooped her up into his arms, cradling her against his chest.

She sighed against him.

"Uh, which way?"

She opened her eyes long enough to point in the direction of her room. It was as if her eyes weighed a ton. So. Heavy.

He carried her down the hall and into her room. She was exhausted from the letdown after the adrenaline rush, but she couldn't even protest when he laid her on her bed, pulled the comforter around her, and smoothed her hair out on the pillow behind her.

Nick planted the softest kiss on her forehead. "Rest now. I'm going to find the man who broke into your house and make sure he never breaks in to anything ever again."

"I need you to pull everything you have on Mark Hubble's accuser as soon as you get in." Nick kept his voice low as he spoke into his cell.

"Of course. How's Maddie?" Timmons asked.

"I heard her shower turn on a few minutes ago, so she's awake."

"You're still there?"

"I crashed on her couch last night. She was too exhausted to think, much less secure the house after the police left. I couldn't leave her alone."

211

And if Timmons didn't like it, that was just too bad.

"I see."

Nick ignored the sarcasm. "We feel like Hubble's accuser is somehow connected. Either directly or a family member. Or it might be one of those women's abuse groups. Whatever, but she was targeted because her testimony set Hubble free."

"I'm on it. Uh, I should probably warn you."

Anything prefaced like that was never good news. "About?"

"I talked with Rafe this morning."

Oh, great. Maddie's brother. And his friend. "Why'd you call him?"

"I didn't. He called me. To ask me to be his best man."

Oh. "Well, congratulations."

"Nick, I told him about her break-in."

And by the tone of his voice, that wasn't all he'd told her big brother.

"He was set to come last night, so I told him she was safe. That you were with her."

Nick could just bet how that information relieved Rafe. "What time should I expect him?"

Timmons gave a nervous laugh. "His flight landed ten minutes ago."

"Thanks for the heads-up. I'll see you at the office. Look for the connection to Hubble's accuser."

"Yes, sir."

Nick shut the cell as Maddie shuffled into the room. She wore jeans and a sweatshirt and socks. Her hair looked darker than light auburn, still wet from the shower.

"I was a little alarmed to hear a man's voice in my living room this morning until I realized it was yours."

Suddenly it felt very intimate to be alone with Maddie, in her house, before morning coffee. "I didn't want to leave you alone last night. I mean, we shut the door to the mudroom, but it's not a secure lock. And the security system, well, we—"

"Thank you. I appreciate your staying. Sorry I was so zonked. Guess after the adrenaline crashed, so did I." She smiled as if unsure of herself. "How about a cup of coffee?"

"I'd love one." Something normal that wasn't intimate. He trailed her into the kitchen.

"I called someone to replace the mudroom door this morning. I won't go with glass this time. It's not very secure. I've learned that the hard way." She put coffee in the filter, poured a carafe of water into the unit, and pressed a button. "They'll be here soon."

"You could always get a dog, you know." He grinned.

She burst out laughing, nearly dropping the cups she'd taken from the counter. "Well, there is that. Remington does love her dog. Although with my schedule . . ."

Oh, yeah. "Speaking of Remington and Rafe . . ."

She set the cups on the counter. "What about them? Cream or sugar?"

"I like it black, thanks." He wished he'd put on his shoes. Standing in the kitchen with her in their socks, waiting for the coffee to perk, still felt too intimate. "Rafe's on his way."

"His way where?"

"Here."

Her eyes widened. "How did—Darren." She shook her head. "When?"

"His plane landed about ten minutes ago."

"Great. He'll be here any second."

"In Darren's defense, he didn't call Rafe."

"Oh, really?" The layers of anger were starting to form. "Rafe just decided out of the blue to visit today, and you, of all people, just happen to know this?"

"No, Rafe called Darren to ask him to be his best man."

She turned her back to him and drummed her fingers on the counter beside the coffeepot. "And Darren just had to tell him about the break-in. I shouldn't have called him last night. He never could keep a secret from Rafe." She was well on her way into working herself into what his mother called a tizzy.

"Hey." He slowly moved up behind her and put his hands on her shoulders. He leaned in, his chest almost touching her back, and put his mouth beside her ear. "I'm glad you called Darren because otherwise, I wouldn't have known."

Maddie turned and gazed into his eyes. She laid a hand against his cheek. "I'm glad you came." Her smile gentled his unease. She licked her lips.

That undid him.

Nick slowly lowered his head and grazed a soft kiss across her lips.

"Hey, what's going on here?"

From the time Maddie had reached the age where she was allowed to date, her big brother had wreaked havoc on her love life.

Rafe hadn't lost his touch.

Maddie pulled free from Nick and turned to face Rafe but kept her hand on Nick's forearm. "Ever hear of knocking?"

"Why isn't your alarm on?" Rafe stormed to her and yanked her into his arms.

He almost crushed her in a tight bear hug before loosening his grip on her. "What is it with my sisters getting into all kinds of trouble when I'm not around to keep an eye on them?" He circled his arms around her waist.

She playfully slapped his bicep. "Hey, I carry a gun. Pulled it last night too."

Rafe's eyes turned serious. "Tell me."

Nick cleared his throat. "Rafe."

Her brother stared at Nick for a long moment. While she couldn't understand guy-ese, they had a long, silent conversation that she wasn't privy to.

Rafe released her. "Sir."

"Good to see you."

Rafe nodded. "Yes, sir."

Nick sighed and looked at her. She so wanted to kiss him, but Rafe would come unhinged if she did. He smiled so sweetly. "I need to get into the office. I'll call you later." He looked at Rafe again. "Come by the office and catch up later, if you feel like it." The invitation had been delivered.

"I'll see you later." The challenge had been accepted.

Naked male ego exhausted her.

She gave Nick a quick, friendly hug. "Thanks for staying last night, Nick. I appreciate it."

He left, the front door's click shut echoing throughout the house.

"He stayed the night? Here? With you? Alone?" Rafe's temper simmered just below the surface.

Maddie grabbed her coffee, handed Rafe a cup of the black java, and sat at the kitchen table. "He stayed on the couch."

"That's no excuse." Rafe reluctantly followed her to the table and sat.

"Not that I owe you any explanation, which for the record I don't because I'm a grown woman, but he did me a favor. I crashed after the adrenaline rush wore off. Purely exhausted. I couldn't even stand up. He took me to my room and tucked me in—"

She wagged a finger at Rafe's expression and open mouth. "He tucked me in, fully clothed, and covered me with an extra blanket. He didn't know the code to set the alarm. The interior door of the mudroom doesn't have a lock. Nick didn't feel like I'd be safe, so he stayed here and kept vigil so I could get some much-needed sleep." She took a sip of her coffee. "Now, are you satisfied?"

"Why couldn't one of your friends come and stay with you?"

She laughed. Such a guy. "Who? Eva? Oh, I can just see that, can't you? She barely qualifies on the range every year at relicensing."

"Well . . . what about Darren?"

"Who couldn't bring Savannah out in the cold. And he's a guy, in case you haven't noticed." She shook her head. "Besides, Nick is a friend."

"Yeah, it looked real friendly when I came in."

And here it was—the real source of her brother's feathers being ruffled. *"Don't be cruel to a heart that's true."* "Are you asking me the nature of my relationship with Nick?"

"No." He paused, staring into his cup. "I think I could figure that one out on my own, Mads."

"I really love you baby, cross my heart." No fair, him using her childhood nickname. The one Dad had bestowed on her when she'd try to follow Rafe as a toddler and couldn't keep her balance long enough. Rumor had it that she'd get so mad, she'd turn beet red in the face and

scream. She thought the rumor had gotten drastically exag-gerated over the years, but the nickname stuck. "Rafe . . ."

"Don't *Rafe* me. He's my boss."

"Was your boss. He isn't anymore." She forced herself to use the tone she reserved for upset children in the church's nursery.

"He's still a SAC, which is an agent's supervisor, whether we work in his field office or not."

"So he's off-limits for me to spend time with?"

"He should be."

She gave a soft chuckle. "Then I should stop hanging out with Darren and Savannah too?"

"They're different." Rafe set his cup on the table. "You don't have *that* kind of friendship with Darren."

Now he was just making her mad. "What about you and Remington? If memory serves me correctly, she was a suspect in the murder case you were working. She wasn't even honest about who she was. You probably shouldn't have *that* kind of friendship with her, yet you're engaged to her now."

"That's diff—"

"Or what about Riley and Hayden? Wasn't he Remington's best friend? He's a police commissioner in another state. Riley probably shouldn't have *that* kind of friendship with him, but she upped and moved to Louisiana to be closer to him. From all appearances, they'll probably be engaged before summer."

"Maddie, I'm not saying—"

She fisted her hands on her hips. "Not saying what, Rafe? That unlike you and Riley, I'm not allowed to choose for myself who I want to spend time with? That you and Riley can date and fall in love and get a happily-ever-after, but I can't? Because *you* think your former boss should be off-limits to me? Are you serious?"

"I'm not saying that." Rafe raised his voice and stood.

She glared at him, her muscles clenching.

"I'm not saying that at all." His tone had gone down a notch.

"Then what are you saying, Rafe?" She struggled to temper her breathing.

"That . . ." He stabbed his fingers through his short, dark hair. "I don't know what I'm saying. I'm sorry, Mads. I just reacted."

His apology erased her anger. She gave him a hug. "I know you were worried about me, and it was a shock to see me with Nick, but Rafe, you have to realize I'm a grown woman who can make my own choices of who I see. Okay?"

He hugged her back. "I don't have to like it, do I?"

She chuckled. "No, but you do have to respect my choices."

"Okay."

Maddie let him go. "How about a fresh cup

of coffee before I have to get ready for work?"

He handed her his cup. "Thanks. Now, why don't you tell me what happened last night with your break-in? And I understand you've had some threatening phone calls too?"

Here they went again.

CHAPTER SIXTEEN

"I like to sing ballads the way Eddie Fisher
does and the way Perry Como does.
But the way I'm singing now is what
makes the money."
ELVIS PRESLEY

"This is Agent Zanca from the Knoxville office. I'm here in the Nashville TBI crime unit." The woman's voice was void of any emotions.

Nick gripped the phone. "Yes?"

"A full report is forthcoming, but I know you're waiting on results."

"Yes?" Why didn't Zanca just spit it out?

"In regards to the DNA sample search in the Ford case, there isn't a full match in CODIS."

Like when a pin is stuck in a balloon, all the air whooshed from Nick's lungs. A dead end. The one area where if he'd gotten a hit, it would have been definitive. Enough for the DA to take to trial. Enough for a jury to convict.

"Having said that, however, there was a potential match from the CODIS search."

"I thought you just said there wasn't a match?"

"There's not a full match, correct, but there was a potential match that popped up."

"I don't understand."

Zanca chuckled over the phone line. "I'm not sure I grasp it all myself. In layman's terms, it's possible your unknown source has a biological relative in CODIS."

Nick took a moment to process that. "So, if we know who is in CODIS, we look at their biological relatives and could possibly find the source of the DNA left at the crime scene?"

"Basically, yes. But the CODIS operator here tells me she can't just run these types of searches without following proper procedures. The tests have to be run through special software that's not CODIS."

"So, how do we do that?"

"According to the operator, the chief law-enforcement officer of the investigating law-enforcement agency joins with the district attorney to file a joint request to run the familial DNA test."

"So, Helm and the DA and I file this request and then we can search for the family member match?" Should be easy enough. They all needed a suspect in this case. Especially before the senator escalated his political maneuvering over his daughter's murder.

"The operator tells me the paperwork for the request is pretty complicated. She recommends you have one of the forensic scientists in your TBI unit help you and the DA. Otherwise, it could be kicked back and forth until accepted and that could take weeks."

"Thanks, Agent Zanca. I'll get on this today. Will you be staying in Nashville?"

She laughed. "Looks like I will. No problem since we're billing your office anyway." She chuckled harder, then cleared her throat. "Just let my SAC in Knoxville know I'm not out recording a country hit and planning to leave the bureau, would you?"

"I will. Thank you. I'll be in touch soon." He hung up the phone. At last, something on the case was going his way.

A knock rapped at his door.

He looked up and into the cold stare of Rafe Baxter.

Nick swallowed. "Come on in."

Rafe shut the door behind him and sat on the chair facing Nick's desk.

Nick waited, giving his former employee the time to work out what he wanted to say. The man had something on his mind, and rightfully so. Nick didn't have any sisters so he couldn't understand exactly what Rafe was going through, but if the feeling he'd had last night when Timmons had called him was even close to the protectiveness Rafe felt, Nick would sit here and take Rafe's disapproval and reproach without argument.

"I know Maddie's a grown woman," Rafe began. "And she has made it abundantly clear she can and will make her own decisions regarding her personal life." He shifted, never breaking eye contact with Nick. "But she is also my sister and I'm bound to look out for her."

Nick waited.

"I respect you, sir, and I appreciate you staying last night to ensure her protection."

Nick nodded.

"But I don't want to see my sister's heart broken. She isn't like the other women you date once or twice, then never see again. Maddie's the type who's in it for the long haul. She wants permanency, a future." Rafe shook his head. "She's had her heart ripped up twice by men she thought were interested in a future with her. After being so deeply hurt, she built up some pretty thick walls to protect herself." He stared openly at Nick. "Apparently you've broken through them."

"Rafe, I respect Maddie very much. Please know that. I would never do anything to intentionally hurt her. We've only gone out twice. I really like her." But it was probably best if he didn't expound to her brother just how much. "I honestly want to see where this relationship will take us. But I also don't want there to be tension between you and her."

What would he do if Rafe asked him to stop seeing Maddie? Could he do it? Would he do it? Just the question tightened Nick's gut.

Rafe let out a long breath. "There's not. Well, not any more than between Riley and me when she started dating Hayden." He tightened his jaw muscles. "I won't see her hurt."

"I understand that. I can't promise to never hurt her, because sometimes, I just don't get the woman psyche, but I won't disrespect her or treat her badly. On that, you have my word."

"Thanks." Rafe visibly relaxed.

Nick released an inward sigh. He'd thought he would have to let Rafe take a swing at him. "I hear congratulations are in order. When's the big day?"

"May fifteenth. It was my parents' wedding anniversary. Remington is set on it."

"That's cool. Congratulations again."

"Thanks."

"Hey, did I hear a groom in here?" Timmons stepped inside Nick's office.

Rafe stood and clapped Darren's shoulder. "How are you?"

"Good. I told Savannah Uncle Rafe would have dinner with us tonight. She's got Kimi cooking already this morning."

Rafe grinned. "And how are . . . *things* with you and Kimi?"

Timmons ducked his head. "Shut up, man. How many times do I have to tell you that she's just my nanny-housekeeper?" He handed Nick a folder. "As you requested, I investigated Hubble's accuser. Seems she has a stepbrother who happens to be very protective of her. He threatened Hubble during the trial so the judge banned him from the courtroom."

Nick scanned the information. Conrad Sloan, thirty-eight, African American. In and out of the system on minor assault charges, petty theft, and one misdemeanor of possession. "Has Hubble received any threats since his release?"

"No, but he's pretty much got a media crew following his every move."

"Maybe Sloan's coming after Maddie first because he holds her responsible for Hubble's release. He might plan to go after Hubble later."

Rafe held up his hands. "Wait a minute. What are y'all talking about?"

Nick closed the file and looked at Timmons. "Bring Rafe up to speed while I coordinate with Memphis PD to have Conrad Sloan brought in for questioning."

Timmons took Rafe from the office. Nick lifted the phone and ordered field agents to bring Sloan in. He'd let the thug cool his jets in the conference room for a while before he questioned him. If he was the man who made those calls to Maddie and broke into her house . . .

Well, he could always turn off the interview camera and let Rafe have fifteen minutes alone with him.

Not that he would, but it was a nice thought.

"Sir?" The rookie whose shift should have ended stood in the doorway.

"Yes, Agent Martin?"

He handed Nick a paper. "I spoke with Mr. Whitlow this morning."

"And?" He glanced at the paper.

"He says he can't recall what day he spoke to Senator Ford. He says it was either Thursday or Friday, but he can't say for certain."

Was everybody's alibi like Swiss cheese?

"Thank you, Martin."

"Yes, sir." The rookie scrambled away.

Nick leaned back in his chair and ran a hand over the stubble on his chin. He hadn't had time to shave last night before rushing to Maddie's, and he didn't take the time this morning before coming into the office.

The weight of the case heaved his chest. So many loose ends. None neat. He didn't like it. Not at all.

He grabbed his cell and punched the number for Maddie. She answered on the first ring. "Hi, Nick."

"Hey. How're you doing?"

"Good. Are you okay?"

"Why wouldn't I be?" He leaned back in the chair again, just her voice easing his burden and lifting his spirits.

"Well, Rafe said he was heading to the office . . ."

He chuckled. "We're fine. He's with Timmons right now."

"Yeah, well, Peter and Eva have gone into pit-bull mode. I can't even go to the ladies' room without Eva joining me."

He could make out Eva's voice in the distance, but not what she was saying. "You're at work?"

"Of course I'm at work. Why wouldn't I be?"

After last night . . . she'd looked so small and helpless, but he wouldn't mention that. "I just thought you might still be tired from last night."

"I'm fine." He heard the smile in her voice. "And my mudroom now sports a nice wooden, *secure* door."

"Good." He paused for a beat. "I actually need to come by your office and talk to you and Eva."

"Oh?"

"About familial DNA?"

"That's cutting edge."

"CODIS got a potential match."

"Ah. I see. Come on over. Eva and I will be happy to help you."

"See you soon." He hung up just as his intercom buzzed.

"Hagar."

"Sir, there is a Ms. Cynthia Mantle here with her attorney to see you."

Ah, so she had lawyered up. "Put them in conference room one, please." He'd let them wait.

He found Timmons and Rafe in Timmons's cubicle. "Guess who showed up?"

Timmons shrugged.

"Cynthia Mantle. With her attorney."

Timmons stood. "Did you ask her in?"

"No, but it saves us a trip."

Rafe gestured to Timmons's laptop. "Mind if I check my e-mail while I wait?"

"Go for it." Timmons followed Nick to the conference room.

"Ms. Mantle." Nick took one of the two chairs on the opposite side of the table. Timmons sat beside him.

"I'm Collette Putman, Ms. Mantle's attorney." The perky brunette was pretty, but you could tell a volume of wisdom hid behind those clear, blue eyes.

"I'm SAC Hagar and this is Agent Timmons." Nick opened the folder he'd brought, pretended to read, then closed it. "I'm sorry, Ms. Mantle, did I miss that we had an appointment today?"

Mantle looked at her attorney, who nodded. "No, sir. But I spoke with my creative writing professor and he told me you'd visited him."

Nick nodded.

"Professor Emmel told me about the recording."

Again, Nick nodded but remained silent.

Mantle looked at her lawyer again. She fidgeted in the chair. "I didn't realize it was so late when I made it to class."

Nick crossed his arms over his chest. Often in cases like this, silence was the best response.

"I forgot I had to stop for gas on Friday morning. After pizza with the study group on Thursday night, it was so late that most of the safer stations were closed. I'd forgotten I needed gas until I got in my car to go to my creative writing class."

"Do you have a receipt? Something with a date and time record?" Nick asked.

She shook her head.

"Did you pay for it with a debit or credit card?"

"I paid with cash."

Nick tapped the file sitting on the table with his index finger. "Let me get this straight—you just remembered you were later to class on Friday morning than you'd originally thought because you had to stop and get gas. You paid for the gas with cash and don't have a receipt. You have nothing to prove you actually got gas on Friday morning. Right?"

Mantle's eyes filled with tears and she turned to her attorney.

"Ms. Mantle is here of her own accord, Agent. She realized she had mistakenly given you inaccurate information and came here to correct the record."

"Only because her professor told her she'd been caught in a lie."

"A mistake, Agent, a mistake. Once her professor brought the actual time of her arrival to class to her attention, she struggled to remember the incidents of that morning." Ms. Putman gave a smile revealing a row of perfectly straight, white teeth. "I'm sure you can understand that after learning of her best friend's violent demise, Ms. Mantle wasn't thinking very clearly."

"I see." Nick opened the folder and stared at Mantle's previous statement. He stared at Cynthia Mantle. Tears still floated in her eyes. Crocodile tears? Maybe.

"Ms. Mantle, it is now your amended statement that you called Gina Ford at 8:04 because you were worried about her. You spoke for six minutes, the conversation, per your previous statement . . ." Nick read from the file. "You said when you spoke to Gina, she claimed she was on her way to have one of the most serious discussions of her life. You stated you asked her was this about the confrontation she'd mentioned the night before and she said yes. She said she'd realized she had to confront two people, and both would leave her scarred."

Nick shut the file and looked her back in the eye. "Is that correct?"

Mantle nodded.

"This call ended at 8:10, correct?"

"So you said the records indicate."

"You then stated you hung up, went and took a shower, then went to your creative writing class."

"Yes." She licked her lips. "But I'd forgotten I had to get gas. After I took my shower, I went to the gas station and filled up my car. Then I went to class, which is why I didn't get there until 8:59."

Nick straightened in his seat. "And you have no proof of buying anything from any station on Friday morning, right?"

Ms. Putman patted Mantle's shoulder. "I believe my client has already answered that question, Agent Hagar."

"Yes, she has. But your client has lied to us before, omitted information in her original interview, and now comes in with as flimsy an alibi as *my dog ate my homework,* and you expect us to just believe her with no proof?" Nick shook his head. "Ms. Mantle, you cannot account for your whereabouts between 8:10 and 8:59 on Friday morning. This is during the window of time Gina Ford was murdered."

"I didn't kill her. She was my best friend."

"To which you were jealous of, and, in your own words, in the middle of a spat with."

"But I didn't kill her." Mantle's tears finally spilled out of her eyes and down her cheeks.

"You have to believe me . . . I would never hurt Gina. She was the closest thing to a sister that I had."

"But she had David. She had good grades. She had money and friends. Everything you wanted but didn't have."

She shook her head, her whole body shaking as she sobbed.

"That's enough, Agent." Collette Putman stood, patting Mantle's shoulder. "My client came here on her own to freely amend her statement when she realized she'd omitted an important fact. She did not come here to be badgered."

She tossed a piece of paper across the table. "Here's the name and address of the station my client purchased gasoline from on Friday morning. I've requested the surveillance footage from the station from eight until nine on Friday morning. I'll be sure to send you a copy." She helped Mantle to her feet. "Come on, Cynthia. Let's go."

Nick watched them leave, gripping the file.

"Do you think she's telling the truth?" Timmons asked.

"I don't know." He handed Timmons the sheet of paper Putman had left on the table. "But you contact this station and get that surveillance tape before she does."

Timmons snatched the paper and rushed from the room.

Nick rotated his neck until it popped. One slice of Swiss could quickly become cheddar if Mantle was on that surveillance video anywhere near eight thirty to eight forty-five.

Chapter Seventeen

"I like entertaining people. I really miss it."
Elvis Presley

She felt his presence as soon as he entered the lab.

Maddie turned to face Nick and Darren. "Hello."

Eva stood as well. "Hi, guys. Peter's on his way."

"Good." Nick crossed the space between them and gave her a quick hug. "How are you?" he whispered in her ear.

"Fine." She wouldn't admit how happy it made her that he didn't act indifferent toward her. Adam had always done that at school. Granted, he was a teacher's assistant and fraternization with students was strictly prohibited, but he'd gone out of his way to ignore her. It had hurt.

Peter entered the lab. "What's this about familial DNA?"

Maddie motioned for everyone to sit. "A familial DNA search is a deliberate search for biological relatives of a contributor of evidence in samples."

Darren shook his head. "In plain English, please."

She grinned. "Okay, you all know that CODIS databases contain the DNA profiles of convicted criminals, reference samples of missing persons and sometimes samples from their biological relatives, and samples from unidentified human remains." Maddie paced as she continued. "When we processed the DNA pulled at the scene, we came back with two separate, individual strands of DNA. One was a positive match to the victim, Gina Ford, the other was determined to be an unknown source."

"Right. With you so far." Nick had a pencil and notebook in hand.

Maddie smiled that he wasn't arrogant that he felt he knew everything and couldn't learn any-thing from her or anyone else. "So we ran the unknown sample we retrieved through CODIS, hoping to find a match with a sample already in CODIS. First on a local DNA index system, then a state, then national. None of these were a match on any level."

Eva stood and took over the explanation. "For there to be a hit, in other words, a match, the samples must both be clearly defined major components of a mixture with all thirteen locations noted."

Darren held up his hands. "You lost me again."

"Okay, you've seen the little model of DNA,

right?" Eva pointed to the basic DNA strand poster on the locker. "That's basically each living organism's genetic instruction holder."

"I get that."

"The structure of all DNA comprises two helical chains each coiled round the same axis. That's why it looks like a really cool diagram. What you're really seeing is the double helix. Each person's DNA is unique. Even identical twins have different DNA. Their strands would be close —meaning, similar, but they aren't a complete and full match."

"Okay."

Maddie sat on the edge of her desk. "So there wasn't a full match in CODIS, but there was one that was close. Not as similar as that would be of an identical twin, but close as in a biological relative."

"I'm not following." Darren furrowed his brow.

"Okay, let's look at it this way. Savannah is your daughter. Everyone says she has your nose and mouth, but her mother's eyes, right?"

He nodded.

"Which is true, because when a child is formed, that embryo takes some of its genetic markers from the mother and some from the father. Each child is different, because at the moment of conception, different markers are pulled. So, in your case, Savannah pulled some markers of facial structure from you and pulled some markers like eye color from her mother. All of this is done in the womb."

Darren nodded. "Okay. Got that."

Eva sat beside Maddie on her desk. "And since your daughter pulled markers from both you and her mother, her DNA strand would look similar to yours and her mother's—the markers she inherited from you in the womb would be almost the same, but her DNA strand wouldn't be identical to either of y'alls."

"Because she took some from me and some from her mother."

Maddie nodded. "Right. But if we ran your DNA profile beside Savannah's, we'd see enough similarities that we'd know you were biologically related."

"Now I understand." Darren grinned.

Nick leaned back in his chair. "So, the sample you got from the back of Gina Ford's shirt wasn't a match to any of the profiles in CODIS, but it showed a potential match to a family member?"

"Exactly." Maddie smiled.

"Can't they just tell us who it is?"

"Familial testing is new. Not every state has legislation that will allow for familial testing. Tennessee just recently got a statute on the books. There are very specific guidelines that must be followed to the letter before the test can be run."

"But it's already in CODIS, right? They already know."

How to explain something so complex? "It's not that easy. They said it's a potential match to a biological relative. Meaning, there are so many markers that matched, but not enough for the system to give them all the information you want. For that, a familial test has to be run, and for that test to be executed, you have to fill out the proper forms."

Nick shrugged. "Okay, whatever. Let's fill out the forms. Agent Zanca said we'd need Eva's and your help and it needed to come from me, Helm," he nodded at Peter, "and the DA. I talked to him today and he'll sign whatever form. He's got the mayor and governor breathing down his neck too."

"I called our Nashville unit and spoke to the CODIS operator. She faxed me the form they're using." Eva passed it to Nick. "Oh, and she wanted me to remind everyone the test is actually conducted with specialized, non-CODIS software specifically designed just for familial testing."

He glanced at the paper, then back to Maddie. "All it basically wants to know is if we received notification that a potential match was obtained from a properly executed CODIS search, if the case is open, and if we agree to follow the TBI's investigative policies and procedures." He read again. "Then it gives some instruction about technical stuff."

"That's the part Eva and I will have to be responsible for."

"But you can do this, right?" Nick's gaze nearly melted her.

She sank back into her chair. "Yes, we can do this."

"How long will it take?"

Maddie lifted a shoulder. "If you get your part filled out, it'll take Eva and me a couple of hours to pull a sample to provide for the analysis. We'll have to send it to our Nashville unit, since it's the CODIS eligible lab. We'll use a carrier, so it could be there for them to start first thing in the morning."

"And once they get it?" Nick moved beside her, so close she could smell his cologne. "How long will it take them once they get the sample?"

Eva answered. "If they get it first thing in the morning, they should start working on it immediately. The actual science of it will take about six hours, give or take. While the forensic scientist in Nashville prepares the sample, your request will be processed by the TBI director here. Once he approves, as soon as the sample is ready, the test can be run."

"And that will take?" Nick stayed beside Maddie but listened carefully to Eva.

"Since the operator in Nashville said the potential match was found on the state level, that will narrow the focus, so it should take about a day."

Nick pushed off the edge of Maddie's desk. "If

it gets there tomorrow and it takes pretty much a whole day to get it ready, then they could load it the next day, and they could get us the information by Friday afternoon, right?"

Eva nodded. "If the director approves the search."

Nick planted a quick kiss on Maddie's cheek. "Then let's do this."

Maddie couldn't find her voice as Eva grinned at her while Peter scowled. It didn't matter . . . Maddie felt as if she could burst with happiness.

Who knew talking DNA could be so romantic?

"Mr. Sloan, I'm Agent Hagar. These are Agents Timmons and Baxter." Nick let Rafe and Darren sit. He chose to stand behind them, staring down at Conrad Sloan. "We're glad you were able to come answer a few questions for us." As he was grateful Memphis PD had allowed them to question Sloan. They stood by the two-way mirror, ready to take the collar if Sloan confessed.

"Didn't know I had a choice." He sat in a classic defensive stance with his arms crossed over his chest and his chin jutted out.

"Do you know who Mark Hubble is?" Might as well hit him sideways right out of the gate.

Sloan's eyes narrowed. "He's the scumbag who attacked my sister."

Timmons leaned forward. "You're angry he's been released, aren't you?"

"Course. What kind of stupid question is that?"

"Angry at the DNA specialist who testified at Mr. Hubble's hearing that got him released?"

"Course. She's wrong. She put that scum out on the street so he can attack my sister or some other woman again."

"Do you know who she is, the DNA specialist?"

Sloan looked down and to the left.

Nick could feel the rage coming off Rafe. It was a very good thing he hadn't seen Maddie last night when she was so exhausted and trembling. Nick didn't know if he was strong enough to hold Rafe back from that anger.

"Agent Hagar asked you a question." Timmons rapped his knuckles against the table.

Sloan jumped. "You ain't got no right to threaten me. I ain't done nothin' wrong."

"Oh, that's where you're wrong." Nick slammed his own hand on the table between Timmons and Rafe, then leaned forward. "Tell me her name. The DNA specialist whose testimony let Mark Hubble, the man who your sister said attacked her, walk out of jail free a little over two weeks ago."

"Maddie. Maddie Baxter."

Nick stood straight and put his hand on Rafe's shoulder. He squeezed. Hard.

"Have you called Ms. Baxter and made any threats?" Timmons gripped his pen so tightly his knuckles turned white.

Sloan slid down in the chair, stretching out his legs to the side of the table. "I ain't threatened nobody."

"Did you call Ms. Baxter?"

Sloan shrugged.

The muscles in Rafe's shoulders bunched. Nick squeezed harder. "We'll get the phone records. Mr. Sloan, where were you last night?"

Sloan's eyes widened. His Adam's apple bobbed. "Last night?"

Rafe sat up ramrod straight. "Where. Were. You. Last. Night? And don't even think about lying to me." His jaw muscles flexed and popped.

"I was out."

"Out where?" Timmons leaned forward, his own hand on Rafe's forearm.

"Maybe I should get a lawyer afore I say anything else."

Rafe slammed the side of his fist into the table. He shot to his feet, the metal chair shooting out behind him before clattering to the cracked floor.

Nick and Timmons each held one of Rafe's arms.

"Maybe you should answer the question before you get pelted." It took everything Nick had not to just let Rafe have at Sloan.

But he was sworn to do his job without prejudice.

Never before had he thought he wouldn't be able to do just that.

"You didn't think anyone saw you when you were at her house, did you?"

Rafe stopped straining against them. Nick couldn't believe Timmons had taken the lead in the questioning. And with a falsehood too. Well, not exactly. Not yet anyway.

"You thought you were safe when you slipped into her backyard and came up the stairs. You didn't consider someone next door to her was on their second-story balcony having a drink and a smoke after a hard day on the golf course, did you?"

Oh, Timmons was a lot better than Nick gave him credit for. Not a lie, but just spinning a hypothetical scenario.

Sloan's eyes grew wider and wider.

"You never saw anyone circle around as you broke the glass on the mudroom door." Timmons leaned across the table, right in Sloan's face. "Did you consider that maybe whoever called the cops wasn't Ms. Baxter? Do you realize that she's a Tennessee Bureau of Investigation officer who carries a badge and a gun? A gun that she was holding just in the hallway when you were stepping through the broken glass. A gun that she knows how to use was pointed at the doorway."

Sloan licked his cracked lips. "I just wanted to scare her. Let her know how wrong she was." He uncrossed his arms and rested them on the table. "It's my sister Hubble hurt. I have to protect her."

Rafe straightened the chair and sat back down. He nodded to Nick and Timmons. "Oh, I understand how hard it is to be a good brother."

"That's all I was trying to do."

"That woman you tried to scare last night? Maddie Baxter?"

Sloan nodded.

Rafe leaned in close, almost nose-to-nose with Sloan. "That's *my* little sister."

Chapter Eighteen

"I never expected to be anybody important."
Elvis Presley

Thursdays shouldn't be such a disappointment. They should be filled with planning for the upcoming weekend and expectations. Not . . . nothingness. Especially when he had a breakfast date with Maddie planned.

Yesterday had been productive. They'd gotten a full confession from Conrad Sloan, charged him, and the prosecution had him in holding pending the judge's sentencing. Rafe had returned to Arkansas this morning. Maddie had helped Nick and Peter fill out the necessary report form that he'd taken to the district attorney, who'd been only too happy to sign the request. Eva had finished preparing the sample for travel and a TBI officer had escorted the sample and request to the Nashville office first thing this morning.

But today? Today, Nick was in a strange mood that he couldn't explain.

"Sir?" Agent Martin stood in the doorway.

"Yes?" Maybe he'd get some good news and break his macabre mood.

"We got the phone records from the senator's home. There was a call to Mr. Whitlow's number at 8:20 a.m. that lasted until 9:04 a.m. last Thursday, not Friday."

Nick nodded. "Thank you." So if the senator wasn't talking to Mr. Whitlow on Friday, who was he talking to? And why weren't there any phone records at all during that time? It was time the senator gave some answers.

He motioned for Timmons to join him as he strode to the car. The bitter cold stung as he started the engine. The storms might have passed, but they left a mean cold front in their wake.

"Where are we headed, Boss?" Timmons blew on his hands.

"To see Senator Ford." Nick eased out of the parking lot and past the gate that bordered the entire building. "Phone records came back. He was, in fact, talking with Mr. Whitlow. Last *Thursday,* not Friday."

"So he still has no alibi."

"Nope, and I'm getting tired of the runaround. This man is calling the mayor daily and the governor every other day, demanding justice be served. He's going on the news and all but throwing whoever we arrest out for the death penalty. No way will there ever be an unbiased jury pool in the whole state. But he flat out lied to us about his alibi for the time of his daughter's murder." Nick turned onto the main highway. "I want the truth and I want it now."

"Who left your box of cereal open to get stale?"

"What? I don't eat cereal. What are you talking about?" Had Timmons been working too hard?

"Well, something's put you in a foul mood this morning."

Nick started to deny it, then stopped. "I know. I don't know what's going on with me. It's like I got to work and this irritation just settled over me."

"You're not at peace."

Really? "Of course not. We haven't a solid lead on the case at this point, we have to wait until tomorrow at the earliest for this familial DNA thing, we seem to be unable to verify a single alibi—"

"Man, have you stopped and prayed about this stress? You aren't going to make it if you don't let go and let God."

Pray about stress? Seriously? "Uh, thanks, but no."

Timmons gave him a funny look. "I know you believe in God. You might not be on the best of terms with Him at the moment, but you believe in Him."

"I don't know what I believe." That wasn't exactly true. At one time, he believed in a sovereign God who loved His children and had plans of good things for them. He didn't plan to kill young men on foreign soil fighting for their country. He didn't plan to rip families to shreds with grief, pain, and guilt. No loving God could allow that. Would allow that.

"You'll figure it out, Boss. I'll be praying for you." Timmons shifted to stare out the passenger's window.

Yeah, pray for him. That'd worked out so swimmingly in the past.

But then there was Maddie, who wore her faith on her sleeve.

Timmons remained silent the rest of the drive and until they parked in the senator's driveway. "Did you call and let him know we were on our way?"

"Nope." Nick shut the car door. "Thought the element of surprise would be fun." He hurried up the stairs.

"Oh, yeah . . . a real ball." Timmons stepped beside him.

"Yes? Is there news?" The senator opened the door to them, showing them into the same, tired formal living room. This time, Mrs. Ford wasn't sitting like an exhibit on display.

"Is Mrs. Ford feeling well?" Nick asked as he sat on the sofa. No way was he going to sit on that uncomfortable chair again if he could help it.

"She's been busy planning the memorial service for Gina. Her funeral will be tomorrow afternoon at two. Memphis Memorial Gardens. Her wake begins this evening, so understandably, Mrs. Ford needs her rest."

"I'm sorry. That must be exhausting for Mrs. Ford."

"It has been. I'll let her know you asked after her." He sat in the hard chair. "Now, how may I help you today?"

Nick inched to the edge of the couch. "Sir, we've tried every way we can to verify your alibi and we can't."

The senator's face twisted. "I've told you several times now, I was speaking with an international investor, Mr. Whitlow. I don't know why you can't call and verify that, and I haven't any idea why the call isn't showing up on my phone records."

"Sir, you did talk to Mr. Whitlow from a little after eight until about nine o'clock—"

"See! Then why are you asking me—?"

"On *Thursday,* sir. Not Friday."

He froze.

"And before you ask, yes, sir, we're sure. The phone records verify that." Nick waited for that to sink in. "Is it possible you just got your days mixed up?"

"Well, obviously."

"Then whatever you were doing on what you thought was Thursday could possibly be what you were doing on Friday." That should have made logical sense and eased Ford's mind a bit, but the senator's facial muscles tightened by the minute.

"Senator, are you okay?"

"Yes, yes. I'm fine." Only he didn't look fine. He looked like a man about to pass out.

"Sir, can you think of what you could have been doing on Friday morning?" Timmons asked.

Ford got up and crossed the room. He closed the French doors to the room, then returned to his seat. "What I'm about to tell you is completely confidential, correct?"

What was the man up to now? "As much as it can be, sir."

"Because if this got out . . . it could destroy me."

"Sir, we don't want to destroy you. We just need to verify your alibi."

"I was on the phone, but not with Mr. Whitlow."

Well, no kidding. Hadn't Nick just told the senator this?

"I was on the phone, but not my cell or the one here at the house."

Oh, this was gonna be rich.

"I have an untraceable phone." Ford shot to his feet again, this time going to his study. He used a key from the key ring in his pocket to open a drawer. He pulled out a pay-in-advance disposable cell phone. "This phone. I was on this phone."

Nick took the phone and inspected it. No SIM card. No account. Not traceable. "Sir, we can't pull records on this to verify when you were on the phone or to whom."

"I know. That's why I *have* the phone."

Nick handed the phone back. "Then why are you telling us this?"

"Because I was on the phone with a certain . . . special friend."

Ahh. A girlfriend.

"You see, my wife doesn't come down until nine or later, so I call my friend every other day around eight. That gives me plenty of time to talk before I walk the treadmill with Gina."

"I see." No wonder he'd looked like he was going to pass out. "Sir, we still can't trace that phone. We're going to need your friend's name and number so we can verify your alibi."

"Why would I make up something that could potentially destroy my career if it weren't true?"

"I've seen people do some mighty strange things in circumstances such as these."

The senator glared at Nick. He stood his ground, staring back, refusing to budge.

"Fine." Ford went to his desk, found a scrap of paper, and jotted down a name and number. He handed it to Nick. "Here. But protect this information. It won't only destroy my career, but will also hurt her."

No mention of hurting his wife. What a piece of work. You think you know someone . . . just went to show that you can never really know someone in public office. All the public sees is the face they want you to see.

Nick folded the paper and slipped it into his pocket. "We'll be as discreet as we can. Thank you."

Timmons stood and followed Nick to the car. As soon as the engine roared to life, Timmons exploded. "I cannot believe him. Can you? I mean, have you seen his wife? She's a beautiful older woman. And he's cheating on her?"

"Now, now . . . you don't know what kind of marriage arrangement they have." Nick pulled over at the end of the driveway and pulled out the paper and his cell. He dialed the number for the office.

"Agent Martin."

"This is SAC Hagar. I need you to get me an address for a Lila Acer with this phone number." He read the number off the paper, gave Agent Martin his cell number for easy reference, then hung up.

"I still can't believe people cheat on their spouses."

"Not everyone has a great marriage, Timmons."

"They should try to make it work. Cheating never helps."

"No, but—" His cell buzzed. "Agent Hagar."

Agent Martin gave him Lila's address, then hung up.

Nick put the car in gear and pulled onto the road. "It's not far from here."

Silence filled the cabin.

"Do you think his wife knows?" Timmons popped his knuckles. "I mean, we always hear that women know, whether they want to or not."

"I don't know."

"It's a whole lot on Mrs. Ford right now."

"We aren't going to leak it, Timmons. We'll just verify his alibi and that should be the end of it."

"But every time I see him on television now, I'll know. And I won't believe a word he says. Because a cheater has to lie. He has to lie to his wife. To his friends. To himself. So why would I ever believe him?"

Nick didn't answer. There was no answer. Funny thing about trust, once it was ripped up, you couldn't tape it back together again.

Soon enough, Nick pulled into the driveway of the address for Lila Acer. Modest, but nice. Stone-front house, manicured lawn. A small foreign compact sat under the carport.

A leggy blonde with startling green eyes answered their knock at the front door. Not at all what Nick had expected. "Uh, Lila Acer?"

"Yes?" She had a Southern drawl that would make a Georgia peach jealous.

Nick flashed his badge. "I'm Agent Hagar and

251

this is Agent Timmons. May we ask you a few questions?"

"Sure. C'mon in." She stepped aside so they could enter.

They followed her into the living room, which was bright with color and blooming plants. "Excuse the mess. I wasn't expecting company." She smiled, her makeup-less face fresh and young. She couldn't have been more than thirty. "Please, have a seat. Can I get y'all some tea?"

"No, thank you." Nick sat on the couch as did Timmons. He couldn't help but draw the comparison between her and Mrs. Ford. The age difference. And the race. Was this why Mrs. Ford had endured a lightening procedure? Did the senator make it obvious his preference of lighter-skinned women?

Lila sat on the love seat diagonal from the couch. "What can I answer for you?" She made *you* sound like it had four syllables.

"Ma'am, we need to know what you were doing between eight and nine last Friday morning."

She went a little pale. "Excuse me?"

"We're investigating a murder, ma'am. Please tell us what you were doing between eight and nine last Friday morning."

"Well, I don't know that I recall, exactly."

"Ms. Acer, please." Nick pitched forward, propping his elbows on his knees. "It's okay. We just need the truth. You aren't in any kind of trouble."

"I-I believe I was on the phone. With a friend." She swallowed so loud it echoed in the room. Her unease was almost palpable.

"Ma'am, were you on your cell phone or house phone?" If they could pull the records, she wouldn't really need to admit to anything.

"I-I don't know."

Nick dug in his pocket and pulled out the scrap of paper and passed it to her. "What number is this? Your house?"

She stared at the paper, her hands trembling. "This is his handwriting. He gave you this." She lifted her gaze to Nick. "This is my house number. That's the phone I was on."

Nick smiled and stood. "Thank you, ma'am. You've been a big help."

"But I didn't tell you who I was on the phone with." She stood, still clutching the scrap of paper.

"I know. We already know." He led the way to the front door. "Thank you, Ms. Acer, you've been a big help."

Once in the car, Timmons let out a long breath. "You let her off easy."

"No, I didn't."

"She's so young. And pretty. It isn't fair."

"It's not our place to judge." Nick raced the engine, but he felt sorry for the senator's wife.

253

"We've verified the senator's alibi. That's all we went to do and we did."

"He's such a fraud. He lectures everyone who'll listen about the inequality for people of color, then has an affair with a white woman." Timmons shook his head. "And his wife getting her skin lightened? Do you think she knows about the affair?"

"I don't know what Mrs. Ford is aware of, and maybe the senator really just wanted to get to know Tiddle better and didn't have an issue with his daughter dating a white man."

"That'd really be hypocritical, now, wouldn't it?"

"We'll pull the phone records for her house, but I think it's safe to say Ford's alibi is confirmed." Nick turned off the highway.

"Yeah. Hey, while we're out, let's run by Ward's. Let's see if we can get anything new on his alibi."

Nick switched lanes. Three turns later, and he pulled up to Leo Ward's house. The garage was closed and no cars sat in the driveway.

They rang the doorbell and waited. Then knocked. Nothing. They knocked again.

"They aren't home."

Nick turned to see an elderly lady in flannel pajamas under a wool coat walking an almost hairless Schnauzer along the sidewalk. "You know the people who live here?"

"Of course I do. I live right across the street.

Betsy Ann McDearmott." She ambled up to him. "I'm a member of our neighborhood crime watch. Who are you?" She put one hand on her bony hip.

He flashed his badge. "Agent Hagar, ma'am, and this is Agent Timmons."

"Is there a problem here?"

"Oh no, ma'am. We're just following up with Mr. Ward. About the satellite dish installer that was at their house last Friday."

"Oh, that. All that drilling so loud. Scared poor Rosie here half to death." She picked up the dog that looked both blind and deaf. Nick doubted poor Rosie even knew what was going on.

"It was loud?"

"Oh my, yes. It was quite disturbing. I called Leo and asked what in the world was going on. I still have cable, you know, but Leo said he couldn't get all the ministry channels he wanted with just cable."

Nick exchanged a look with Timmons. "You called Leo? That morning?"

"I sure did. I hadn't really a choice, not with all that ruckus going on. I wanted to know what was happening. Me and poor Rosie couldn't even hear our morning show."

"Mrs. McDearmott, do you happen to recall what time you spoke with Leo?"

"Why I sure do. Right about eight thirty."

"Are you sure?"

She set the dog on the sidewalk again. "Of course I'm sure. It was just as my morning show was about to start and it comes on at eight thirty every weekday."

"And you called the Wards' house?"

"Yes. Leo apologized profusely and explained the technician would be inside soon and not making any more noise. That Leo is a nice man. His wife too. He even sent his son over that evening with a fresh batch of those tea cakes his wife makes."

Another alibi sewn up.

"Thank you so much, Mrs. McDearmott. You've been so helpful."

"Happy to help, Agents." She tugged on the leash. "Come on, Rosie. It's almost time for our afternoon stories."

Nick stared at Timmons once they were back in the car. "That's strike two. We're running out of suspects."

"Maybe we'll get the info from the familial earlier rather than later tomorrow."

Nick turned over the car's engine. "Be sure and wear a clean suit tomorrow."

"Why?"

"We're going to a funeral."

Chapter Nineteen

"I'll never feel comfortable taking a strong
drink, and I'll never feel easy smoking a
cigarette. I just don't think those things
are right for me."
Elvis Presley

The omelet melted in her mouth. Maddie moaned
aloud.

Nick grinned. "Good?"

"Oh. My. Goodness. This is truly a master-
piece." She'd ordered the portobello mushroom-
and-roasted pepper omelet. The perfect blend of
portobello mushrooms, and Swiss and mozzarella
cheeses exploded in her mouth with just the
right kick of roasted red peppers.

He chuckled. "Nothing beats Brother Juniper's
breakfast. It's the best breakfast in Memphis."

"I can't believe I've lived here all my life and
never eaten here." Not really surprising. She
normally didn't get out for breakfast often, but
she'd never have stumbled upon the house with
the white picket fence as a breakfast culinary
delight.

"My brother adored this place, so my family
used to come every Sunday after church." Nick
shook his head. "I think Roger just liked that it

was a house and he loved the cheery walls. Or could've been he had a crush on the waitress. At any rate, I fell in love with the food." He scooped another bite of his Hungry Tiger open-faced omelet.

Church every Sunday . . . so was he a Christian? That would be number one on her list of requirements for a man. She wiped her mouth. "What church do you attend?"

His fork froze midbite. He swallowed and lowered his fork. "We attended Crossway Church."

"Over on Altruria?"

He nodded, shoving the bite into his mouth.

"I know it." She smiled. "I've visited there a couple of times. I liked it."

He chewed.

"I attend the Life Church and love it. The schedule is great for working around if I have to work on Sunday. For instance, I'm planning on attending service tomorrow evening at six. Would you like to join me?"

Nick took a long sip of coffee. "I think I'll be working. If we get that info back from Nashville TBI."

She swallowed her bite, the omelet suddenly not as flavorful as before. "I understand. The offer stands, though." She pushed away her plate. Disappointment didn't mix with mushrooms.

Nick's cell phone broke the uncommon, uncomfortable silence with its buzz. "Excuse me," he said before answering the call. "Hagar."

Maddie sipped her coffee. No doubt about it, Nick didn't want to come to church with her. Maybe he really liked his own church, but he hadn't invited her to go with him. Maybe he'd been burned by a church as a young man and never reconciled himself. The reason didn't matter, only that it didn't appear he was a godly man as he never broached the conversation, even when she opened the subject matter wide.

Lord, if Nick's strayed from You, I pray You will draw him nearer to You. Not just so we can have the relationship I really, really want, but for his eternal life. Amen.

She contemplated in silence, catching his part of the phone conversation.

"Great. Set it up in my office and we'll view it when I get in."

She drank the rest of her coffee.

"Yeah. I'll let her know. Thanks." He hung up. "Sorry about that."

"It's okay. Anything urgent?"

"No, just an alibi verification, maybe."

"Good."

"Oh, and the judge has set the date for Conrad Sloan's sentencing. It'll be Monday at nine."

She still didn't know exactly how she felt about Sloan. She could certainly understand him being upset because of his sister, but retaliating against her served no purpose except for his idea of vigilante revenge. While she'd done her job and done it well, she couldn't help feeling much like Sloan—that because of her, a terrible monster had been set free.

But science didn't lie.

"Are you planning to go? I'll be there. I'll have to testify since I took his statement, but I won't be able to sit with you."

"It's okay." She probably wouldn't go. She hated courtrooms. Hated to testify. It was the one part of her job she didn't like.

He frowned. "How about I get Timmons to testify, and I'll sit with you?"

"No, really. I probably won't be able to go anyway, unless I have to." She shrugged. "I'll be busy at work."

Nick gave her a funny look. "Okay." He nodded toward her plate. "You didn't eat half of your omelet."

"I'm full." She set down her cup. "I know you need to get to work. I do too." She stood. "This was really nice, though. Thank you."

He stood as well and tossed a couple of twenties onto the table. He took her elbow and led her out of the diner-style restaurant. "Is everything okay?"

"Yeah. My mind's already on work." She smiled past her disappointment.

"I know, how about dinner tonight? The Rendezvous?" His smile danced in his eyes.

"I thought you didn't eat ribs in public?" She

couldn't help responding to that smile of his.

"For you, my lady, I'll disgrace myself with barbeque-sauced cheeks." He wagged his eyebrows.

She laughed. "How can I resist?"

"You can't. That's the point." He hugged her. "How about I pick you up at six?"

"Sounds great to me."

They stopped beside her car. He leaned down and kissed her temple. "See you tonight."

Her heart didn't stop thumping despite the unsettling disappointment until she reached the office.

"Deus, cujus miseratióne ánimæ fidélium requiéscunt, hunc túmulum benedícere dignáre, eíque Angelum tuum sanctum députa custódem: et quorum quarúmque córpora hic sepeliúntur, ánimas eórum ab ómnibus absólve vínculis delictórum; ut in te semper cum Sanctis tuis sine fine lœténtur. Per Christum Dóminum nostrum. Amen."

Nick stared at the priest, vested in a black cope at Gina Ford's gravesite. He lifted the collar of his coat to ward off the wind. While sunny with temperatures in the thirties, there was a gusty wind rattling through Memorial Gardens Cemetery.

The second priest—or was it an assistant?—turned toward the crowd of mourners and translated the Latin. "O God, by Your mercy rest is given to the souls of the faithful, be pleased to bless this grave. Appoint Your holy angels to guard it and set free from all the chains of sin and the soul of her whose body is buried here, so that with all Thy saints she may rejoice in Thee forever. Through Christ our Lord. Amen."

Nick drew in a quick breath. God's mercy? Where was His mercy when Roger had been killed? Where was His mercy when his mother had to stand over a casket and peer down into her son's lifeless face? Nick shook his head. He needed to concentrate. He was here to do his job, not look for an epiphany.

Mrs. Ford stood beside the senator, her face covered by a black veil. She leaned against the senator as the priest splashed water over the gravesite, then swung a canister of incense over the casket.

"*Réquiem æternam dona ei, Dómine.*"

"Eternal rest grant unto her, O Lord."

"*Et lux perpétua lúceat ei.*"

"And let perpetual light shine upon her."

"*Requiéscat in pace.*"

"May she rest in peace."

"Amen."

"*Anima ejus, et ánimæ ómnium fidélium defunctórum, per misericórdiam Dei requiéscant in pace.*"

"May her soul, and the souls of all the faithful departed, through the mercy of God rest in peace."

Nick's heart thudded. Was Roger's soul at peace? Was his brother in the presence of God? Strange how just the idea made him feel . . . well, hard to explain. Not as angry?

"Amen."

The crowd formed a line to address the senator and Mrs. Ford. Some offered hugs, some a handshake, but all offered some form of condolence. The senator spoke to every person while Mrs. Ford merely nodded or accepted the offered embrace.

Nick ignored his own burning emotions as he noticed a few people from the very back of the crowd slipping away toward the row of vehicles lining the cemetery. One he recognized—David Tiddle. Nick stiffened, his mind and concentration solely on David. He motioned for Timmons to stay and monitor those offering condolences to the grieving parents, then moved to follow Tiddle.

He had to sprint the last few yards, all uphill, so as not to shout after the younger man. "Tiddle."

The man turned, then stopped. "Ah, hello." His eyes were bloodshot and swollen.

"Agent Hagar."

"I remember. Well, I didn't remember your name, but I remember who you are." He stared down the hill toward Gina's casket. "I probably shouldn't have come. Her father will have a cow if he sees me. But it seemed wrong not to pay my last respects to someone I loved." Moisture filled his eyes.

By all accounts, Gina had loved Tiddle very much and vice versa. Nick recognized the grief Tiddle wore like a favorite jacket. "I'm sorry for your loss."

"Thank you." He swiped the back of his hand across his face and cleared his throat. "I didn't think it'd be this hard to stand there and stare at that box, knowing she was inside. I didn't think it'd be so painful to tell her good-bye in my heart."

Nick understood. He hadn't been prepared to tell Roger good-bye at the funeral. His actual final words to his brother had come much later, when he was on a nature walk in Shelby Farms Park. Alone and in the quietness only nature could provide, Nick was able to empty his heart and let Roger go.

Tiddle used his chin to gesture toward the graveside. "I heard on the news the senator said you had some forensic evidence?"

"I can't discuss an open investigation, Mr. Tiddle."

"But the senator can?"

He wasn't supposed to, but apparently a gag wouldn't keep the politician's mouth closed. "I have no idea where Senator Ford received his information." Although the Medical Examiner suspected one of his clerks to have been the leak. A clerk who had since been let go.

"I see." Tiddle nodded. "I figured the old man was just blowing smoke when I didn't hear about any arrest being made."

"No, no arrest. We're still actively investigating, though."

"I can't believe you had the nerve to show up here." The woman's voice grated from between two cars.

Nick and Tiddle both twisted toward the voice.

Cynthia Mantle pointed at Tiddle as her spiked heels punctured the carefully groomed ground. "You aren't welcome here."

This could be very interesting. Nick leaned against Tiddle's car.

"More welcome than you." Tiddle's eyes narrowed. "At least Gina loved me. She didn't even like you anymore. She wanted to get away from your jealousy and pettiness. Get away from you clinging to her coattails."

Mantle glanced at Nick, then stepped closer to Tiddle. "We were having a rough patch, yes, but it was brought on by you."

"Me?" Tiddle chuckled, cold and humorless. "Please. I didn't have to do a thing. You were so jealous of her that everyone saw it for a long time. Gina was so good, she chose to believe the best about people, even you. Until you showed your true colors."

"You poisoned her against me. Told her your filthy lies."

"Lies?" Tiddle crossed his arms over his chest and leaned against his car, opposite side of Nick. "You did make a move on me."

"Before y'all were dating."

"No, it was after we'd already gone out several times."

"But you weren't exclusive."

Nick digested the information. No one had mentioned this little tidbit before. That would explain some of the bitterness between them.

"Didn't matter. I wasn't interested, and you didn't like that. Couldn't stand that I preferred Gina over you." He waved a hand up and down in front of her. "But really, who could blame me?"

Nick pressed his lips together and waited. Most of the women he knew would dole out a slap for that one.

"Oh, puh-leeze. Get over yourself, David. Every-one knew you were just a gold digger. It was only a matter of time before Gina figured it out. Once she did, you'd be nothing but a flash in the pan." She leaned closer to Tiddle. "But I think she did find out. She told me that morning she was going to confront two people in her life and it would hurt her, but that she'd do it. I think one of those people was you."

Tiddle's snide expression slipped just a fraction. "Like she would talk to you?"

"She did. Ask Agent Hagar there. He has the

phone records that prove I talked with Gina."

Tiddle glanced at him. Nick kept his expression neutral.

"Even if you did talk to her, she probably told you to leave her alone and stop calling her."

Interesting. Mantle hadn't said she'd called Gina. How did he know she'd been the one who called and not Gina calling her? Had he just assumed?

Tiddle shook his head at Mantle. "You just can't accept that Gina was done with you. She'd had enough of you using her."

"Me using her? Don't you mean you?"

"Cyn, Cyn, Cyn . . . we all know your poor father got caught embezzling three years ago and is spending time in a federal camp. Poor, little disgraced Cynthia needed big-hearted Gina with her father's political influence to make sure she wasn't ostracized by everyone in Memphis."

Mantle's face went fire-engine red. "I wasn't using her for money. Who did she hand money to all the time, David? Huh? You. *Loans* you called them. Did you ever pay her back?"

More interesting stuff. He should've brought a recorder. Who knew a funeral could provide so much information about suspects.

"Yes. Yes, I did pay her back. With interest."

"Sure you did."

"I did, but I don't have to prove anything to you."

Nick's cell phone vibrated. He moved to the back of the car to answer the call. "Hagar."

"Nick? It's Maddie."

"Hey."

"Guess what I'm holding?"

"Um . . . a leash?"

She laughed, throaty and soft. It did strange things to his gut. "No. I'm holding the results from the familial DNA test. An Agent Zanca just hand delivered the sealed envelope to me. And she said to tell you that you owed her one."

Yes! "I'll round up Timmons and we'll head that way now." He squinted down at the mourners, trying to spot the agent. "Thanks for calling me."

"See you soon."

Nick hung up and walked back to the bickering couple. "Excuse me, but this is neither the time nor the place for your discussion." Although he'd enjoyed the results.

"Sorry." Tiddle dug in his pocket and pulled out his keys.

"Yeah. Sorry."

Nick looked from one to the other. "As the investigation is still ongoing, I'm going to remind you both to remain in town in the event we have more questions."

"Of course. Thank you." Mantle stalked off.

"Sure." Tiddle unlocked his car and climbed behind the wheel.

Nick caught Timmons's attention and waved him up before heading to his car. Timmons slipped in the passenger's seat. "What's up?"

"The DNA results are back. We're heading to the lab now." He cranked the engine and pulled free from the line of cars snaking throughout the cemetery. "Did you catch anything down there?"

"Not really. Lot of people there who didn't know Gina at all."

"Just wanting to be seen here to get on the senator's good side?"

"Something like that. What about you?"

Nick gave the condensed version of Mantle and Tiddle's argument.

"That adds to both of their motives."

"Right." Nick picked up speed as he nosed the car onto the highway. "What about the gas station's video?"

Timmons shook his head. "Martin and Salman both watched it twice. There is a blond woman who goes in and comes out during the time in question, but her face is concealed both times, so no positive ID."

"Maybe one of them will be the hit. Especially since Cynthia Mantle's father is in prison. His DNA profile should be in CODIS."

Timmons snapped his fingers. "This could be it, Boss. This could be it."

Nick could only hope so.

CHAPTER TWENTY

"I'm trying to keep a level head.
You have to be careful out in the world.
It's so easy to get turned."
ELVIS PRESLEY

"You can't read the contents by osmosis, you know." Eva chuckled as she passed Maddie's desk.

Maddie didn't bother looking up from the sealed envelope propped on her desk. "Nick's on his way."

"So you'll know the contents soon enough." Eva plopped onto her own chair.

Maddie drummed her fingers. "Aren't you the least bit excited? This is the first time we've been a part of using familial DNA on a case. It's really cool." She sat up straight. *"Long distance information give me Memphis, Tennessee . . ."*

Eva shook her head. "Yes, it's terribly exciting."

"Not even the Nashville TBI has gotten to actually work a case with familial DNA." *"Help me find the party trying to get in touch with me."*

"Groundbreaking."

"Eva, what's wrong?"

"Nothing."

Ah. *Something* was on her mind. Maddie

propped her chin in her hands. "Come on, what's going on with you? It's like one second you're excited, then you get around me and you aren't." She sat up straight. "Have I done something to upset you?"

"No, no. Nothing like that." Eva crossed her arms over her chest. "I'm just a little sad this investigation will end soon."

What? "You don't like all the investigation part? You like the serology stuff." Had all the chemicals finally warped her head?

"Well, this case is different."

"Who are you and what have you done with my friend?"

Eva smiled, one of those I-have-a-secret-I'm-not-going-to-share smiles. "Forget it. No big deal."

Maddie stood and crossed the room, plopping down on the middle of Eva's desk. "Now you must tell me."

"It's nothing."

"Eva!" Maddie leaned and got nose-to-nose with her friend. "Tell me or else. Remember, I know how to hide bodies and not leave evidence."

"Okay, I give." Eva laughed. "It's just that I've enjoyed working with Darren. A lot." Her face reddened. "A whole lot."

Dawning hit Maddie like a freight train. "You have a crush on Darren?"

Eva's face turned as red as a candy apple.

"Don't you dare tease me about this or I'll have to take you out."

Eva . . . and Darren? Eva and Darren. Eva and Darren. Yeah, it could make sense.

Maddie smiled. "I'm not going to tease you. I love Darren like a brother. Sometimes I like him more than Rafe." She thought about that for a second. "Actually, most of the time I like him more than Rafe."

Eva grinned. "He's pretty great. He's sweet and funny and good-looking as all get-out, but you already know that."

Well . . . it was kind of that she didn't. Growing up, all her friends had been gaga over Rafe, but he was just Rafe to her. She thought the same about Darren.

"And he's a perfect gentleman."

Maddie swung her dangling legs. "Uh, I didn't realize you two had grown so . . . uh . . . aware of each other." At least she hoped it wasn't one-sided. But Darren had been seeing Kimi, his nanny-housekeeper. Hadn't he?

"We've just formed a really nice friendship. Mainly just talking on the phone and e-mails. Texts."

She had to ask. "What about Kimi?"

Eva shook her head. "Everybody assumed they were dating. They weren't. Never have. Kimi actually has a serious boyfriend, but he's in the service and is overseas at the moment. Stationed in Korea for six more months. So Darren takes her out to dinner and the movies at times, just so she isn't so lonely. He's so sensitive like that."

That was true, Darren was very sensitive. "You do remember he has a daughter, right? He's a single parent?"

Eva frowned. "Of course. I'm not stupid."

Maddie held out her hands. "Sorry. You've just steered clear of single daddies in the past."

"They aren't like Darren."

Oh no. Maddie recognized the over-the-moon look in her friend's eyes. The problem was, Darren was her friend too.

She loved Eva, she did, but the woman went through men like Maddie went through Elvis songs: She loved so many, she never could pick just one favorite. She didn't want to see either Eva or Darren hurt.

Creak.

Maddie hopped off Eva's desk just as Nick and Darren strode into the lab, Peter matching their strides. She grabbed the envelope from the desk and handed it to Nick. "Special delivery, sir."

Nick held the envelope, paused, then handed it to Peter. "It's officially your case."

Maddie had never seen Peter so impressed before. He nodded to Nick. Maddie just wanted to kiss Nick smack on the lips right then and there. What an amazing man he was. Showing such respect.

Peter opened the envelope and pulled out the pieces of paper. His lips moved as he read silently.

"Well?" Eva had come around from behind her desk and stood beside Darren.

"There are a lot of law enforcement policies we have to follow and investigative regulations, but according to this record, the unknown DNA sample we submitted is a familial match to one Brody Alexander."

Maddie blinked. No, that couldn't be right.

Nick shifted. "Who's that?"

"Brody Alexander is the biological relative of the person whose DNA was recovered from Gina's back," Eva explained.

"So, we find this Alexander character's blood relatives and that's who left the blood on the victim at the scene?" Darren asked.

No!

"That's it, in a nutshell." Eva smiled at Darren.

"Then let's go find out who Alexander's blood relatives are." Nick nudged Darren.

"Wait a minute. There's policy on how we find that out." Peter flipped the page and read. "To determine possible familial relationships, the investigator shall conduct a full background check of the identified individual and family members, including but not limited to: criminal history checks, inmate profiles from Department of Corrections as well as visitor logs from DOC, presentence investigative reports, prison telephone logs, and other public records."

"So we have to run a background check on this Brody Alexander first, then narrow down his blood relatives. Maybe we'll find a connection between one of them and Gina Ford."

"I already know the connection." Maddie finally found her voice. Her entire body trembled.

Nick moved to take her elbow and helped her to her chair. "What's wrong? You're so pale . . . like you've seen a ghost."

In a way, she had. "I know who Brody Alexander is and who his immediate family members are."

"And that's what's got you white as a sheet?" Darren hovered behind Nick.

"Well, who is he?" Eva asked.

Maddie struggled to control her racing pulse. Not even an Elvis song could comfort her right now. "Ten years ago, he was released from federal prison. He did a short stint for selling junk bonds or something."

"You know him?" Nick asked quietly.

"I've never met him personally."

"So why are you still pale?" Eva asked.

"Brody has two children. A daughter, Tammy, who should be in her early thirties about now. I don't know much about her."

"And his other child?" Peter asked.

"He has a son, Adam, who is thirty-four."

"And how would either of them connect with Gina Ford?" Nick asked.

She licked her lips. "Adam is a teacher at the college."

"At University of Memphis?" Nick's eyes lit up.

"Yes, but it can't be Adam."

"How's that?" Nick asked.

She couldn't go into this right now. Not here. Not now.

Eva moved beside her. "Adam started out as a TA at the University of Tennessee, didn't he?"

Maddie locked stares with Eva.

"*That* Adam?" Eva barely whispered.

Maddie gave a slow nod.

The room grew still and close. Maddie found herself struggling to breathe. To even catch her breath. It was as if someone had poured glue into her lungs.

"Would someone mind enlightening the rest of us as to what's going on?" Nick boomed.

Just when she'd been happy, when a chance for a true happily-ever-after was within her grasp, her past came up to smack her upside the head.

"Okay, let me wrap my mind around this." Nick worked through the information. "Whoever left the blood drop on the back of Gina Ford's shirt is a blood relative to Brody Alexander. Brody has a son, Adam, who just so happens to be a teacher at the university Gina attended."

"Right." Timmons had joined Nick, two steps away from the woman-whispers between Maddie and Eva.

"That's a pretty strong connection to me. We need to see if Gina had Adam for any classes. Talk with her friends and see if they'd ever seen them together around campus."

Maddie stood. "It's not Adam."

"How do you know?" She seemed pretty adamant about the guy.

"I just do." Maddie ran a hand through her hair. It caught the light and picked up the highs and lows of the red.

Nick curled his hand so he wouldn't touch it. "The connection's too strong. We'll look into it."

"No, you have to believe me, Nick. It's not Adam. He wouldn't hurt anyone. He couldn't."

The pleading in her voice yanked his chest. But it also . . .

"How do you know?"

She let out a shaky breath. "I know him. Or I did."

"People surprise each other all the time, Maddie. You know this."

"Not Adam. He wouldn't."

Why was she so staunchly defending him? "How do you know this Adam character so well that you can be so positive it's not him?"

She swallowed, then licked her lips. "I dated him. Back in college."

Nick's chest tightened like a vise grip had it in its claw. Tighter. Tighter. "That was . . . how many years ago?"

"Eleven." She kept her eyes focused on his.

"That's a long time ago, Maddie. People change."

"Not like that. Not Adam."

She sounded so sure. "Have you spoken with him recently?" *Please say no.*

Maddie shook her head. "Not in several years."

At least there was that.

She held up her hands. "I know what you're going to say, that he could've changed, but I'm telling you, there's no way. Adam might be a cheater, but he abhors violence."

Cheater? Ah. He understood that all too well. Joy. She'd done a real number on him. Made him doubt himself. Nick would bet his badge Adam had done the same kind of number on Maddie. Something they had in common: the firsthand knowledge that you can't ever trust a cheater because a cheater has to lie.

He caught Timmons's eye over Maddie's head. Yeah, he thought the same thing . . . as Timmons had just said recently, you can't ever trust a cheater because a cheater has to lie.

"When his father went to prison, Adam was furious. So upset. He wouldn't visit his father in prison and hasn't spoken to him upon release."

"Still?" Nick asked.

She shrugged. "I guess. I don't know."

"So, as far as you know, father and son could've patched things up and they're a happy, cozy family now. Right?"

"I guess but—"

"And as far as you know, Adam could have become some deranged killer, stalking women, right?"

"No, he couldn't. It's not in Adam. It's just not. He's a very gentle soul. A kind spirit."

Nick fisted his hands, not at all familiar with the feelings surging through him. He couldn't even process them as fast as they whipped through him. Anger. Jealousy. Disappointment.

Fear.

"Well, I'm sure Charles Manson and Jeffrey Dahmer's ex-girlfriends thought they were gentle souls and kind spirits too." Nick hated the way the sarcasm rolled off his tongue, but it was out of his mouth before he could stop it. "We'll just do our job and check out Adam Alexander and see what we find."

Maddie blinked and jerked back as if he'd slapped her. Her face colored right back up. "You do that, Agent, and see if I'm right." She stood and headed to the door. "If you'll excuse me." She marched from the room.

Eva gave him a glower, then rushed out the door as well.

Helm glared at him. Even Timmons stared at him funny.

"Aw, come on. I'm not the bad guy here. This is our job, guys."

"You were mean to her. She doesn't deserve that." Helm shook his head. "She said nothing offensive to you."

Everything she said was offensive to him. She took up for her ex-boyfriend. A guy who cheated on her *eleven years ago,* yet she still defended him. Eleven years.

"The point is, guys, she didn't even want us to look into Alexander." He stared at Timmons. "You know that's basically the point she was making."

Timmons nodded. "That's true." He looked at Helms. "We can't do that. We have to check out everyone."

Helm continued to frown. "Doesn't mean you have to be rude to her."

And he was right. "You're right. I'll apologize to her. That was uncalled for."

Helm hesitated, sighing. "Okay. What do we need to do first?"

CHAPTER TWENTY-ONE

"I'm so nervous. I've always been
nervous, ever since I was a kid."
ELVIS PRESLEY

If she'd ever been madder in her adult life,
Maddie couldn't remember it.

Eva had spent the better part of the last three
hours attempting to make excuses for Nick's
blatant rudeness. Maddie hadn't accepted any of
them.

Now, an hour at home to unwind, and she was
still furious. Even worse, she had a date with him.

Not that she should keep it. She shouldn't—she
knew that, but she had to be ready in case. As
clueless as the man was, he'd probably show up
and be confused why she wasn't raring to go out
with him.

In a moment of normalcy, Maddie realized
Nick was probably hurt because of her defense of
Adam. But their past relationship aside, Nick
should trust her judgment. On the other hand, she
couldn't help being baffled by the familial DNA
results.

Science didn't lie.

But she was positive Adam wasn't involved in
Gina's murder. Knew it in her gut. Maybe it was

Adam's sister, Tammy. She could have known Gina, had a problem with her. Maddie had never met Tammy since Adam's and her relationship had to remain primarily a secret—him being a teacher's assistant and her being a student.

The doorbell buzzed at six o'clock, on the dot.

Nick was punctual in addition to being clueless.

She took a deep breath before she turned off the alarm, then opened the door.

A huge bouquet of roses with a pair of legs stood on her doorstep. Red, white, yellow, pink, orange, and purple—all mixed together with greenery and baby's breath. There had to be at least four or five dozen.

"Oh. My."

A hand extended, holding an envelope the size of a greeting card.

Maddie pressed her lips together and opened the envelope. Metallic confetti scattered all over the stoop of her front door as she pulled the card from the envelope.

I'M SORRY covered the front of the card. Big, bold print. Little print. All different colors.

She opened the card.

A picture of a teddy bear holding a sign that read FORGIVE ME? filled the interior of the card. Nick's name was scrawled across the bottom, barely legible.

It was too cute. She let out a giggle.

Nick peeked at her from around the massive rose bouquet. "I'm really sorry for being such a rude jerk."

"You were rude. And you were a jerk."

"I know. I'm sorry." He pushed out his bottom lip. "Forgive me?"

Like she could resist that sad, puppy dog face? Grinning and shaking her head, she stepped aside. "You'd better come in before those roses drive you into the ground."

In the kitchen, she dug around in cabinets until she found six vases. She filled vases with water, split the roses among them, and distributed the arrangements between the dining room, living room, bedroom, and office. She returned to find a sheepish Nick in the kitchen.

"I really am sorry. Cross my heart." He held open his arms.

She smiled and stepped into his embrace. As he hugged her, she inhaled. His cologne soothed her frazzled nerves. "It's okay." She squeezed him back, then stepped out of his touch. "But don't do it again."

"Yes, ma'am." He bowed low, then straightened. "You ready for some finger-licking-awesome ribs?"

"You bet. Getting angry makes me hungry." She chuckled at his feigned shocked expression.

Within moments, she'd let him help her into her coat, set the alarm, and sat in the front seat. The sweet aroma of roses hung in the car. She smiled to herself.

"Hey, what are you doing tomorrow night?"

Was this a trick question? "Um, I don't know."

"I do." He hummed as his fingers tapped on the steering wheel.

"Oh, really?" He seemed mighty cocky.

"Yep. I do."

"Do tell." She crossed her arms over her chest.

"Nope. You gotta guess."

A game? He was normally a serious type. But the roses, the silly card, and now the guessing game . . . he was showing her a totally different side to his personality. She liked it. "Dinner?"

"Nope."

"Great, I'm gonna go hungry." She chuckled.

"Stop trying to distract me . . . you have to guess." He merged the car onto I-40 west and picked up speed.

"Um, a movie?"

"No way. Too dull. I don't like dark theaters much."

"I don't either. But I love watching DVDs at home with a big bowl of popcorn."

"With so much butter it drips down your elbow."

She laughed. "Now I'm really, really hungry."

"You still have to guess." He changed lanes.

"Bowling? I hope it's not bowling because I'm really awful at it." She made a face.

He flashed her a smile. "Nope, not bowling, but I'll make note to bet you per pin."

She gave him a slight shove.

"Guess again."

"Am I even close?"

He shook his head. "Not even."

"Give me a hint."

"No way. You're a smart cookie. You can figure it out."

"Come on, just a little hint." She leaned closer so he could see her by the dashboard light. She pouted, pushing her bottom lip out.

"That's pathetic."

"A hint. A hint. I want a hint," she chanted.

He took the Second Street exit. "Better hurry. We're almost to the restaurant."

"Dancing?"

"No. I don't dance."

"What do you mean you don't dance?"

He shrugged. "I just don't."

"Everybody dances."

He shook his head as he took a slight left onto North Second Street. The Crowne Plaza Hotel blazed on the corner. "I don't dance."

She leaned her head back against the headrest. "Well, I love to dance. I'm making a note that you have to take me dancing if I have to go bowling."

"Tick-tock. You're almost out of time." He pulled into the Rendezvous parking lot and found a vacant space, not such an easy task.

He turned off the engine, undid his seat belt, then turned to face her. She unclicked her seat belt and faced him.

"Okay, here's a clue. It was my backup to the roses in case you needed more coaxing to forgive me."

How sweet. She snapped her fingers. "Man, I knew I should have held out for more." But she grinned, loving this game and loving this playful side of him.

He let out an exaggerated groan. "Fine. Maybe you'll figure it out over dinner." He got out of the car and rushed around to open her door for her. "I can't wait for you to figure it out or I'll die of starvation."

"Yeah, you really look like you're starving with those muscles." She froze as he shut the car door. Had she really just said that out loud?

He chuckled.

Yep, she'd said it aloud. Heat filled her cheeks. Good thing it was dark outside. And cold enough to cool her flushed face.

They entered the restaurant. On a Friday night, the place was packed and hopping. The mix of spices and grilling welcomed them and made Maddie's stomach growl. Not that Nick could hear it over all the people talking.

They didn't have to wait long. Soon, they crossed the wood plank floor and were seated in the main dining room, right under the big

American flag. The red-and-white checkered tablecloth always reminded Maddie of the picnics her family used to go on.

After they'd ordered soft drinks and both a full order of the world-famous Rendezvous charcoal-broiled pork ribs, the waiter left them alone.

"Guess." Nick smiled across the table at her.

"A picnic."

"No, but that's a good suggestion. We should go on one sometime."

Her heart pounded at the way he seemed to be making future plans with her. "I like picnics."

"We'll leave the ants out of our picnic, though."

"Definitely."

"Okay, another guess."

"Give me another hint."

"You'll love it."

She laughed. "So you think."

"I know you will. Okay, you get three questions as your hints."

"Goodie." She took a sip of her drink that the server set at her elbow. "Okay, do I have to travel far to get there?"

He shook his head. "Nope. Less than an hour. That's one."

"Is it indoors or out?"

"Indoor. It's too cold outside. That's two."

"Hmmm." She truly had drawn a blank.

The waiter appeared with their ribs and sides. Maddie offered up grace, then took a bite. The ribs were as melt-in-your-mouth-wonderful as she remembered. She closed her eyes and chewed, savoring the flavor. "This is smack-your-momma good." Maddie took another bite. Then another.

They didn't talk, just enjoyed the flavorful food cooked to perfection. Their drinks were refilled as quickly as they were depleted. And again. Soon enough, Maddie wiped her mouth and tossed the napkin onto the table. "I'm stuffed. I can't eat another bite."

"Me too." Nick tossed the last rib onto his plate. He grabbed the napkins and went to work cleaning his face.

He looked mighty cute with barbeque sauce on his chiseled cheeks.

After he paid the bill, they walked arm in arm across the parking lot. "You have one more question."

"You have me stumped for sure, Agent Hagar." Not to eat, a movie, dancing, bowling, or a picnic . . . inside and close by.

They reached the car, but he didn't open the door. Instead, he placed a hand against the passenger window, one on either side of her, trapping her against the car. He leaned in, putting his mouth right beside her ear. "One. More. Question." He pulled back, stopping when they were eye-to-eye.

Like she could think with him this close? "Um." She licked her lips. "Is it a concert?"

He shifted, not releasing her, but putting a little more space between them. "Mmm-mmm." His affirmation growl was low, guttural.

Her heart raced. She licked her lips again. "I like concerts."

His gaze locked with hers. "What's your all-time favorite Elvis Presley song?"

" 'Amazing Grace,' hands down. Something about that song . . . and the way he sings it." She sighed. "Reminds me of my mom."

His stare burned through her.

Heat flooded her face. "Uh, which concert?"

His fingers found their way into her hair. Gently, barely tugging, he pulled them through the length of her hair. His fingertips caressed the ends as he reached them. "The Elvis Lives, Ultimate Elvis Tribute Artist Event tour."

Her heart stopped. She grabbed hold of his arms. Her eyes went wide. "Are you kidding me? The Elvis Lives concert? Here? Tomorrow night?"

He nodded.

"That's been sold out forever. It sold out within thirty minutes of the tickets going on sale. I know, I tried to buy them an hour after they opened." Her heart started again . . . racing double-time. "You're kidding, right?"

His gaze never left hers as he shook his head.

"You're serious?" She couldn't help that her voice rose like that of a schoolgirl's.

He nodded.

"Oh. My. Gosh. I'm going to see the Elvis Lives concert?" She couldn't stop her legs from bouncing.

"*We're* going to see the Elvis Lives concert. Tomorrow night. Eight o'clock. At the FedEx Forum."

Maddie jumped up and down, making Nick drop his arms. She threw hers around his neck, still bouncing. "I'm going to see Elvis Lives. I'm going to see Elvis Lives." She'd wanted to see this concert for years, but it never worked out.

"Thankyouthankyouthankyou." She squeezed his neck harder.

"You're welcome, you're welcome, you're welcome."

She stopped jumping and grabbed his face. Holding it between her hands, she stood on tip-toe and planted a firm kiss against his lips.

Nick froze. Did he dare move? Dare to deepen the kiss?

Maddie stepped back, her hands dropping to her sides. Her mouth opened, then closed. She smiled, then pinned her bottom lip with her top teeth. "I'm sorry."

"For what?" Driving him crazy? Making him realize he had some strong feelings for her? Very strong feelings.

"I just really wanted to go to this concert and you got us tickets and I don't know how and I'm so excited and I love Elvis and—"

Enough.

Nick leaned down and gently rested his lips against hers. The scent that was uniquely Maddie filled his senses. He wrapped his arms around her, pulling her closer.

She moved her lips against his.

He froze again, not even breathing. Did she not want him to kiss her? Was he holding her too tight? Too close.

Her hands wound around his neck again, her fingertips grazing the skin above his collar.

His heart jackhammered.

He pulled away, resting his forehead against hers, staring deep into her beautiful brown eyes.

She'd done it again—made him go stupid.

CHAPTER TWENTY-TWO

"I've tried to lead a straight, clean life,
not set any kind of bad example."
ELVIS PRESLEY

"A moment, please, Professor?" Nick rushed to Professor Emmel's side, walking with him to his car.

"How did you know where to find me, Agent?"

Nick grinned. "Wasn't too hard to learn you belong to a writers' critique group that meets every other Saturday morning at this bookstore."

"We writers can be quite predictable."

"I was wondering if I might have a moment of your time, please."

The professor glanced at his watch. "Well, I'm free until lunchtime."

"Great." Nick gestured to the hole-in-the-wall coffee shop. "How about I buy you a cup of coffee?"

"That would be lovely."

Nick opened the door for the older gentleman. They placed their orders at the counter, then found an open table in the corner. "How was your meeting?"

"Very well, thank you. I've almost completed the manuscript I've been working on since summer. Soon, I'll send queries to a round of agents."

Was that good? "Uh, congratulations."

"Thank you. It's been a lifelong dream of mine to publish a novel. I'm very pleased with this draft and my critique group loves it."

The young barista delivered their coffee to the table.

Professor Emmel took a sip. "So nice to have coffee in real ceramic mugs, unlike the big coffee-house chains with their protective sleeves." He set his mug back on the table. "But I'm fairly certain you didn't hunt me down to talk about my manuscript or coffeehouses, did you, Agent Hagar?"

"No, I didn't."

"As I'm sure you are aware, I spoke with Ms. Mantle regarding our conversation. You didn't advise me not to."

"No, I didn't." It had actually worked out just fine that he had. She'd lawyered up and came in on her own. "But I'm not here to discuss Ms. Mantle."

"Then how may I help you?"

"Professor, the discussion we're having now *is* confidential. Do you agree not to discuss anything we talk about with anyone outside of law enforcement?"

"Certainly."

"This is an official investigation. Discussing details would be considered hindering an investigation."

"I understand, Agent." He took another sip of his coffee.

"Do you know Adam Alexander?" He lifted his own cup.

"Adam?"

"Yes. I understand he's a fellow teacher at University of Memphis?"

"Correct. He teaches Earth Sciences over in Johnson Hall." The professor creased his nose like he smelled something that stank.

"What can you tell me about him?"

"You already know he's a teacher. Our classrooms aren't in the same building. We don't exactly run in the same social circles."

Nick detected the harsh tone in that last sentence. "Oh?"

"For one, Adam is much younger than I."

"Only by about ten years or so. That's not much these days, Professor."

Emmel smiled indulgently as he took another sip of coffee. "Perhaps not, but he socializes with a much younger crowd than his own age. Much younger, if you get my drift."

"Are you implying he hangs out with student-aged people?"

"Exactly. Not just that age bracket, Agent, but actual students."

"Are you sure?"

"Of course I'm sure. I wouldn't say it otherwise. I've seen him out at restaurants with students. Always female students, to be sure."

Ah, a womanizer. And this was the man Maddie dated and she still took up for eleven years later? Nick couldn't get it.

"Oh, I'm sure you're thinking that I'm not being entirely forthcoming. Let me assure you, I am. He's even been warned by the provost twice to mind his Ps and Qs regarding the young ladies on campus."

Interesting. He'd ask Helm to question the provost.

"The last time, from what I understand, the provost told him if another complaint was filed on him at the university, he'd be reprimanded."

"So, this is definitely a habit of his?"

"Did you know he used to work at the University of Tennessee?"

Nick did. "Really?"

"He worked at the Health Science Center campus here in Memphis."

"So he switched to University of Memphis?" Nick left the door wide open for Emmel.

"Well, the way I understand it, he was asked to leave." And the professor walked right through it. "He had gotten himself into an, ahem, delicate situation with a young lady whose father called the board of directors. He was given the choice— leave with a good letter of recommendation on his teaching abilities, or stay and face disciplinary actions. He came to our campus about ten years ago."

The professor took another hit of coffee. "It's a disgrace, if you ask me."

"I think so too." Truth be told, everything Nick learned about Alexander disgusted him. "Do you happen to know if Gina Ford was in Mr. Alexander's class?"

"I don't rightly know, Agent. As I said, his classroom is in a different building than mine and I didn't know Gina Ford." He stood. "If you'll excuse me for just a moment, please." Emmel headed to the restrooms.

Nick pulled out his cell.

"Agent Timmons."

"It's Hagar. I need you to get Gina Ford's appointment book. I need to know if she took Adam Alexander's Earth Sciences class."

"Yes, sir."

"And please ask Helm to speak to the provost of the University of Memphis regarding any disciplinary warnings or reprimands given to Mr. Alexander."

"Yes, sir."

Nick hung up just as Professor Emmel returned to the table. "Excuse me."

"No problem. Just one more question, if you will, Professor."

"Yes?"

"Have you knowledge of any instance in which Mr. Alexander exhibited violence?"

"Not personally, no."

Nick leaned forward. "But you've heard of such instances?"

"Purely hearsay, Agent."

"I understand."

Emmel drained his cup. He set it on the table and absently traced the lip. "Some of the faculty members get together on weekends and watch sports or play cards. At one of them, he and one of the other teachers, Mr. Doak, had an altercation. This occurred just last week."

"Did you hear what the altercation was about?"

"I understand it began as a political discussion, then the debate became heated. I was told Mr.

Doak gave up arguing and went to leave the gathering. To go outside, get some fresh air to cool off." Mr. Emmel lifted his gaze to make eye contact with Nick. "But Mr. Alexander followed him outside and proceeded to hit him from behind."

"Was Mr. Doak hurt?"

"He was able to throw Mr. Alexander off of him. They tussled and Mr. Doak ended up getting the better of the deal." Emmel shrugged. "Still, Mr. Doak had to have two stitches on his temple where Mr. Alexander's ring caught him." He glanced at his watch, then stood. "I'm sorry, Agent Hagar. I really must keep my lunch date." He paused as he lifted his briefcase. "By the questions you asked, I'm assuming Mr. Alexander is a suspect in Gina Ford's murder? What about Hailey Carter's?"

"I'm not at liberty to say. Thank you, Professor Emmel. You've been an enormous help. I'll call you if I need anything else."

"Happy to help." He lifted his briefcase and hurried from the coffee shop.

Nick stared out the window as people walked by, seeming to enjoy the warmer weather for a change.

A ladies' man. Violent. Would attack a man from behind. How had Maddie ever gotten involved with such a creep?

His phone buzzed. "Hagar."

"It's Timmons, sir. Mr. Helm just checked Gina's appointment book. She did have Adam Alexander as her Earth Sciences teacher. Get this . . . so did Cynthia Mantle. That study group that met on Thursday night? It was for Adam Alexander's class."

"Call Collette Putman and see if she and Mantle can get into our office as soon as possible on Monday morning."

"Yes, sir. Mr. Helm is going to call the provost Monday morning."

"Good work, Timmons. Make a note for Helm to also try to meet with another faculty member, a Mr. Doak. See if he'll talk about his altercation with Alexander."

"Thank you, sir. Is there anything else I can do?"

"You're off this afternoon, aren't you?"

"Yes, sir, but if you need me . . ."

"No. I'll talk with Tiddle. See if he remembers hearing Gina mention anything about Alexander, then I'm cutting out for the day as well. See you Monday."

Nick drove to Tiddle's apartment, hoping against hope he'd be home and not at work. He glanced at the clock on the dash. He had plenty of time to get back and get ready to go hear Elvis tonight.

Maddie had been so excited. The pure joy in her expression, almost childlike . . . it was worth the exorbitant price to get the sold-out tickets. He couldn't wait to see her tonight. He'd just avoid talking about the case or Adam Alexander. That was definitely a hot button of hers.

But why? She admitted he'd cheated on her. From everything he'd learned, the guy was a louse. Maddie was beautiful, smart, funny—why would she even be with such a loser?

Tiddle's car was in the lot. Nick bounded to the door and knocked.

"Yeah?" Tiddle answered the door wearing jeans and no shirt. "Oh. Hang on." He pushed the door closed before Nick could say anything.

A minute later, he opened the door. This time, he wore a pullover. "Sorry about that. We had a late-night shoot and I didn't get home until four this morning. I just woke up." He waved Nick inside. "Come on in."

Nick noticed the apartment was messier than on his previous visit, but at least the suitcase wasn't packed and ready to go by the door. The stench of dirty dishes assaulted Nick's nostrils. He coughed and breathed through his mouth. "Sorry to barge in unannounced like this."

"It's okay." Tiddle sat on the edge of the chair. "Is there some news?"

"Actually, I need to ask you a few questions. About Gina."

He sat a little straighter. "What about her?"

"I know this is hard, but I need to know if she

ever mentioned one of her teachers to you. Particularly her Earth Sciences teacher."

"Hmmm. Let me think." Tiddle rubbed his chin. "That's not the Asian chick? No, that was one of her math classes. The stuffy woman with the blue hair? No, that's not it." He grinned. "Wait, I remember. He's the hot-for-teacher dude."

"Hot-for-teacher dude?"

Tiddle grinned. "Based on the classic Van Halen song? Anyway, that's what Gina called him because Cyn used to have a crush on him."

Oh, this was very interesting. "Cynthia Mantle had a crush on Adam Alexander?"

"That's his name—Alexander." Tiddle shrugged as he propped his feet up on the coffee table. "Yeah. But don't hold that against the dude. Cyn had crushed on just about all her male teachers under fifty."

"Did Gina ever mention anything specific about Mr. Alexander? Anything you can remember?"

"I can't think of anything right now." Tiddle's face puckered. "Why? Do you think he had something to do with Gina's murder?"

"I can't say at this time." Nick pushed to his feet. "Thank you."

Tiddle got to his feet as well. "Sure. If I can help any more . . ."

"I know where to find you." Nick let himself out before he passed out.

Even in his roughest college days, he never let

the dishes pile up enough to smell that bad. Good thing he had a cast-iron stomach.

His mind raced through possibilities as he strode to the car. What if Alexander had an affair with Mantle and Gina found out and threatened to go to the university about it? Alexander risked losing his job if another report was made on him. Maybe she went to confront him and they got into an argument. He shoved her, then killed her to keep her quiet so he wouldn't lose his job.

His phone buzzed. "Hagar."

"Hello, Nicholas."

As if his day just had to get worse. He laid his forehead against the steering wheel. "Hi, Dad. How's the weather in Florida?"

"Fine. Listen, your mother is worried about Ashley. She hasn't heard from her in almost a month, and you know how your mother frets."

They couldn't hold on to Roger's fiancée forever. It was bad enough that they'd been so disappointed when Nick wouldn't step into Roger's shoes and ask her out. She'd been trying to disentangle herself from his mother since their move.

"Dad, I've tried to tell Mom that Ashley's moved on with her life. It's time to let her go." Last month, he'd run into Ashley and her new man. She had a ring on her finger. Seeing her with a guy other than Roger had struck Nick, something he hadn't considered. What would his

301

mother say if she knew Ashley was engaged, and would be, heaven forbid, married?

"But your mother loves Ashley so much."

And holding on to her was a way of holding on to Roger.

Nick sighed. "Ashley's a beautiful woman who is pushing forty. Mom can't expect Ashley to remain Roger's girlfriend forever. It's time she accepts that."

Disapproval hung heavy over the phone.

"Look, I'll try to get in touch with Ashley and have her call Mom. I'm just in the middle of a very important case and—"

"Just ask Ashley to call your mother. I don't like to see her upset."

"I'll try. Listen, Dad, I've met a—"

"I'm sorry, Nick. Your mother's calling for me. She needs me to open a jar. I'll talk to you later. Good-bye." And the phone went dead.

Nick resisted the urge to bang his head, hit the steering wheel, or get out and kick the tires. Nothing he did, no measure of success, would ever measure up to the memory of Roger. At least not to his father. He should be used to it by now.

Coming in second best was never something you got used to.

Now he needed a very hot, very long shower before his date with Maddie. Could he measure up to her memories of Adam Alexander?

CHAPTER TWENTY-THREE

"Until we meet again, may God bless you
as He has blessed me."
ELVIS PRESLEY

Maddie joined Darren as he headed to the church's Kid's Life area. "It was a good service this morning."

Darren smiled. "I really liked the praise and worship songs today. Really inspired me." He rounded the corner of the hallway.

"Yeah. Me too."

He stopped and put a hand on her arm. "Are you okay, Maddie? Are you worried about tomorrow? Nick asked me to be available to testify about Sloan if needed. He said you'd decided not to attend."

"I'm not planning on it."

"Then what's wrong?"

"Do you have a second?"

He shifted out of the walkway, tugging her with him so others could get around them. "Sure. What's up?"

"I'm confused, Darren."

He leaned against the wall. "About?"

"Nick."

He pushed off the wall and stiffened.

"Look, I know he's your boss, and I shouldn't talk to you about him, but I've got no one else." She felt so alone in this . . . like she was swimming against the current.

"What about Eva? Don't you ladies normally talk about us guys and how clueless we are?" He waggled his eyebrows.

"What I need advice on about Nick, Eva can't help."

"You need a guy's perspective, huh?"

"I need a male Christian's perspective."

"Oh." He looked about as uncomfortable as Elvis in a room full of female fans.

"I'm sorry. I shouldn't have said anything. I don't want to put you in a sticky position. Just forget it."

His hand on her shoulder stopped her from moving away. "No. It's fine."

"Are you sure?"

"Yeah. What's on your mind?"

"Nick's salvation."

He nodded. "I hear you. I've been praying for him."

Her entire insides crushed.

Darren smiled. "You're falling in love with him, aren't you?"

She blinked back the tears. "He's generous and funny and strong and gentle. He makes me laugh and stupid and happy. He even took me to the Elvis Lives concert last night, and didn't make fun of my singing along with the artists onstage at the top of my lungs." And he had stood right beside her, clapping his hands and making himself have fun, just because she loved it.

"He's pretty taken with you as well, Maddie." Darren pulled her from her memories of last night.

"But if he doesn't have a personal relationship with Jesus, Darren . . . there's no chance for us to be together." There went her true chance at a happily-ever-after. She would mourn the loss of this relationship like no other. She feared she might never recover.

"I think he has hit a fork in his spiritual road. I think he's at the crossroads, still trying to decide which way to go." He smiled. "He has a strong moral fiber, doesn't even like to mislead suspects when we're questioning them, even though the law certainly allows—in fact, encourages that to get suspects to tell the truth."

"But strong moral fiber isn't enough. You know what Scripture says."

Darren nodded. "I do. But here's the kicker for me, I wasn't a Christian when I met Georgia. Heck, neither was she. But Jesus called her and she listened." He smiled as his eyes took on that faraway glaze. "She came to me and Rafe in our college dump and said, " 'Darren, Rafe . . . y'all have to understand. Our lives have purpose. Meaning. We aren't just here by some fluke.

God's been orchestrating our lives from before we were born.' " He grinned at Maddie. "Georgia's smile . . . her enthusiasm—she hadn't stopped until both Rafe and I had followed her to church and met with the pastor."

She'd never realized Rafe hadn't been a Christian before then. Their parents had been missionaries for goodness sakes.

"I can see by your expression that you didn't know that about your brother, huh?"

She shook her head. "But we were raised in the church, Mom and Dad—"

"Did their job as parents. They told you the gospel, they took you to church, they gave you all the information you needed. But, and this is true for every Christian, the choice to follow Christ has to be each person's own decision. Rafe had to make his own." Darren chuckled. "Although Georgia made it hard. She was bound and determined we get as passionate about Jesus as she."

Maddie smiled. "That's a nice story. Thank you for sharing it with me."

"My point is that I wasn't a Christian when I fell in love with Georgia, but it was God's plan that we be together in this life. I know He has a plan for everything. He loves Nick more than you or anyone else can. He hasn't given up on Nick . . . I don't think you should either."

"You've given me a lot to think about."

"To pray about. I'll keep praying for Nick. And I'll pray for you as well over this matter. For both of you to have wisdom."

"Thanks, Darren. I really appreciate it."

"Let's go get that little blond dynamo of mine and see if she wants some lunch." He headed down the hall to Savannah's Sunday-school classroom.

"Speaking of dynamos, want to talk about Eva?"

He only hesitated a moment. "There's not really much to tell."

She fell into step beside him. "Are you sure?"

Darren turned outside of Savannah's class. "For right now, I'm just enjoying getting to know her. Who knows what tomorrow will bring?"

Savannah came to the doorway, bouncing up and down like only a five-year-old can. "Daddy! Daddy! Daddy! Oh, Aunt Maddie!"

He lifted his daughter and snuggled her neck until she laughed. "I learned that we should live for today because tomorrows aren't guaranteed."

"Thank you for coming in so early on a Monday, Ms. Mantle." Nick pulled out the chair across the conference-room table from the two ladies and sat. "Ms. Putman."

The lawyer nodded.

"I just have a few questions, Ms. Mantle. I'm hoping you'll be able to shed some insight on one of yours and Gina's teachers."

A confused expression marched across Mantle's face. "Our teacher?"

"Yes. Mr. Alexander. I believe he's your Earth Sciences teacher, correct?"

"Yes."

"And his class is the subject matter for the study group you and Gina both belonged to that meets on Thursday nights, correct?"

"Right. We meet at McWherter Library at eight, then stop studying around eleven. We usually go out for pizza at Garibaldi's after."

"Ms. Mantle, what is the nature of your relationship with Mr. Alexander, your Earth Sciences teacher?"

Her face grew taut and pale. "He's my teacher."

Putman sat up straighter. "I'm not sure how this relates to your investigation, Agent." She leaned over and whispered in Mantle's ear.

"Oh, I think Ms. Mantle knows exactly how this relates to my investigation." He stabbed her with his stare. "I'm not asking these questions out of the blue, Ms. Mantle. Do you need me to repeat the question?"

"No." She whispered in her attorney's ear.

Putman looked at Nick, then whispered back.

"I went out with Adam a couple of times." Mantle looked like she'd eaten something that didn't agree with her.

"Adam Alexander, your teacher?"

"Yes." She swallowed. "I'm an adult, you know. There's nothing wrong with it."

"Were you aware that Mr. Alexander had been warned by the university not to fraternize with female students?"

She shrugged and looked at her lawyer.

"That's hearsay, Agent."

"We aren't in court, Counselor. I'm just asking if she knew."

Putman nodded at Mantle.

"He told me we had to keep our relationship a secret on campus because the provost would fire him if he found out."

Even stronger motive. Losing his livelihood was powerful incentive for Alexander to keep his relationship with Mantle a secret. "But he didn't end your relationship? You just exercised caution on campus, correct?"

"Right. We avoided going to the regular hangouts. We went places where there were fewer students."

Something Tiddle had said to Mantle about her using Gina raced through his mind. "So, where did you go? You and Mr. Alexander?"

"Just places."

"For instance?"

Mantle looked at her lawyer.

"I don't see how this is relevant," Putman said.

"Did you go to Gina Ford's town house? With Mr. Alexander?"

Mantle swallowed and stared at her attorney.

Ah, he'd scored. "Ms. Mantle, did you and Mr. Alexander go to Gina Ford's home?"

"Yes."

"What was Gina's reaction?"

Mantle's face went red. She leaned over and whispered in her lawyer's ear again.

"Ms. Mantle, I'm asking what Gina's reaction was to your bringing Mr. Alexander, her teacher, to her town house."

"One moment." Ms. Putman put her head beside Mantle's. The whispering back and forth was fast and furious.

Nick swallowed the urge to smile. This could nail Alexander's coffin. At least be enough to bring him in for questioning.

Ms. Putman glanced over him, then went back to her whisper-fest with her client.

Maybe Mantle was in on the murder with Alexander. Maybe she'd helped him, or at least covered up for him.

"The first time, she wasn't very happy with me. She told me she didn't approve of such a relationship as it was wrong."

"And the next time?"

Mantle suddenly became very interested in the table's scratches. "She told me I couldn't bring him over there again." She ran her fingernail over the notches.

Nick studied her. The way she slumped in the

chair. How she wouldn't even glance up, not even at her lawyer. "Did you bring him over to Gina's house again, after she told you not to?"

She nodded.

"What did Gina say?"

Mantle looked at Putman, then back at him. "She didn't know. At first."

Interesting. "At first?"

"She wasn't there when we were."

Ah. Now it made sense. And whether she realized it or not, she'd just cemented her own motive. "But she found out later?"

Again, Mantle glanced at Putman before continuing. "She wouldn't have. She had class for another hour or so—"

Putman put her hand on Mantle's arm and looked at Nick. "My client is answering your questions in this line against my advice."

Now it was *really* interesting. "So noted." He nodded at Mantle. "But she found out?"

"We were leaving when David pulled up."

"David Tiddle?"

"Yes. He knew Gina hadn't approved of my relationship with Adam."

"So he knew about it?"

"Yes, but . . ." She looked at Putman for a brief moment, then continued. "He told me he wouldn't tell her if I stayed away from her. He was determined to cut her off from her family and friends so she wouldn't realize what a jerk he really is."

311

Back up. "He told you he wouldn't tell Gina if you stayed away from her?"

"Right."

"But he told her anyway?"

Mantle swallowed. "I didn't believe him. Adam said he'd seen the look of guys like him before and they were cowards. I thought David was just trying to manipulate me."

With blackmail? "So you didn't stay away from Gina?"

She shook her head. "I went to her place that same night to borrow a sweater I loved and he was there. As soon as I saw him, I knew he was going to tell her. He did."

"What happened?"

"She went ballistic. Said she was so disappointed in me and mad that I would use her house as a no-tell motel." Mantle's face went red again. "She told me what hurt her the most was that I had totally disregarded her wishes." Big tears slid down her cheeks. "Gina asked for my key to her house back and then told me to get out."

This was solid motive. He stared at Putman, who did a slight shoulder lift. "When was this?"

"About two weeks ago." She dabbed at her tears with her shirt sleeve.

"This was that *spat* you told me about?"

She nodded. "I'm sorry I didn't tell you everything, but I knew it made me look bad."

Did it ever. "So why are you telling me all this

now?" He nodded toward Ms. Putman. "Especially against your lawyer's advice?"

"Because I'm convinced David's the one who killed Gina. If he found out she and I were talking again, he'd know I would tell her about his attempts to manipulate her. He couldn't afford to have her dump him."

"Why is that, exactly?"

Mantle continued to sniff between statements. "He was totally obsessed with her. He changed his work hours so he could be with her when she didn't have classes. After he dropped her off at her place after a date, he'd sit in his car, parked on the road, until she turned out all the lights. It was like if she was awake and not in class, he just had to be with her. I don't think he could've handled it if she had broken up with him."

Sounded like an abuser . . . trying to cut her off from her family and friends. "Did he ever hit Gina that you're aware of?"

Despite her obvious dislike of Tiddle, she shook her head. "Oh no. He was too scared to lose her."

Yet she sat here and accused him of murdering Gina. If anything Mantle said was the truth. At this point, Nick just wasn't sure.

"One more question, Ms. Mantle."

She wiped her nose with her sleeve and nodded.

"What did Mr. Alexander say when you told him that Mr. Tiddle had called your bluff and told Gina?"

"He said David was trouble with a capital T and I should stay away from him."

"And Gina? What did Mr. Alexander say about Gina?"

Mantle sniffed. "He asked if she was angry enough to go to the provost and tell on us. He was worried about that, naturally."

Of course, but how worried was he?

"How did you answer him?"

"I told him she was pretty mad. He said he'd talk to her after class on Thursday."

Gina Ford was murdered the next morning.

CHAPTER TWENTY-FOUR

"I was training to be an electrician.
I suppose I got wired the wrong way
round somewhere along the line."
ELVIS PRESLEY

The courtroom was more elaborate than it'd been for Hubble's hearing. This was open court, complete with members of the press sitting in the back benches.

Despite the chill of the February morning, Maddie was burning up. She clasped and unclasped her hands in her lap. She could make out Darren sitting just behind the prosecutor's table.

"Return to sender, address unknown."

Opposite the prosecutor's table sat Conrad Sloan and his defense attorney. Conrad Sloan, the man who had called and threatened her. The man who'd come to her house to—what? Traumatize her? Terrify her? Would he have stopped there? Maddie shivered.

"No such number, no such zone."

What if he had come out of the mudroom . . . would she have pulled the trigger? Would she be the one before a judge now instead of him? Self-defense was a legal term. It didn't change the fact that a person was dead. Would she have been able to live with herself?

The courtroom deputy entered the room from the door behind the judge's platform, the judge behind him. The deputy called the court to order and read the case number. The judge took his seat and instructed everyone else to as well.

As she sat, Maddie noticed the young African American woman sitting behind the defense table. At first, she wondered why a teenager would be in the courtroom, then realized the girl was actually much older but had a very slight build.

The prosecutor stated the charges, mentioned Darren being prepared to testify, along with the arresting officers from Memphis Police Department, and noted the signed confession.

She could make out the flipping of pages from the reporters seated behind her.

Soon enough, the prosecutor sat.

The judge leaned forward and peered down his nose. "Would the defendant like to address the court prior to sentencing?"

The defense attorney shot to his feet. "He would, Your Honor." He nodded for Conrad to stand.

He was a lot shorter than she'd expected, this man who had deliberately set out to scare and possibly harm her. He wasn't that stout either. Actually, he was built a lot like Peter, now that she evaluated him without emotion.

"Your Honor, I did call Ms. Baxter to scare her. I did go to her house. I didn't plan to actually break in, but I got so worked up thinking about what she done that I just did." He glanced over his shoulder at the young woman sitting behind him. "See, Your Honor, a man attacked my little sister some time ago and went to jail for it. We thought it was done. But then, Ms. Baxter comes into court and says that man's blood DNA don't match the man's who hurt my sister. So the court lets him go."

The young woman bent her head. Her body shook in silence.

"That man who attacked my sister, he's out free now. All because of Ms. Baxter saying so. My sister's scared he's gonna come after her and hurt her again. I just wanted Ms. Baxter to know what it felt like for my sister to be so scared."

A sob escaped from the woman.

"I'm very sorry for breaking into Ms. Baxter's, Your Honor." He nodded. "Thank you." He sat beside his attorney.

The judge continued to stare at Conrad. "You do understand, Mr. Sloan, that Ms. Baxter, your intended victim, is a TBI officer, and as such, an officer of the court?"

The defense attorney motioned Conrad back to his feet. "Uh, yes, sir, Your Honor."

"And you understand that you are charged with a Class C felony, is that correct?"

"Yes, sir."

"And your attorney has explained to you what your guilty plea means?"

"Yes, sir."

Maddie only heard the judge's voice speaking, not the words. Her focus remained on the young woman. She had to be Conrad's sister . . . the one who accused Mark Hubble.

The judge's voice rose, seeming to bounce off the paneled walls. "In accordance with the gradations of criminal offenses under Tennessee law, I hereby sentence you, Conrad Sloan, to eight years in prison and a fine of eight thousand dollars." He asked for the financial information from the pretrial services desk, but Maddie stopped listening.

The young woman ran from the courtroom. Two members of the press pursued her.

Maddie grabbed her purse from the bench beside her and burst out of the courtroom. She looked up and down the hallway, finally spying the woman. The reporters had her flanked on either side while she covered her face with her hands.

"Leave her alone." Maddie advanced on them.

The blond reporter glared at her, his expression clearly displeased at her interruption. "We're just asking her some questions."

"I don't think she wants to answer any of your questions." Maddie stepped between the woman and the reporters.

"Hey, I know you." The second reporter, a pudgy sort, nudged the first one. "It's Maddie Baxter. You're the one whose house was broken into."

The young woman gasped behind her.

They had to get away from them. Where? How?

Maddie grabbed the woman's arm and led her down the hallway, across the corridor, and into the ladies' room. She shut the door and leaned against it. "There. They can't get to us in here." She straightened. "At least they'd better not."

The young woman stared at her. Disdain lined every pore of her face. "You're the one who let Mark out. He attacked me."

The accusation cut through Maddie. "I'm sorry, but science doesn't lie. I ran that test multiple times to be sure."

The woman's eyes were pools. "You don't think I know the man who attacked me?"

Maddie's own eyes burned. "I read the transcript of your trial. It was dark. You were scared. You were crying. Isn't it possible you were mistaken?"

The woman trembled.

"I didn't want to set him free. Don't you see? I hate that he's out. I know he's a creep. But, ma'am, Mark Hubble's DNA did not match what was taken from the scene of your attack." Maddie shook her head, willing her emotion to settle back down.

The woman glared at her. "And now my brother, who has been eaten with guilt that he couldn't protect me since the attack, is in jail for eight years." She shook all over. "Eight years in jail, while Mark Hubble is free." She reared her hand back and slapped Maddie across the face.

Stinging pain shot throughout Maddie's entire head. She lifted her hand to her cheek, which felt as hot as scalding water.

"Live with that." The woman marched from the bathroom.

Leaning over the row of sinks, Maddie stared at her reflection in the mirror. The woman had left a defined handprint on her right cheek.

Live with that?

Maddie didn't know if she could. *Oh, God, please help me.*

. . .

"Hagar." Nick wedged the phone between his chin and shoulder as he finished typing his case file notes on his computer.

"It's Peter Helm. I just finished speaking with Mr. Doak."

Ah. The teacher who got tangled up with Alexander. "And?" Nick reached for a pen and a scrap of paper.

"They were at a fellow teacher's house, playing pool and shooting darts. Some in attendance were playing canasta. The topic of politics came up and Doak and Alexander found themselves on opposite sides of the fence. The exchange between them got heated so Doak went outside in the backyard to cool off a bit."

Pretty much what Emmel had already said.

"Here's where it gets interesting. Doak says he was out there alone for a good three to five minutes before Alexander came out. He says he apologized for getting hostile and assumed that's why Alexander came out. But it wasn't."

Helm cleared his throat. "Doak says Alexander began insulting him on a personal level, making rude and crude statements about Doak's wife. Naturally, Doak got angry. He made a comment to the effect of 'at least I can get a real woman instead of having to settle for young college girls who only sleep with me to get a better grade,' and then Doak implied Alexander would soon lose his job because of his actions."

"And that's when the fistfight broke out?"

"Not exactly. Doak said Alexander laughed and told him he didn't know what he was talking about and implied he knew how to handle his problems. And then he punched Doak."

Handle his problems . . . might be referring to Gina. "Helm, did you get the day this all went down?"

"Yes. It was Friday night."

The day Gina Ford was murdered.

"Agent Hagar?"

"Yeah?"

"I think it might be best if you speak to the university's provost."

"Is something wrong?"

"No, not at all. I just think the FBI carries more weight than the TBI, and I've been asked to look into something this afternoon."

"Okay. I'll head that way now." He hung up the phone and buzzed Timmons. They met at the car.

"How'd court go this morning?"

"Sloan got eight years, eight thousand dollars."

Nick cocked his head. "About right." But he would've liked to have seen the scumbag who scared Maddie get the maximum sentence of fifteen years.

"I wanted to talk to Maddie after it was over, but she'd already left."

"Maddie was there?" She'd told him she

wasn't going to go. Said she didn't want to be there.

"Yeah. I guess she changed her mind."

He'd ask her about that later, but for now, he pulled up into the parking lot of the University of Memphis's main office.

The afternoon sun slipped further toward the horizon as the wind skittered an empty paper cup across the asphalt.

They were sent right in to see the provost, who stood to greet them. "Welcome." He extended his hand across his desk. "I'm Archibald Roman."

Nick introduced himself and Timmons, then they sat in the plush chairs facing the provost's elaborately detailed desk. Diplomas and certificates decorated the walls behind his desk. Photos of Roman with various political and famous personalities littered the office in their snazzy brass frames.

"How may I help you, gentlemen? Is there any news on Gina's or Hailey's deaths?"

Nick leaned forward. "Actually, Mr. Roman, we'd like to ask a few questions regarding a member of your faculty. Adam Alexander."

The provost's upper lip stiffened. "What about him?"

"We understand there have been several complaints made against him."

"In what manner?"

Nick rested his right ankle on his left knee. "We hoped that information would come from you, sir."

"Employee files are confidential."

"This is a murder investigation, Mr. Roman. Here. On *your* campus. Surely the alumni and trustees would love for there to be some sort of resolution to avoid the fear of young women moving to other campuses, fleeing for their safety?"

A line of sweat on the man's brow glistened in the lights. "Well, yes." He paused, looking past them before seeming to reach a decision. He leaned forward. "I can tell you that Mr. Alexander has been warned several times regarding his alleged involvement with students." He withdrew a cloth from his pocket and daubed his forehead. "Understand it's alleged. Nothing has been substantiated."

"If you receive another complaint on Mr. Alexander of the same nature, what will happen? Probation?"

"No. He's already on probation. That goes with the second warning."

Nick waited.

"This university is over a hundred years old. We are well respected in the education community. Our motto is *Dreamers. Thinkers. Doers.* Our reputation is always on the line in these kinds of situations."

Still silent, Nick continued to wait.

The provost sweated more profusely. "Just between us, the man is a womanizer. If I receive a third complaint of this nature, he'll be fired."

The motive for Adam Alexander to shut up Gina Ford just went platinum.

"Mr. Roman, do you know if Mr. Alexander has any classes on Friday mornings?"

"Let me check." He lifted the receiver, asked the question, waited a moment, then hung it up. "He doesn't have any classes on Fridays."

"I have one final question for you." Nick sat up, placing both feet firmly on the ground. "Why did you hire Mr. Alexander when he'd had trouble with this exact issue at the University of Tennessee Health Science Center campus here in Memphis?"

The provost's face puckered as if he'd eaten a Sour Ball. The sweat covered not just his forehead, but his upper lip and bridge of his nose as if it were the middle of summer instead of winter. "That's confidential information."

Ah, so there was more to the story. It didn't matter at the moment. If they needed it to indict Alexander, Nick could get a warrant. But he was fairly sure it wouldn't be required to get the indictment. For now he had enough to bring Adam Alexander in for questioning.

He couldn't wait to see the man who'd broken Maddie's heart yet left her still inspired to take up for him.

CHAPTER TWENTY-FIVE

"I've been getting some bad publicity—
but you got to expect that."
ELVIS PRESLEY

Nettie Sloan. That was the name of the accuser in the Mark Hubble case. The name of the woman who'd slapped her yesterday.

Maddie sat across the table from Peter, each of them reading parts of the Hubble file. There had to be something there that was missed the first time. She had no doubt Nettie believed Mark Hubble had attacked her. But the DNA . . .

Science didn't lie.

She had the motto inscribed on a plaque over her desk and on the posters hanging in various places in the lab. It was a fact. Eyewitnesses could —and usually were—mistaken, testimonies could be twisted, and facts could be distorted. But science? Science was the one steady . . . the one constant. It couldn't be manipulated. Not when she broke it down to the barest and the DNA strands were the foundation of life.

"I'm not seeing anything." Peter set down the page he was reading and rubbed his eyes. "If something was missed, I'm missing it too."

"Thanks for getting these files from Memphis

PD and reviewing them with me. I can't accept not knowing who really attacked Nettie Sloan."

"I understand, and you're welcome." Peter smiled. "Okay, let's brainstorm. Look at the facts of the case. Nettie was at home, alone. Her electricity went out, so it was dark. In November at ten p.m., it's dark. So she's alone in her house and it's pitch black. She said she didn't have a flashlight, so she lit a single taper candle and set it on her kitchen table."

Maddie pulled another document from the folder. "Her kitchen is separated from the living room by a wall with just a double-door opening. Between that single candlelight and the actual scene of the attack, there lay seven feet and a couch with a three-foot-high back."

Maddie stood and paced. "Now, I'm scared, it's dark, and I can only make out dim outlines because the only candlelight source is in another room, and tapers don't give off much light anyway. I hear something. I start to cry and my eyes fill with tears. So everything I see at this point is a blur."

Peter nodded. "A man storms in through the front door and pushes her off the couch. He attacks her on the floor of the living room."

"With the couch now blocking most of the light from the candle in the kitchen."

"She's crying harder now."

"Which blurs her vision even more."

Peter pushed his glasses back up his nose. "So there's no way she could make a one hundred percent positive ID on visual."

Maddie sat down and grabbed another file. "He had no alibi. Said he was hanging out at his house, having a drink or two." She flipped pages. "So why did the police focus on you as a suspect, Mr. Hubble?" Although, she'd looked into his eyes in the courtroom and seen the evil lurking there, that didn't mean he'd committed this crime.

She turned the page. "Because he has a record of breaking and entering a sorority house, indecent exposure to a bunch of college girls, and being a Peeping Tom at a girls' dorm. Minor charges. Never did any time behind bars."

"Did the police look at anyone else?" Peter shoved papers about. "Yes. Matter-of-fact, their primary suspect was one Bobby Rust."

He shifted as he read. "Bobby was seen lingering around the Sloan house in the weeks before the attack. Had asked Nettie out on a date but been rejected. And get this: he and Conrad Sloan used to have a small-time drug business on the side together until Conrad did some time for possession and supposedly cleaned up his act."

Sounded like a primary suspect. "Did he have an alibi?"

"He was with friends. Verified by two ex-cons."

"Such reliable witnesses."

"Bobby Rust doesn't have a rap sheet at all."

Peter flipped page after page. "He's clean. Not so much as a parking ticket." He shook his head. "Not even a single drug charge."

"That is odd." A guy like that, he should at least have some sort of record. But nothing? "Nettie picked Hubble out of a police lineup." She pulled the photo of Hubble and set it beside Rust's picture. "They have similar haircuts. Are about the same height and build."

She stood and tacked the pictures side by side, on the wall, then stood with her back against the opposite wall. "I'm not crying to blur my vision, it's not dark in here, and the only way I can see is through shadows, and I'm not scared, and those two men look really similar to me."

Peter straightened papers and slipped them back into the file. "Since Bobby Rust had an alibi, weak as it is, and has no record, the police didn't even put him in the lineup against Hubble."

Maddie leaned against the table and stared at the two photographs. It was here. She could feel it. What was she missing?

She flipped through papers again. "What does Rust do? For a living, I mean? Nine years ago when Nettie was attacked."

"Uh . . ." Peter flipped through papers. "He worked as a mechanic at a chop shop."

Something about that . . .

"Hang on a second." She rushed into the lab and accessed her computer. She ran an Internet search for Memphis news regarding a drug bust nine years ago. Four clicks later, and she set the article to print.

Her adrenaline surged as she returned to the meeting room down the hall from the lab. "Peter, have you ever had a CI before in an investigation?"

"A confidential informant? Sure. Once or twice. Why?"

"As a matter of courtesy, when all is said and done, don't most law-enforcement agencies clean the CI's record of minors like misdemeanors and such?"

"Most times, but not all. Why?"

"If that CI was extremely valuable to you in your case but he was a suspect in a different, minor case, is it plausible someone might have pushed a different suspect?"

Peter shook his head. "Don't think so, Maddie. I think you're off base."

She waved the printout. "Am I? This is the news article from nine years ago, a mere three months after Nettie was attacked. It's about an undercover operation by Memphis PD narcotics unit in which they worked with DEA to uncover a drug-trafficking ring where drug suppliers from foreign countries were hiding drugs in vehicle parts and shipping them to auto shops in the United States."

She tossed the paper onto the table. "The article

stated that undercover agents and *confidential informants* were vital in bringing down this drug ring."

"I can't believe that."

"Think about it for just a minute. You're working undercover alongside a vital CI. You're right there, elbow-to-elbow with criminals. If you help bust this ring, you're a hero in the eyes of your superiors and the DEA. This is huge." She paced, gesturing with her hands as she talked.

If only her glasses wouldn't keep slipping. She shoved them back to the bridge of her nose. "But now your vital CI has gone and done something stupid, like attack a girl who rejected him and whose brother just happens to have a little bad blood between them. But hey, the girl's basically okay. But if your vital CI gets charged, your undercover operation is done."

"I see where you're going, Maddie . . . I just can't believe this could happen."

"Oh, this kind of stuff can and does happen. Hello? Innocence Project? Even my testimony at Hubble's hearing."

"But it wouldn't work."

"Okay, back to my scenario. You can't let your operation go bust. The girl's okay, on the outside. If your CI can't do it himself, you help get some lowlifes who'll agree to back up the CI's alibi. You find someone who looks enough like your CI, who has a record for something similar to attacks on women, and have him put in the lineup in place of your CI."

"That's reaching."

Maddie stopped and faced him. "You think?" Because everything in her said she'd hit the nail square on the head.

She needed to ask Nick for his help.

Just after lunch, Agent Timmons escorted Adam Alexander into the interrogation room. Not much to look at, honestly. Brown hair cut short but not a crew cut. Green eyes that were a little too close together. He had a high forehead and his mouth was a little too wide. Nick didn't see the attraction for him to be such a womanizer.

The district attorney stood beside Nick on the other side of the two-way mirror. "You better make sure he doesn't have an alibi. This familial DNA thing is too new."

"I'll ask for the sample. He might give it up."

"If he doesn't, remember I can't get a warrant for his DNA sample if you blow this."

"I got it."

The DA nodded. "You're up."

Nick headed into the room. "Hello, Mr. Alexander, I'm Special Agent in Charge Nick Hagar." He set the large stack of file folders he'd borrowed from the records room on his side of the table, then made a point of sliding them to the end.

"The agent who brought me here said you wanted to ask me a few questions about the murders of two of our students at the university where I teach."

Nice work, Timmons. "That's correct. You are an . . ." He shuffled through the top folder, set it aside, then did the same with the folder beneath. "Ah, you're an Earth Sciences teacher, correct?" He stared at the man across the table from him.

"Yes."

"And you've been a teacher at the University of Memphis for how long?"

"Almost ten years."

Not quite enough to have tenure, so he could easily be fired with a third complaint. "Was Hailey Carter in any of your classes?"

He shook his head. "No. My particular class is an advanced one, for seniors and the occasional junior."

Nick closed a file and reached for another. He opened it slowly and moved his eyes back and forth, then looked at Alexander. "What about Gina Ford? Was she in any of your classes?"

He nodded. "She was in my Thursday class."

Leaning back, Nick let the folder fall facedown against his chest. "What was your impression of her?"

Alexander blinked rapidly. "Excuse me?"

"Your impression? As her teacher, what was your impression of Gina Ford?"

"Uh, she was smart. Friendly. Everyone seemed to like her. I didn't know her that well. She made straight *A*s in my class."

"I see." Nick sat up, closed the folder, and grabbed another that he opened and pretended to peruse. "Ah, what about Cynthia Mantle?"

The man's Adam's apple bobbed repeatedly. "What?"

"Cynthia Mantle, Gina Ford's best friend. She's also in your class, isn't she? The same class as Gina?"

He nodded. "Yes."

"And your impression of Ms. Mantle? As her teacher?"

"Uh, she's bright. Completes all her assignments. Makes good grades in my class."

Of course she did.

Nick transferred folders again. "Mr. Alexander, where were you last Friday morning between eight and ten?"

"Excuse me?"

"You. Friday morning. Eight and ten."

"I teach at the university."

"You have no classes on Friday. None at all." Nick shoved the folder he'd been holding back onto the stack. "I'll ask again, Mr. Alexander. Where were you between eight and ten last Friday morning?"

"Um . . . should I get a lawyer?"

Nick leaned forward, tenting his hands over the

table. "Do you *need* a lawyer, Mr. Alexander?"

"No, but the way you're questioning makes it seem like I do."

Nick waved to all the folders on the table. "If you'd like to call a lawyer, I'll bring you a phone and be happy to wait for him to get here."

Alexander jerked his head a little, as if popping it. "No. I'm good."

"Are you sure you don't want a lawyer?"

"No."

Nick stood and faced the two-way mirror. He winked before turning back to Alexander. "I'm a little confused."

"About what?" Alexander jutted out his chin.

Good. His defensiveness was kicking in. About time. "If you had to leave the University of Tennessee Health Science Center campus here in Memphis because of alleged improper behavior with a student and had received two similar warnings from the provost at your current place of employment, why would you start a relationship with your student Cynthia Mantle?"

"I-I—"

Nick sat up straight. "Isn't it true that you knew Gina Ford threatened to go to the provost about you and Cynthia after she found out the two of you had used her home as a meeting place?"

"That was just once!"

"Weren't you so desperate to keep your job that you'd do anything to shut up Gina Ford?"

"No! Are you implying I had something to do with her death? You're crazy. I had nothing to do with that."

"Then where were you last Friday morning?"

"I was . . . I was . . . I think I was with Cynthia."

"No, you weren't. She was on the phone with Gina before Gina's murder, then at a gas station, then in Professor Emmel's class. Unless you two were working together and she called Gina to make sure she was where you could kill her."

"That's a lie!" He raised his voice as he jerked upright in the hardback metal chair.

"Then where were you?" Nick leaned across the table, invading Alexander's space.

"Give me a second to think." The man's voice remained loud and higher pitched than normal.

Nick turned and stared at the two-way mirror. He needed more. He could feel the DA shaking his head, letting him know Alexander hadn't incriminated himself or proven he didn't have an alibi. Nick turned back to Alexander. "So? Where were you?"

"I can't remember. I can't remember right now." Alexander had turned a little pale. "I swear to you, I had nothing to do with Gina's death. Nothing."

Moving in for the kill, Nick sat in the chair beside him. "Listen, let's make it easy." He made his voice low, his tone conversational. "Voluntarily give me a DNA sample and we'll compare it to what we found at Gina's crime scene. If you had nothing to do with her murder, as you claim, then there won't be a match."

He had no alibi. That combined with his motive and the familial DNA match, should be enough to get a warrant for the DNA sample. He almost clapped his hands and rubbed them together. Charging this character would be the highlight of his Tuesday.

"Okay."

He coul—"What?"

"Okay. You can have the DNA sample. Blood? Hair? What do you need?"

He'd agreed! "You just wait here. I'll get someone to collect a sample from you here." He turned and rushed from the room.

The DA and Timmons met him in the hallway.

"Un-canny-believable." Timmons shook his head. "I can't believe he agreed."

The DA clapped Nick's shoulder. "Hurry up and get someone to get his sample before he has time to think about it and lawyer up."

Not Maddie. He'd call Eva.

Nick nodded. "Let me make a phone call."

Agent Martin waved his hands. "Agent Hagar." He rushed toward Nick.

"Not right now, Mar—"

Maddie came rushing down the hall beside Agent Martin.

He took the biggest sucker punch in history right square in the bread box.

Maddie grinned. "I'm sorry to bother you, but I have something I need your help on."

Timmons joined them. "Perfect timing, Maddie. We were just about to call someone to collect a DNA sample for us. You saved us some time."

"Time we don't have." The DA stuck his hand out to her. "District Attorney Jones. Nice to meet you."

"Maddie Baxter, TBI, forensic scientist." She shook his hand, then smiled at Nick. "Happy to help out. What kind of sample do you need? Your crime scene unit should have everything I need."

Nick swallowed hard. "Maybe we should just have one of our team collect it."

Jones gave him a quizzical look. "No. We need to get that sample now, before he changes his mind."

"It's fine, Nick. I don't mind." She smiled. "What kind of sample do you need?"

"Which one is best for DNA extraction that will be compared against DNA from blood?"

"Any will work for comparisons, just a matter of preference."

"Get blood. It's easier to explain DNA to a jury when you're comparing blood against blood," Jones said.

"Okay." She looked at Timmons. "Just call your CSU and tell them I'm taking a blood sample and to send me a pack. They'll know."

Timmons nodded.

"Oh, and tell them to make sure there are gloves too."

Timmons acknowledged and headed to the office.

Maddie turned back to him. "Is there a place I can set this?" She held up a purse-briefcase combo thing.

He had to tell her but didn't want to in front of Jones. "Over here."

She frowned. "Is everything okay?"

"Please excuse us," he said to Jones, then took her gently by the arm and led her a little away.

"What's wrong, Nick?"

"About that DNA sample . . ."

"Yeah? You know I can take it."

"It's not that."

"Then what is it?"

"Maddie, we need it from Adam Alexander."

CHAPTER TWENTY-SIX

"I've tried to lead a straight, clean life,
not set any kind of a bad example."
ELVIS PRESLEY

"Adam's here?" Maddie nearly swayed, but she forced herself to stand firm.

Nick opened a door off the hallway. The room was dark, but there was a big window and Adam sat on the other side. Nick led her inside. She set down her briefcase and hauled in a deep breath.

She'd always known she'd see him again. She just hadn't been prepared to feel . . .

Such overwhelming relief.

Happiness bubbled in her chest. All these years, she'd imagined he had some magical hold on her. Like if she ever saw him again, she'd fall under his spell again. Not true.

She looked at him through the window. What had she ever seen in him? Maybe he'd aged poorly, but he wasn't even all that attractive. Not like Nick.

She turned to Nick, grinning. "You mean I get to stick him with a needle?"

His brows furrowed. "I don't understand . . . you were so adamant he's innocent."

"Oh, I still believe he's innocent." A cheat and a jerk, yes, but not a murderer. "The DNA sample will prove which one of us is correct."

Nick crossed his arms over his chest. "Then why are you acting almost giddy?"

He'd never understand, even if she tried to explain it. "Let's just say that seeing him again makes me so glad I'm not dating him any longer."

Nick grinned and pulled her into a hug. He planted a quick kiss on her lips just as Darren entered the room. He coughed.

She stepped out of Nick's embrace and laughed. "It's okay to come in, Darren."

"CSU sent your packet." He held up the bag.

"Good."

District Attorney Jones stepped into the room. "Are you ready?"

She took the bag from Darren. "You betcha."

He nodded at Nick. "You have to go in with her, in case he's changed his mind and lawyered up."

Nick opened the door for her and let her precede him into the room. "This is Ms. Baxter with the Tennessee Bureau of Investigation, and she'll be taking a blood sample from you for DNA typing purposes."

Adam nodded, then glanced at her. His eyes widened. "Maddie?"

"Hi, Adam." She set the bag on the table and pulled on the latex gloves.

"It's been a long time."

"Eleven years." She reached for his arm. "Can you pull your sleeve up, please?"

"Wow. How have you been?"

She took the blue strip of rubber and tied it tightly around his bicep. "I'm wonderful. Make a fist for me, please."

"You look amazing."

Nick slid the chair against the floor. It made a long, scraping sound.

Maddie smiled as she bent her head and felt for Adam's largest vein on the inside of his elbow.

"So you work with the cops? That's cool."

She found the vein and reached for the syringe.

"I actually *am* a commissioned law-enforcement officer." She slid the needle under the skin and into the vein.

He winced.

She pulled back the plunger. Blood began to fill the tube. "I get to carry a gun and everything."

"You really look great." He moved a little. "I don't see a wedding ring. You still available?"

Nick coughed.

She released the rubber strip around his arm, still smiling to herself. "I'm not married but I am seeing someone." Maddie filled the rest of the vial, then eased the needle out and put a wad of gauze against the hole. She secured the tube of blood. "Keep pressure on your arm and it won't bruise."

"You turned out to be one beautiful woman, Maddie. Interested in getting together sometime?"

She collected all of her items and stood, looking down at him and shaking her head. "No, I wouldn't. I don't even know what I saw in you back then, Adam. I sure don't know why I beat myself up that you cheated on me." She headed to the door, Nick on her heels.

As soon as he shut the door she turned to Nick. "Kiss me."

"What?" He glanced toward the door to the viewing room.

"I said, kiss me."

He planted a quick kiss on her cheek.

"Thank you. I feel so much better now."

Darren and the district attorney met them in the hall. Neither smiled.

"Did you have a personal relationship with Adam Alexander?" Jones asked.

She blinked. "We dated eleven years ago."

The district attorney looked at Darren, who turned to her. "I'm calling Eva to get her over here now."

"What's wrong?" She'd done everything by the book. Even told him how to avoid bruising.

"You could have just blown our case." The DA scrunched his face. "If the DNA matches and he gets a good defense attorney, they'll throw out the sample saying you contaminated it because of your past relationship."

"You know he's gone, gone, gone . . ."

"You were witnesses through the two-way mirror that I followed proper protocol in drawing his blood. I would never tamper with the chain of evidence. That's my reputation on the line."

"Hip shaking King Creole."

"But if you process it . . . Agent Timmons says there's another forensic scientist in your lab who can run the tests?"

Maddie nodded. "Eva."

"Good. Then we'll let her take it and process it. How long until we can run it against the sample taken from Gina Ford's murder scene?"

"Since Adam's sample is a known sample, we

can compare the two for a match. That can be done within about thirty-six hours."

The DA nodded. "So you should know if it's a match—?"

"Thursday morning."

"Very well." DA Jones held out his hand. "I'll take custody of the sample until your co-worker gets here."

"Okay." She handed it to him.

"Thank you. Is there any way you could take tomorrow off from work? Just so you won't even be in the lab? I don't want to risk giving a defense attorney any ammunition."

"That's fine. Peter will let me have a day off."

"I'm glad you understand."

She nodded, then touched Nick's arm. "Can I see you for a few minutes? There's something I need your help with." She could only pray he'd be willing and able to help her. "I have every-thing here in my briefcase."

To see Alexander didn't have an effect on her . . . Nick's heartbeat held steady and firm. She'd done her job without batting an eye. Even deflected Alexander's innuendos and blatant interest. He couldn't remember the last time he'd been so attracted to a woman.

"Okay, are you ready?" She sat in front of his desk, the one she'd cleared off to make space.

"Ready."

She handed him a piece of paper. "That's the crime-scene report of an attack on one Nettie Sloan nine years ago."

Sloan? "Maddie, what are you doing?"

"Just hear me out. Please." She pointed at the paper. "Read it."

He scanned the information. Woman's electricity goes out at night. Man breaks in and assaults her, then leaves. "Okay."

Maddie handed him another sheet of paper. "Here is the initial suspect. Read it."

He'd have to humor her or he'd hurt her feelings, so he read. Bobby Rust. Had previously been rejected by the victim. Had allegedly previously been engaged in drug dealing with the victim's brother, but they'd had a falling out. Alibi stated he was with friends. Two collaborated his story, both ex-cons. Rust had no record. Worked at an auto shop. "Okay."

She handed him another piece. "Now, here is the next suspect the police came up with."

He took it and read. Mark Hubble. No previous contact with victim or her family. As far as records went, he didn't even know the victim. He had past record including sexual misdemeanors. Alibi could not be confirmed. Unemployed. "Okay."

"Now, stay sitting there." She went to his office door and shut it. She taped two photographs up on the door, then turned out the overhead light.

Maddie turned on his desk lap and situated its beam until it pointed to the ceiling. "Now, squint your eyes and look at those pictures."

He did. Couldn't tell a single thing about them except both were black men and both had big heads.

She turned on the lights. "Look at the pictures again. Can you tell me anything that you see that could distinguish one from the other?"

"No."

Maddie smiled and pulled the pictures down. She handed him the two pictures.

"These guys look pretty similar."

"That's my point."

He looked up at her. "Maddie, honey I want to help you, I do, but I'm not getting what your point is."

"Why would the police not put both men, both suspects, in a lineup for the victim?"

"Well, he has an alibi and no record."

"He has the word of two ex-cons and don't you find it strange he has no record? Nothing at all? No minor possession, even though according to the investigating officers, he had been engaged in drug dealing with the victim's brother. He doesn't even have a speeding ticket."

"That is a bit unusual."

"Hubble had a habit of sexual deviation, yes, but it was always directed to college girls. Never some-one off campus. Why change his MO *that* night?"

"Good point."

She smiled and he knew he was supposed to concentrate on the scenario she laid out, but his mind wandered to the passion in her eyes. How she'd been so confident and assertive after seeing Alexander.

"Nick?"

He focused back on her. She held out yet another sheet of paper. A copy of a newspaper article about a big drug-trafficking bust. Memphis PD in partnership with DEA. Undercover stuff. Put over ten suppliers and dealers in prison and confiscated drugs with a street value over two and a half million dollars. He remembered something about this. Mexican cartels would put the drugs in car parts and ship them to auto shops in the states.

Wait a minute . . . "Let me see the sheet on Rust again."

She handed him the entire folder.

After the initial investigators questioned Bobby Rust, he was omitted totally from the investigation. No further mention of his name was made. It was as if he'd never been a part of the investigation. Had the original investigators' notes not been in the file, Bobby Rust wouldn't have even been a part of the file.

It was common practice for the two prime suspects, if they didn't have iron-clad alibis, which the word of two ex-cons wasn't, to be put in the lineup for the eyewitness. Especially when they had such similar features and builds.

Furthermore, Nick couldn't see what led the police to consider Hubble a suspect in the first place. He had no connection to the victim or her family, nor had his MO led the investigation to Hubble. The only thing was his sexual record and the victim's positive identification.

Which in Nick's experience, was about as reliable as a city bus.

It was as if someone handed Hubble to the authorities as a suspect and swept Rust under the rug. Add in the element of the drug bust and Rust's employment . . .

"Did you find out the name of the auto shops busted in the undercover operation?" he asked Maddie.

"No. I didn't even think to."

He tapped the copy of the article. "Contact the reporter. They usually keep their notes. If not, you can find it in the arrest records."

"You're thinking the same thing I am, aren't you—that Rust was a CI or somehow valuable to the drug-trafficking operation?"

"It looks suspicious. If the name of the auto shop in the bust is the same one Rust worked for, then you have something you can take to the DA and ask them to look into. Especially since DNA has proven Hubble wasn't guilty of that crime."

She smiled, and his entire world righted. "The man who attacked Nettie Sloan was never Mark Hubble. It was Bobby Rust."

"You don't know that. You can only take to a judge what you can prove. You've proven Hubble wasn't her attacker, so you need to offer up another suspect."

She nodded. "But I'm right. I know it." She grinned wider. "Call it a hunch."

"A hunch, huh?" He wanted to kiss that cute little dimple in her right cheek that rarely came out to play. "You could be right. Wait and see what you can prove." He handed her back her file. "Why are you doing this? You said Hubble creeped you out in court."

"This isn't about him. It's about Nettie Sloan and giving her peace of mind. It's about giving her justice against the man who really attacked her."

He stood and leaned over his desk toward her. "You're awfully cute when you're fighting for justice, you know that?"

She leaned toward him until their noses were almost touching. "I am, am I?"

He nodded, then planted a kiss on the tip of her nose. "Very cute."

Chapter Twenty-Seven

"Whatever I will become will be
what God has chosen for me."
Elvis Presley

TCB Auto Repair.

That was the name of the shop shut down in the drug-trafficking ring operation. Owned by one Thomas Bruster.

It was also Bobby Rust's place of employment nine years ago.

Maddie debated for the umpteenth time about asking Nick to go with her to see DA Jones. She didn't need him, though. She was well within her rights to take a matter such as this to the district attorney.

When she'd called this morning, his secretary had told her, "You're in luck. His nine o'clock canceled. But you'd better hurry. He plays golf on Wednesdays at eleven if at all possible."

So Maddie had gotten dressed and hurried down to the DA's office, where she now paced outside of his office.

"Ms. Baxter, come in." He greeted her in the hall- way and escorted her into his office. "Such a pleasure to see you, although I have to admit, I wasn't expecting to hear from your office before tomorrow."

"This is a different case, sir. Since I'm not working in the office today."

He smiled. "Very good. Now, what can I help you with today?"

She laid out the case and her concerns, much as she had to Nick. DA Jones gave Maddie his full attention. "I think this definitely should be considered. Take your file to Captain Moore at the main precinct. Tell him I sent you. He'll listen and if he thinks it's worth looking into, he'll make it happen."

She stood and shook his hand. "Thank you."

Maddie went directly to see Captain Moore, who agreed it looked suspicious enough for further review, so he assured her it would go to his best team. If they found something substantial, they'd also turn the incident over to Internal Affairs to investigate as well.

Barely eleven thirty, and she had nothing else planned for the rest of the day. Maybe she'd cook Nick dinner. She almost laughed. She'd have to go grocery shopping first. She needed to do that anyway. She couldn't remember the last time she'd gone. It would serve her better to make a list before going. Otherwise, she could end up without half the stuff she needed.

Did Nick like lobster? Grilled lobster tails

were amazing. The weather was nice enough to fire up the grill. If she wore her coat.

She'd just pulled up in her driveway and opened her garage when her cell rang. She had to dig around in her purse to find it. "Hello?"

"Where are you?" Eva sounded both excited and upset at the same time.

"Just pulling in my driveway. Why? What's up?"

"We just got a call from Memphis PD. Their CSI finally processed forensics taken from the Hailey Carter crime scene. They think they have a clean latent. Peter sent Ivan over to assist and bring it back to run through AFIS."

"Oh, I pray they get one."

"Yeah. And guess what else?"

"You won the lottery?" Maddie chuckled as she pulled her car into the garage and pressed the remote to shut the door.

"Could be better than that."

"Really?" She headed into the house, tossed her purse and keys onto the table, then put her gun and badge in her bedside table.

"Darren asked me out."

Maddie plopped onto the bed. "Darren asked you out?"

"Yeah. It's not a real date-date or anything. He invited me over to his house for spaghetti Friday night. Give me a chance to get to know Savannah a little better too. Then we're going to watch a DVD. Isn't that cool?"

Eva sounded so excited. "That is cool."

"I can't wait."

Maddie knew how she felt. She couldn't wait to see Nick again. "How's the testing going? I really hate not being there."

"I know. It's good. Results should be up around three in the morning. I'll be in at seven to analyze so I should be able to compare no later than nine."

"Thanks, Eva."

"No worries."

Her call-waiting beep sounded. "Hey, my other line's ringing."

"I'll talk to you later."

Maddie pressed the button to answer the other call. "Hello?"

"Maddie?"

"Riley!" She rolled to prop up on her pillow. "How are you?"

"I'm wonderful. Couldn't be better." The pure joy in her sister's voice struck a chord.

"Oh?" But Maddie had a feeling she knew what was coming next.

"Hayden proposed! Over breakfast!"

"Aww, Riley! I'm so happy for you. This is awesome." Tears filled her eyes. Happy, joyful tears that felt amazing.

"I can't believe it. I'm so happy I can't even describe it."

Maddie laughed. "Coming from a journalist, that's pretty bad."

"I know, right?" Riley laughed. "My ring is beautiful."

"Text me a picture."

"I will! Oh, Maddie, I'm so happy."

"Baby girl, I'm happy for you." And she was. So very happy for Riley. And for Rafe and Remington.

"We aren't like Rafe and Remington, though. We aren't going to have a long engagement."

"You aren't?"

"No." Riley giggled. "Hayden says he's waited too long for me."

Maddie smiled. Her sister was in good hands. "So are y'all thinking of a date?"

"I think June brides are beautiful."

"June! That's in four months."

"I know. It's crazy, but Hayden can take his vacation then so we can have a real honeymoon."

"That's wonderful, Ri. I think you'll be a beautiful June bride."

"You'll be my maid of honor, right?"

"I wouldn't miss it."

"Oh, Hayden's telling me we have to call Rafe and Remington now. I'll talk to you soon. I love you."

"Love you too." Maddie hung up the phone and held it close to her chest.

Was it wrong for her to be delighted that she'd been the first one Riley had called? Probably, but she didn't care. This was a happy day indeed.

• • •

"Hagar." Nick shoved the cell to his ear without checking the caller ID.

"Nicholas."

Nick couldn't stop the internal groan. "Hi, Dad. Listen, I've been working on a tough case and haven't had a chance to track down Ashley to—"

"Nicholas, it's your mom."

His heart seized. "What about Mom?"

"She fell. It's her hip. She's going into surgery in an hour or so."

"What happened? How'd she fall?"

"She was going down the back steps to prune her flowers and slipped and fell."

"What hospital?"

"You don't need to rush down here. She just wanted you to know." Of course. She wanted him to know. Dad wouldn't even have thought to call.

"What hospital, Dad?"

"Wellington Regional."

"I'll see you soon." Nick disconnected the call and dialed the number for his friend Stan.

"Yo."

"Stan, it's Nick."

"Yo, dude. It's been a while since we kicked it. What's up?"

"I need a favor."

"Name it." Many a time, Nick had helped Stan out by getting his brother into various rehab centers.

"Can you fly me to Florida now? My mom's about to have surgery. They think she'll need a hip replacement. I can't fly commercially because I'll need to come right back if she's okay."

"No problem. Meet me at the airport."

"Thanks."

Nick let Timmons know he was leaving, then called Maddie as he drove to the airport.

"Hello." Her voice soothed his nerves.

"Hi there."

"Hey, you. What're you doing?" She sounded happy. And relaxed. Maybe the day off was doing her a world of good.

"I'm about to head to Florida."

"What's going on?"

"My mom fell. They're taking her into surgery on her hip in an hour or so. A friend's flying me."

"Oh, Nick. I'm so sorry." She paused. "Are you okay?" It was as if she could sense his turmoil over the phone.

"I will be. I just wish I'd get to see her before her surgery."

"I know. I'm sorry. Is there anything I can do for you?"

If she could hold him right now, he might believe everything would be okay. But she couldn't. "Thanks for asking. I'll probably be back late tonight."

"Call me if you need anything, Nick. And know I'm praying for your mother."

Strange how that comforted him. It'd been a long time since the thought of prayers brought him such relief.

Four and a half hours later, Nick headed into the surgical waiting area of the hospital. His father sat in a corner, reading a Bible.

Had he ever seen his father reading a Bible? Nick couldn't recall. Certainly not since Roger had died.

"Dad."

He looked up, then smiled as he stood and grabbed Nick into a hug.

It'd been a long time since Dad had hugged him. Nick hugged him back before sitting in a chair beside him. "How's Mom?"

"She's out of surgery and in recovery. The doctor said they were able to replace her right hip."

Nick let out a heavy breath. "I was so worried about her."

"I know I told you not to come, but I'm glad you did."

His heart a little lighter, Nick smiled. "Me too. I never did mind well, huh?"

"Oh, you were always the one who minded like you were supposed to. I never had to worry about you going off and breaking the rules."

"Really?" Nick was truly shocked.

"Yeah. Roger? We had to watch that boy like a

hawk. He was always doing something he wasn't supposed to. Always getting in trouble."

Dad admitting Roger got into trouble? That wasn't like him.

Dad furrowed his brows. "Only the Marines could straighten him out."

"But Roger was your golden boy."

Dad gave him an incredulous look.

Had he said that out loud? Finally?

"I loved Roger very much, that's true, but he was never a *golden boy*."

"You always favored him, Dad. You let him play in your office, took him to work with you, things like that."

"Son, don't you understand? He was always a bit of a handful for your mother, so I had to help her out with him more. Keep him out of trouble."

Nick let it go. He tapped the Bible. "Doing a little reading?"

Dad actually blushed. "Your mom. Said she hadn't put up with me all these years not to see me in eternity." He lifted a single shoulder. "So I've been doing some studying these past few months."

Nick's emotions threatened to choke him. "How do you get over God taking Roger?"

"Your mom finally got me to understand . . . God doesn't like war. He doesn't like all the discord. Man starts war, not God. So it was man's fault and not God's that Roger was in Iraq. Man killed your brother, not God."

"I know God's all-powerful, so He could've stopped it. And He didn't."

"There must've been a reason."

"Yeah, Dad, what?"

"I don't know."

"And you're okay with that?" How could he be? Yet Nick recalled his gut feeling when he'd heard the priest at Gina's funeral. The peace.

"I have to be, son. I may not understand, I don't even want to, but I have to accept that. Otherwise, as your mother says, I'm just going to be nothing more than a bitter man who won't get to see Roger again."

But . . . Nick had some serious thinking to do.

CHAPTER TWENTY-EIGHT

"There are too many people that depend on me. I'm too obligated. I'm in too far to get out."
ELVIS PRESLEY

Moment of truth.

Maddie held her breath as Dr. Sebrowski verified Eva's results. In moments, Peter grabbed the report and brought them into the main room and handed them to Eva.

"Well?" Nick was as anxious as she.

"Mr. Adam Alexander is excluded as a match for the blood sample extracted from the back of Gina Ford's shirt at the crime scene."

Maddie released her breath.

"What?" Nick shook his head.

"It's not a match. It's not Adam's." Eva handed the report to Darren.

"Are you sure?" Nick asked.

Eva popped her hands on her hips. "Of course I'm sure. They aren't a match."

Darren looked at Nick. "Now what? I didn't think past Alexander."

"I hate to say it, but I told you so." Maddie reached for the report.

"Oh, you don't hate to say it. You enjoy being right." Nick nudged her.

She grinned. "Yeah, I do." Then she frowned. "Eva, do you still have Adam's sample up?"

"Yeah. What's wrong?"

"Pull it on your screen, then, split screen it and put it beside the familial one."

Eva sat in front of her computer and did as Maddie instructed.

Leaning over Eva's shoulder, Maddie eyeballed the double helixes. She pointed to the screen. "Superimpose them."

"What?" Nick asked.

"Hang on."

Eva did.

Maddie and Eva both gasped in unison.

"What?" Nick asked again.

"We can't be sure unless we run it through CODIS as a familial search again, and I don't even think that would be allowed, but I'd bet my next paycheck that whoever left that blood on the back of Gina's shirt is related not just to Brody Alexander, but Adam Alexander as well."

"So it's still someone who is a blood relative of Brody Alexander, but it's not Adam?" Darren asked. "This is getting complicated."

"I won't even try to explain on the diagram. But the DNA from Gina's shirt is similar enough to both Adam's and his father's."

"That leaves, who? The daughter?" Nick shook his head. "The daughter, right. She's the only one left."

"That's all in their family." But Maddie couldn't imagine a woman killing Gina and then stabbing her, then staging her in the car. Not unless she had help.

"And the daughter is younger than Adam?"

Maddie nodded. "By two years, I think."

"This is crazy." Darren shook his head. "I mean, Adam Alexander had motive, no alibi, and definitely the means."

"Who knows? Maybe Mom or sis helped him, same motive and means." Nick shrugged. "But we need to check it out."

He looked so tired. He hadn't gotten back into town until the wee hours of the morning. "How's your mom?"

"Good. Dad says if all goes well, they'll move her to the rehab center on Monday."

"I'm glad." Maddie smiled.

"I'll call you later." Nick and Darren left the lab.

"How do you feel about being right?"

"Good that I'm right, but I feel like every time we're close to justice for Gina, it slips away."

Eva nodded and leaned back in her chair. "I know. It's discouraging."

Wasn't that the truth.

"Oh, here's some good news."

"Yeah?"

"Ivan was able to help Memphis PD's CSI pull the print they lifted from Hailey Carter's crime scene. He'll run it through AFIS as soon as he's finished cleaning it up." She tapped her pen on her desk. "He says it wasn't high enough quality."

They laughed together. Ivan was many things, but mostly, he was extremely persnickety about latents. That's what made him the best.

"Brody Alexander?"

"Yes."

Nick flashed his badge and introduced himself and Timmons.

Brody waved them inside. "Can I get you something to drink? I apologize for the mess, but my wife and daughter are out of town."

"No, thank you. Actually, we have a few

questions for you, your wife, and your daughter."

"Well, my wife and daughter are on a mother-daughter cruise at the moment."

"A cruise?" Nick wanted to pound something. If this was another dead end, he'd give up on that whole familial DNA thing.

"Yes. Our women's ministry sponsors the cruise every other year. This year, they're sailing in the Caribbean." He grinned. "I'm jealous."

"I am too." Nick pulled out his notebook. "When did your wife and daughter leave, Mr. Alexander?"

"It will be two weeks ago tomorrow. They'll come ashore on Saturday and fly home on Sunday. I sure have missed them."

"I imagine so." Two weeks . . . they left before Gina Ford was murdered.

That only left Brody Alexander, but it wasn't a perfect match to him, personally. So either the familial DNA was a bust, which Maddie swore science didn't lie, or they'd missed something.

"Is there something I can help you with?"

"Sir, if you don't mind, can you tell me a little about your past imprisonment? I know it might be uncomfortable to discuss, but I believe you have some information we need for an open investigation, and I suspect you aren't aware of it."

"I don't mind at all. But I need to back up and tell you my whole life story for it to make sense. Okay?"

Nick nodded. "Go ahead."

"Back in college, I fell in love with Leslie, who was a devoted Christian. She still is, of course, but she made me want to be a better man. She led me to become a Christian. I had been a huge party guy, but after dedicating my life to Christ, I let go of the college fraternity and parties."

Nick noticed Timmons taking notes just as he was.

"I was honored that Leslie agreed to marry me. The very next year, we were blessed with a baby boy, Adam. My career took off and I joined a large stock-brokering firm. Two years later, we were blessed again, this time with our daughter, Tammy."

The man wasn't kidding—he truly was going to give his life story.

"We went through our twenties and thirties as movers and shakers. I made good money. A lot of money. When I turned forty, it's as if God put His hand on me to move me. I felt strongly that I was led to quit my job at the big brokerage and go to work at a smaller similar company."

He smiled. "I loved it. I only had two bosses and I had time for more personal interaction with my clients as well as a slower pace. I loved selling securities and bonds to locals, turning a very nice profit, which allowed me to give back more to the community and church."

Nick fought against yawning.

"Unfortunately, unbeknownst to me, my bosses

created bogus securities for us brokers to sell. An FBI investigation silently progressed until I was indicted. I went to trial, but although I'm innocent, I was found guilty and sentenced to four months in a federal prison camp."

Now they truly did know his life story.

"But God has had His hand on me all the time. Every step of the way, my faith has increased and the Lord continues to bless me in ways I never even thought of."

So how does this man's DNA click with another blood relative that's not his son or daughter? Even if his parents were still alive, Nick seriously doubted they'd have means or motive to murder Gina Ford.

"Mr. Alexander, do you have any brothers or sisters?"

"I had a brother, but he was killed in an auto accident some six years back."

This did not make any sense.

"Agents, I know you don't have to tell me anything, but if you'd narrow down what you're looking for in connection to me, perhaps I could help you."

How had this man raised such a womanizing louse of a son? Unless the apple didn't fall far from the tree? After all, he hadn't expected to learn Senator Ford was having an affair.

"Mr. Alexander, we mean no disrespect, but is it possible you fathered another child?"

364

The man visibly stiffened his entire body. "I've never cheated on Leslie."

"We're not accusing you of any such thing, sir. But as you said, you were a bit of a party guy in college before you met your wife."

Brody squirmed just a bit. "Well, I suppose it's possible. It was back before I met Leslie. Before I became a Christian."

"Any names?"

"Oh. I'd have to really think about it. That's been such a long time ago."

"No woman ever contacted you? Maybe asked you for money?"

"No." The man's face didn't reveal any of the markers of dishonesty. "I met Leslie in my junior year of college, so if this occurred, it would have to have been in my freshman or sophomore year."

Nick stood. "If you could give it some thought and get back with us." He handed Mr. Alexander his card. "We'd really appreciate it."

"Of course." Mr. Alexander showed them out.

"What do you make of that?" Timmons asked once they were in the car.

"I don't know. Either that familial DNA is bogus, or he has a kid he's not aware of." Nick turned the car toward the office.

"You think he's on the up-and-up . . . that he doesn't know about another child?"

"I've been surprised before, but I don't think

he's hiding anything. The man embraces his past, even the bad parts, way too much. I don't think he'd deny it."

Timmons grinned. "That's a man following God."

"What do you mean?" He remembered his father had been reading a Bible at the hospital. Had he somehow missed the Christian revival train?

"Learning from the mistakes of your past. Growing. Praising God during the hard times. It's all part of your spiritual walk."

"You really believe all that?" Nick knew that all from church, but somewhere along the road . . . between Roger getting killed and the horrors he saw every day . . .

"I do. And I know what you're thinking."

"Oh yeah? What am I thinking?"

"We're in a job where we see the true evil nature of men day in and day out. It's hard not to become jaded. But that's not God's fault."

"It's not? I thought God was all-powerful, able to do whatever He wanted."

"Man, how long has it been since you read your Bible? Have you even done that since you became an adult?"

"Well, after Roger died, we kinda stopped going to church."

"You should remember this because it's taught in Sunday school: free will. Yes, God is all-powerful and could do whatever He wanted, but He gave each one of us free will. The choice to follow Him and have eternal life is our choice. He loves us and wants us all to share eternal life with Him, but the choice is always ours."

"So the evil we face in our jobs—"

"Is because some people choose to move out of God's will for their lives and what we have to clean up are the consequences of their bad decisions."

"That doesn't seem right. To the victims, I mean."

"Okay, let me put it this way. Parents tell their kids not to drink and drive all the time. We have laws against it. But say a kid defies his parents and the law. He goes to a party and drinks. It was his choice to drink, not his parents'. He has a girlfriend who is at the party. She's not drinking as much, but when it's time to go home, she gets in the car with him. It's her choice to get in the car, not her boyfriend's, not her parents'. On the way home, they get in an accident and both are killed. Everyone calls it a great tragedy, which it is, but it's also the consequences of bad choices. The consequence of sin is death."

"But Roger didn't choose to get shot defending his country."

"No, and sometimes consequences are ripples you can't see. And sometimes my bad choices cause effects to other people. For instance, if I choose to go out and rob a bank, then I might get caught. If I do, I go to jail. Savannah would suffer because I made a bad choice. But God can use that to teach her about consequences that might stop her from making a really bad choice that could cause her harm. We just never know. Not this side of paradise anyway."

Nick pulled the car into the parking lot of the FBI. He killed the engine but didn't get out. His mind was tripping over what Timmons had said.

"Being a Christian doesn't always mean doing the right thing. But it does mean we're forgiven. We get that second chance."

"That part I got. We see some bad characters. If they apologize, then their slate is wiped clean too. That's a hard one for me."

Timmons chuckled. "Well, it's not just an apology. There's a process. Recognizing what you did is wrong. Admitting it. Then taking it to God and confessing you did it. Then you turn away from it, making a conscious effort not to repeat it. Then there's God's forgiveness, but you have to accept it too. And that means not carrying it around with you all the time. It means letting God heal your heart and move on."

Even more to think about. "Thanks, Darren."

"No problem."

Nick followed Timmons into the office, but his mind was heavy. What bad choices had he made that had caused innocent people to be hurt? What were the consequences of the sins he'd committed? Was he ready to truly go through the stages of forgiveness?

CHAPTER TWENTY-NINE

"I hope I didn't bore you too much
with my life story."
ELVIS PRESLEY

"Maddie. You aren't going to believe this." Ivan ran into the lab, his hair sticking up even more than usual.

"Whoa, where's the fire?" She looked up from her inventory sheet.

"The print we got from Memphis PD crime scene unit from the Hailey Carter crime scene?"

"Yeah. You helped save it."

"Right. I cleaned it and brought it here to run through AFIS. I got a hit. A perfect match." Ivan's eyes were wide with excitement.

"That's awesome, Ivan. Have you called the investigator working the case?"

"I did, but I wanted to tell you too."

She smiled, as did Eva. "Knew if anyone could do it, it'd be you."

"Maddie, the print matched to Mark Hubble."

It was like the lab had gotten caught in a vacuum. All the air sucked out of space. Maddie had to remind her lungs to push the air in and out. "Are you telling me there's forensic evidence that links Mark Hubble to Hailey Carter?"

"That's *exactly* what I'm telling you. I'm going to meet the detectives." Ivan rushed out of the lab as quickly as he'd rushed in.

She was going to be sick.

"Maddie . . . Maddie, it's okay." Eva rushed from her desk and grabbed her. Shook her a little.

"It's my fault. It's my fault he got out. My fault he was put out on the streets to kill that poor, young girl." The room seemed dimmer. Darker.

"It's just his print at the crime scene."

Maddie's eyes burned. "Science doesn't lie, Eva."

"And you're working to find out who really attacked Nettie Sloan. You're doing good work, Maddie."

"My testimony set him free. Because of me, Hailey Carter is dead." The tears burned but she didn't care.

"No, because of Mark Hubble, Hailey Carter is dead."

Maddie shook her head, her stomach twisting and turning like worms in a can. "Don't you see? If I wouldn't have testified, he wouldn't have been let out. If he wouldn't have been let out, Hailey Carter would still be alive."

"Stop this. Snap out of it." Eva flicked her

forehead. "You did your job. Nobody made Hubble kill anybody, just like nobody made Rust or whoever assault Nettie."

"Everything is wrong, Eva. Why do I even bother?"

"Because sometimes, we do it right. We were able to prove Adam wasn't Gina's killer. That's something, right?"

Maddie shrugged. It didn't seem to matter. A young girl was dead because of her. Because of *her*.

"We can, and will, find Gina Ford's killer. We will help Nettie Sloan see justice served to whoever attacked her. This is our job. We don't make anything happen . . . we simply interpret the science. That's it. We're spectators, not participants. You taught me that when I started here."

"Maybe I was wrong."

"No, you weren't wrong. You were right. People can and do the unreasonable and the unthinkable. That has nothing to do with us."

The door to the lab swung open and Nick swaggered in.

Maddie's heart leapt.

He took one look at her and rushed to her side. "What's wrong?"

"Oh, Nick." And the tears fell.

He held her tight. "Honey, what's wrong?"

Maddie couldn't speak. The guilt formed more tears that spilled out. She could hear Eva's voice, knew she was telling Nick what had happened, but Maddie couldn't stop the tears. All that mattered at this moment was Nick was here. He was holding her. And she drew comfort from his strength.

The lab door creaked open as Eva left.

Finally, the well of tears dried up enough for her to untangle from his embrace. She looked at his shirt, now wet. "Sorry."

"Don't you be sorry. I'll never mind holding you when you need me." He put his finger under her chin and raised her face so he could look her in the eye. "Are you okay?"

"I set him free and he killed Hailey Carter. Because of me, she's dead."

"That's not true."

"It is."

"No, it's not. If you hadn't testified, some other forensic scientist would have. Either way, Hubble would've gotten out because he shouldn't have been in there in the first place. And who knows, it's possible he would have never escalated to murder from his other charges had he not had to serve six years in prison for a crime he didn't commit."

Well, that sounded logical. She sniffed. Her nose was probably red. She knew her eyes were. She must look a total mess.

"You know, someone very wise told me today that sometimes innocent people get hurt by the consequences of someone else's bad choice to move out of God's plan for them."

She went still. Was Nick really talking to her about faith?

Lord, if he's there, please, please, draw him closer to You. As close as You can.

He kissed her forehead. "I wish I knew the right thing to say to you, but I don't. All I can tell you is that you did nothing wrong, you're a wonderful woman, and I'm crazy about you."

Nick pulled her into his arms and held her again. She sighed against him and whispered up prayers for the peace that only God could provide.

"We're missing something." Nick stared at the case board.

"I'm not seeing it." Timmons stood back, staring at the board from different angles as if Gina's killer hid in one of the corners of the dry-erase board.

"Adam Alexander's not the killer. DNA proved that, so we can mark him off." Nick drew a line through Adam's name with the black marker. Even though Nick really liked him for the crime. He had the strongest motive. And he was a louse.

"Leo Ward's alibi was verified, so we can X him out too." Timmons drew a line through his name.

"Cynthia Mantle. Her alibi hasn't been confirmed and she lied to us, but I don't think she's the killer."

Timmons tilted his head. "So do we mark her off or not?"

Nick really didn't believe she killed her best friend, but if he was wrong . . . "Leave her there for now." He pointed at the next name. "Senator Ford's alibi has been verified, so mark him off."

Timmons did. "That leaves Gina's boyfriend, David Tiddle."

"His alibi could fall through. Don't know that a trip to Clarksville would be useful. Most cleaning crews don't remember the trash left behind."

"Right. He's probably clean, but his eyes are a little too close together for my taste."

Nick froze. "What did you say?"

"I was talking about Tiddle. His eyes are too close together, in my opinion."

"Wait a minute." Nick flipped through the folders and grabbed the photo of Tiddle and placed it beside the one of Adam Alexander. "Both of their eyes are too close together."

Timmons moved to stand beside Nick and stared at the pictures.

Both Tiddle and Alexander had brown hair. Both had green eyes that were too close together. Both stood almost six feet tall. Both had high foreheads and widow's peaks.

"Tiddle's thirty years old."

Timmons nodded. "Which would mean he was conceived before Brody Alexander married his wife."

Was it possible? Were they reaching for straws out of desperation?

"I'll pull a full background on Tiddle."

The dossier—he'd never given it back. "I have one from the senator." Nick dug around in his desk drawer until he found it. "Here's the background info we have: Parents died when he was ten. No other living relatives could be located, so he was put into care of the state. Bounced around foster homes, making appearances in juvie a handful of times, then dropped out of the system's paperwork trail at sixteen. Tiddle didn't show back up on the report until his late twenties. A couple of pleas for minors, but all probation or warnings. Nothing serious. Work record read sketchy, at best. Waiter. Maître d' at several restaurants. Assistant to various professions. No stability. No permanency. Hit or miss."

"Parents died when he was ten?" Timmons asked.

"Why don't you start there? If he's Brody Alexander's son, either he's adopted or his mother lied on the birth certificate."

"I'm on it." Timmons rushed out.

Nick held up Tiddle's picture.

Was he looking at Gina Ford's killer?

"You look beautiful." Maddie stared at her soon-to-be sister-in-law in her wedding dress. "Simply stunning."

Remington smiled, her long, blond hair shining under the lights of the bridal shop. "Thank you."

"You will be a gorgeous bride. My brother's a lucky man." Tears filled her eyes. "Oh, look at me. I'm such a sap. I'm the one who always cries at weddings."

Remington stepped out of the dress and hugged her. "I'm so happy I'm going to be in your family."

"Me too." Maddie dried her eyes. "And your best friend too."

"I can't believe Hayden and Riley are getting married just a month after us. It's crazy. Oh, do you remember Hayden's sister?"

"Emily?" The poor thing had been involved with one loser guy after another.

"Yes. She got married about three months ago, and they just found out they're expecting."

"I didn't even know she got married."

"She did. A really nice guy from up north. Dylon. They're so happy it's wonderful. Hayden's mom, Ardy, is so anxious to hold a grandbaby, I don't know if she'll make it until Emily gives birth."

Maddie smiled as Remington went to get dressed. Emily married and expecting. Rafe and Remington getting married. Riley and Hayden getting married a month later. It seemed as if everyone was moving forward into a new stage of life. They'd all reached for and got their happily-ever-afters. Would it ever come for Maddie?

Remington stepped out of the dressing room. "Let's go have a coffee before Rafe and I have to head back."

They headed down the street to the little coffee shop wedged between boutiques. After getting their lattes, they found a table.

"Rafe's worried about you." Remington took a sip.

"Why?"

"Because he knows you're seeing Nick and he's too pigheaded to ask you how that's going."

Maddie smiled. "So he sent you to ask instead?"

Remington grinned. "Something like that. He's worried Nick will break your heart."

"Tell Rafe that Nick is wonderful, a perfect gentleman, and one of the kindest men I know. He won't hurt me. And if my heart gets a few more cuts and scratches, well, that's just part of living."

"Here. Here." Remington tapped her coffee cup against Maddie's.

That was the truth. After seeing Adam and not feeling anything, Maddie realized she didn't need to protect herself. Oh, she might get hurt, but it was part of the process.

Like Eva said, if she wasn't going to try, how would she ever have a chance at her happily-ever-after?

CHAPTER THIRTY

"The Lord can give, and the Lord can take
away. I might be herding sheep next year."
ELVIS PRESLEY

"It took some creative investigative work, but here it is: the full history of David Tiddle." Timmons entered the office wearing a smile.

Nick leaned back in his chair. "Lay it on me. It's Friday and I'm ready for the weekend. Would be really nice to have a good lead."

"Well, here you go. Finally got the name of his birth mother, Priscilla Jones. She literally sold him to Sherwin and Velma Tiddle. While extremely wealthy, the Tiddles had been turned down by every adoption agency due to their advanced age. Sherwin was sixty-four and Velma, sixty-two." He set a picture of a young woman, smiling, on the desk. That smile looked very similar to David Tiddle's. "This is Priscilla Jones. Her college photo."

"Pretty." He nodded at the folder. "Wow, that is a little old to start with a newborn."

Timmons nodded. "According to everything I can find, the Tiddles had concentrated on their careers in their twenties and early thirties, then decided to start their family only to have problems. They spent their late thirties and early forties in fertility treatments to help Velma conceive."

Nick had heard of people so desperate for children, they'd try just about any route they could.

Timmons continued. "They even went so far as to try in vitro fertilization. In her midforties, an emergency hysterectomy was needed. In her early fifties, they began to look into surrogates, but none were interested. They tried all the adoption routes, but by now they were in their midfifties, and state agencies weren't interested. By their late fifties, they opted to go private adoption with less-than-standard options for which they paid handsomely, and they were given a baby boy they named David."

"It's almost like black-market baby brokering." Nick actually felt sorry for the Tiddles, except there were thousands of others who wanted children just as desperately but didn't have the money to buy a baby.

Timmons nodded. "They doted on their son and spoiled him rotten. When David was seven, Sherwin died from a sudden massive heart attack. It was the first time David realized his parents were much older than those of his classmates. Every time Velma came to a school function, everyone thought she was his grandmother, at least, that's what his school records claim."

"I can understand that. Kids can and do just

spout out the first thing that comes into their heads." Nick was glad his parents had been, for all practical purposes, normal.

"When David was ten, Velma had a stroke and had to be put in a facility for twenty-four-hour care. At this time, the state took custody of David and worked him into the foster-care system. Barely a year later, Velma died. The social worker informed David that there was no money left in the estate as it all went to Velma's care."

"That's harsh."

"Yep. David was moved from foster family to foster family. With each foster family who was mean to him or abused him, David grew a bit angrier . . . a bit meaner. At sixteen, he had enough and ran away to live on the streets. The system lost track of him from then on until he became an adult."

Nick shook his head. The things people did . . . "Whatever happened to Priscilla?"

"She died of a drug overdose the year after she gave her baby up for adoption."

"So, the moral to this sad story is we go ask Brody Alexander if he remembers a Priscilla Jones. Why don't you do that and I'll go see if I can round up David. Maybe he'll surprise me as well and offer up a DNA sample."

Timmons laughed. "Yeah, I don't think you're that lucky. I'll call you if Brody remembers Priscilla."

Nick drove to Tiddle's apartment with his adrenaline spiking. This was it. He felt it. Knew it in his gut. Now he just had to prove it.

Tiddle's car sat in its parking space. Nick parked beside it, then rushed to the door. The chill in the air had become all too nippy.

"Hello, Agent Hagar." Tiddle opened the door and waved Nick inside. "It's getting colder out there."

"Weather forecast says we might get snow tonight."

"I'd believe it."

Nick noticed the suitcase in the hall. "You going somewhere?"

Tiddle followed his line of vision. "Maybe." He shrugged and smiled, but beneath his smile, fear snuck in. "Gotta be ready in case the boss needs me to scout."

"I see."

"Please, sit down." Tiddle motioned toward the couch.

Nick sat in the chair. "I have a couple of questions for you."

Tiddle took a seat on the couch. "Shoot." He grinned, nerves tugging at the corners of his mouth. "Not literally, of course."

"When did you learn you were adopted?"

As if time suddenly moved at the slowness of frame by frame, Tiddle's upper lip quivered, then his chin wobbled, and finally, his face flushed. "E-Excuse me?"

"When did you learn you were adopted?" Nick watched every nuance of Tiddle's expression and body language and would bet the man hadn't known. This could be useful. "Come on, David. Surely you realized you couldn't be the biological son of Sherwin and Velma?"

"Uh, I guess I never thought about it."

"I guess you heard the senator spouting off to the media that we'd brought a suspect in Gina's murder in for questioning."

"I did hear something about that on the news." Tiddle's foot bounced. "So, who is it?"

"Well, as usual, the senator got some of his facts wrong."

Tiddle's laugh came out forced. "Yeah. He does that."

"See, we found a familial DNA match in the system to the blood left on Gina."

Tiddle's eyes widened. "There was blood left on Gina?"

With his focus there . . . Nick leaned forward and lowered his voice to a stage whisper. "And we haven't released this just yet, but those stab wounds? Not her cause of death."

"Really?" Tiddle blinked. Once. Twice. And again.

But he never asked how she died.

"Matter-of-fact, there's been new evidence in the Hailey Carter case that proves irrefutably that these murders were not executed by the same person. The arrest in the Carter case should occur any moment now."

Tiddle's Adam's apple worked overtime. "T-That's good."

"Yeah. But back to that family DNA thing. It's ironic. We did think we had the killer pegged by it. At least I thought so."

"It wasn't?" Tiddle fidgeted on the couch.

"No. And for a few moments, it really confused me. I'd looked at the information until it was embedded in my brain. You ever do that? Look at something so long and so hard that you can no longer see what's right there in front of you?"

Tiddle fingered the edge of the ugly and knotted throw pillow on the couch. "Uh, I guess so."

"That's what happened to me. I became so focused on that particular aspect of the case, that I overlooked some other details. Threw me totally off track."

Tiddle remained silent.

Nick stood and went to the front window. He eased back a curtain and looked out, nodded as if gesturing to someone, then turned back to Tiddle. "I know you travel a bit, for work and all, so you probably know this, but I just recently found out what express checkout is. Do you use that? It's incredibly cool."

"Yeah. I've used it on occasion. It's convenient."

"I agree. But the thing is, David, they slip your

bill under the door. If you forget it, like I'm always forgetting things as I get older, housekeeping finds it when they come to clean the room. Some zealous worker—probably one itching for a promotion—can turn it in to the manager and it just might be put in a file in case that person comes back and wants a copy."

His cell phone buzzed. "Excuse me just a minute." Nick stepped into the little dining area. "Hagar."

"It's him. Brody remembers Priscilla. It was a one-night stand, he didn't even know her last name. Frat party. He never saw or heard from her after that night, but he recognized her picture." Timmons nearly tripped over his own words.

"Oh, I see. That's interesting."

"I'm on my way to meet you at Tiddle's now. I should be there in fifteen minutes or so. Stall."

"Thanks." Nick hung up and turned back to Tiddle. "Sorry about that."

"No problem."

Nick glanced into the kitchen. There weren't dirty dishes, but the stench of just that hung in the room. He returned to the living room. "Anyway, I wondered if you ever knew who your birth parents were."

"Uh, no." Tiddle shook his head and blew air.

"Really? You never wanted to know? You could possibly have siblings or half-siblings running around in the world. Wouldn't that be interesting?"

"I never thought about it. I guess that might be."

"You know, my girlfriend is a DNA specialist. I bet she could get your DNA and process it and help you find out if you have some living relatives."

"That's okay. I'm not fond of needles." Tiddle stared at his suitcase waiting in the hall.

Nick would bet his next paycheck that the man was about to leave town.

"She can do that DNA thing with your spit. No needles."

Tiddle stood. "I appreciate it, but not right now." He glanced at his watch. "Matter-of-fact, I really need to run a few errands before I go into work, and I don't want to be late."

"We don't want that." Nick's hand rested on the butt of his handgun on his hip. "Mr. Tiddle, I really must insist you come with me to answer a few more questions."

He froze. "I've cooperated with you all along."

"Yes, sir, and I do appreciate that. But I need you to come with me to answer a few official questions regarding Gina Ford's death."

His gaze darted to the suitcase to the door to Nick to the suitcase to the door to Nick—

"David, it's really in your best interest if you come with me now and answer a few questions."

"Sure. Let me just go to the restroom and brush my teeth." He moved toward the hall.

Nick grabbed his shoulder. "Your teeth are fine. Let's go."

Tiddle tensed.

Nick tightened his grip on Tiddle's shoulder. "Don't do it. I'm armed. I will shoot you if you run from me because I'm too old and too tired to have to chase you. I'm trying to help you here. I can make it easier on you if you tell us the truth. My partner is right outside. You have zero chance if you run. Do you understand what I'm telling you?"

"Maddie?" Peter stood in the doorway of the lab, a man wearing a cheap suit hovering at his elbow. "This man needs a word with you, please."

She glanced at Eva, shrugged, then went into the hall.

"I'll be in my office if you need me." Peter squeezed her arm as he passed.

"Ms. Baxter?" He flashed a badge. "I'm Jeffrey Melendez with Memphis PD Internal Affairs. Can we talk?"

"Sure." She led him to the break room. They sat across the table from one another, the aroma of recently popped popcorn lingering in the air. "How can I help?"

"Captain Moore sent us the Nettie Sloan file and filled us in on your hypothesis. Very interesting."

"I thought so." Her breathing hitched. "I'm

almost positive Bobby Rust's DNA will match that taken from the Nettie Sloan crime scene."

"And we're working on attaining such a sample through the proper, legal channels."

Was Nettie's attacker finally going to be brought to justice?

"I just wanted to touch base with you. Assure you that we're looking into the investigators who handled the case nine years ago." Melendez tapped his notebook. "Based upon the case files and my initial interviews, Captain Moore is reopening the Nettie Sloan case."

Maddie wanted to cry. "Thank you."

"There's no guarantee, you know that, but I've also put my investigators on the case to monitor the detectives."

This was the best she could hope for.

He stood. "I just wanted to bring you up to speed. If this goes the way I think it will, I'm sure you'll be getting a DNA sample to run against the one from Ms. Sloan's crime scene."

She stood, wanting to dance. "Thank you, Mr. Melendez."

"No, thank you. If you hadn't reviewed this case so diligently, it probably would remain nothing but a file in a cabinet."

As soon as he left, she raced back to the lab. She filled Eva in on the conversation.

Eva's eyes widened. "That's so awesome, Maddie. I know how important this is to you."

Maddie nodded. "I just can't let Nettie Sloan down again."

"You didn't let her down the first time, Maddie, someone else did. Someone messed with her life, and Hubble's too, for that matter. It wasn't you."

"I know." She smiled at Eva. "I do. But I still want her to have justice. I want her to see there are people who care about the truth and work for the victims, not for the system."

"You're a good person, Maddie."

She sat straighter. "Thanks, Eva. You are too."

"Hey, can I interrupt this love fest?" Peter stood in the doorway.

They laughed.

He stood at Maddie's desk. "You okay? The IA guy looked a little tense when he left. Was on the phone talking low and fast."

She told him what she'd told Eva. "I'm so excited that the truth will finally come out."

Peter smiled. "I have even better news. Just heard from the deputy director. Our funds came through! The expansion for the lab is back on track."

Maddie grinned. "This is wonderful. I can't wait to tell Nick about it tonight. I invited him for dinner."

"Then let's get outta here." Eva turned off the light in her desk's overhead. "I'm having dinner with Darren and Savannah."

They walked out together. A few snowflakes drifted in the air.

"Snow! Oh, I hope Savannah wants to dance in the snow with me. I love that." Eva twirled.

Maddie smiled. She, too, loved snow. It was like God's way of cleaning with beauty.

CHAPTER THIRTY-ONE

"They put me on television. And the whole thing broke loose. It was wild, I tell ya for sure."
ELVIS PRESLEY

Evening settled over Memphis as Nick and Timmons stood in the viewing room. David Tiddle sat on the other side of the two-way mirror, his feet bouncing his knees up and down. The technician straightened. "It's recording now, sir."

"Thank you." Nick nodded and the man left.

Tiddle chewed his fingernails.

"Think he'llconfess?"

"I think he wants to. I think he needs to."

Tiddle spat the nail on the floor.

Nick pointed. "Send someone in with some water for him and have them as discreetly as possible, retrieve that nail. We might need that DNA."

Timmons went to find someone while Nick continued to stare. The mayor had called again today. The senator was pushing hard for something to be done on his daughter's case. The DNA would prove Tiddle killed Gina, Nick was sure, but that would take a few days. He wanted this over, and now.

As soon as Timmons returned to view, Nick took a deep breath and entered the room. "Sorry to have kept you waiting. Do you need more water?"

"No, I'm good." Up and down went his knees, like a piston in an engine.

"Look, I'm not gonna lie to you, David. I know you killed Gina. My problem is, I don't understand why. If I can get the why, maybe I can talk to the DA for you. See if he can do something. The senator's pushing for the death penalty."

Tiddle's face whitened.

"By electrocution, not lethal injection." Nick leaned back. "I've never seen either in person, but I had to watch the videos of both. If it were me, I wouldn't want to be electrocuted."

"I don't want to die." Tiddle's expression was one of pure horror.

"Then talk to me. I can't make any promises, but I'll do my best. If you don't lie to me. Shoot me straight, and I'll see what I can do." He looked Tiddle in the eye. "Deal?"

If he lawyered up at this point, everything went south. He needed the confession. The proof would be in the DNA and that would come later, but what he'd said about the senator pushing for the death penalty was true.

"Okay."

"We know about your childhood. About being in the foster-care system after your adoptive parents died. About your juvie record." Nick's heartbeat drummed. "So start at the beginning. Friday morning."

Tiddle shook his head. "It starts before then. Before I even met Gina."

"Then tell it your way." Nick leaned back in his chair.

"I didn't know I was adopted until you told me. You say you know about my childhood? You don't. Let's just say that moving from one family who doesn't want you to another isn't exactly a self-esteem builder."

He took a sip of water. "I wasn't the most masculine of guys, and violence never turned me on. But I needed to learn how to make a buck. I knew I didn't have the guts for drugs, didn't have the ability for burglary—I have a hard time unlocking my door with a key—so I focused on scams. Blackmail being the easiest and least messy."

Moving from blackmail to murder was quite the reach.

"I made my way through my twenties with little blackmail schemes here and there. Enough to survive, but not big time. Until one day, as I was getting some photos on another gig, I happened to spot Senator Ford sneaking into a house that wasn't his. And he was following a woman that looked nothing like the photos I'd seen on the news of Mrs. Ford."

Lila Acer.

"I began to watch that house. I took photo after photo of the two of them together. Some that there was no way he'd be able to explain his way out of. I figured I'd hit the big-time. But he's a senator so getting to him and getting the demand letter to him past his flunkies would be impossible on my own."

Like Ford's security team had held the threats from Ward's people.

Tiddle shifted in his seat. "So I researched the senator to see a time when I could get through to him. And I found Gina. I began to research her, learn her schedule, figure out where she hung out. I waited for the opportunity to *run into* her. I finally did. We became friends, then started dating. I knew if I could just get close enough to her, she'd eventually take me to her father's house. I'd planned to slip copies of the photos and the demand letter in his room to find when I wasn't there."

What a calculating scumbag.

"But then I started having real feelings for Gina. I wanted to spend more and more time with her and cared less and less about her father and the blackmail. I got the photographer's apprentice job and really applied myself to learn the trade." His eyes glassed over as he stared at Nick. "I didn't lie to you about loving Gina. We were in love. We planned to get married."

A marriage based on blackmail, that was rich.

"Gina made me a better man. I looked forward to a future with her. I gave up my blackmail plan and concentrated on building a future with her."

Sounded like a beautiful story. "What happened?"

"She went to my place to study while I was out of town. The whole Hailey Carter murder had her shaken up and she wanted to stay farther away from campus to feel safer. She was looking in drawers for a highlighter as hers went out and she found the pictures of her dad. Naturally, she got upset and left."

"I have to interrupt to ask. If you loved her and were going to start a life with her, why'd you keep the pictures?"

"Honestly? I forgot about those copies. I'd destroyed the negatives and the other set, along with the demand letter. Those were extras and I'd shoved them in that drawer months ago."

Nick nodded.

"That Friday morning, she came here, furious, but more hurt than anything." Tears shone in his eyes. "I tried to explain but she was despondent. Not just about her father, but she'd figured out I'd intended to blackmail him." He shook his head as he cried. "She wouldn't let me explain. We argued. She threw the pictures down and stormed toward the door."

Nick could see it.

"I couldn't let her leave. Not like that. I'd never see her again. I tried to stop her. She struggled against me. She came at me like a cat, ready to claw my eyes out. I shoved her off of me."

That explained the bruising around her collarbone.

"She shoved me back, then turned to grab the lamp in the bedroom. I pushed her. She fell backward and over the bed." His tears fell freely. "She landed on her neck. I heard it crack. Knew she was dead."

Nick's stomach turned.

Tiddle sniffed. "I knew I couldn't explain her death. Knew the whole blackmail thing would come out. I panicked. I remembered all the news about Hailey because Gina was almost obsessed with it. She freaked, terrified someone would attack her. And that's when I got the idea to make it look like Gina had been killed by the same guy."

"How could you do that?"

"It wasn't easy. Remember, I don't have the stomach for violence."

Yet he stabbed his dead girlfriend and staged her body.

"It was the hardest thing to do. Stabbing her. I

threw up so much that I started throwing up blood." He shook his head. "I can't get the stink of vomit out of my house."

"Where's the knife?"

"I tossed it in the Mississippi River. I knew the boyfriend is always the first person the police look at. I couldn't risk anyone finding it."

"You drove her to the place where you left her?"

"I put her in her car, drove her there, and left it as close to what Hailey's had been, at least what the news had said. When I got back home and was cleaning up, I noticed I'd nicked myself on the knife."

"You left a drop of blood on the back of her shirt when you placed her in the car."

Tiddle nodded. "And that's what happened."

Nick stared at the man. Cold. Heartless. Unforgiving. Nick couldn't help but wonder if he'd be that way in a few years if he didn't change his attitude. Change his life. Change his anger at God. He could easily end up just like Mom had warned Dad: bitter without hope. Speaking of Dad . . . without excusing himself, Nick headed out into the hall and lifted his cell.

"Hello?"

"Dad, I think I owe you an apology."

"For what?"

"All these years I've believed you favored

Roger. That you loved him more. That nothing I did could ever measure up to him."

"Oh, son. That's not even close to the truth. You were always the easy one to be so proud of. Great grades, a true gentleman, never giving your mom the rough times. You were always so respectful and honest." Dad's voice cracked. "You two were as different as night and day. There was no comparison between you."

Nick's chest constricted. "I guess I just never realized."

"Son, we've always been proud of you. So proud of the man you've become. You are a good man, Nicholas. I love you."

Nick's throat threatened to close. "Love you too, Dad. I have something I need to do. I'll call you later."

Nick stepped outside, his mind and heart both overwhelmed. Despite the myriad emotions and thoughts overtaking him, Nick knew one thing for certain: he didn't want *not* to spend eternity without Maddie.

EPILOGUE

Six Months Later

Maddie walked out of the courtroom, her arm linked through Nick's. Bobby Rust had just been found guilty of sexual assault on Nettie Sloan nine years ago. Maddie's heart pounded. "Finally, she's getting justice."

"It was nice that she apologized to you." Nick kissed her forehead. "I'm not quite sure what she was apologizing for."

"Doesn't matter. It's all okay."

"I have a surprise for you."

She turned and smiled. "I love surprises."

"I know you do. Come on." He put her in the car, then held up a blindfold.

"You've gotta be kidding me."

"Nope. If you want your surprise, you have to put it on."

Maddie jerked it from him and secured it over her eyes. The car started. "This feels weird to be riding and not be able to see."

"Not too far."

"You're a man of mystery, Nicholas Hagar."

"Hey, speaking of mystery, do you mind if I go to church with you on Sunday morning?"

Her heart thrumped. "Of course. Yes. I'd love for you to come." *God, I don't know what You're doing, but thank You.*

She spent the next several minutes praising God for pulling on Nick's heart. He was now truly the perfect man. At least for her.

The car stopped. "Hang on, I'll come around and get you."

His door slammed. Hers opened. His touch made her smile as he helped her from the car. With him leading, she walked over asphalt, then ground. "I'm feeling a little wobbly."

"Just a little bit farther."

Finally, he stopped her. "Here we are. I'm going to help you sit."

Talk about blind trust. She let him ease her onto what felt like a bench.

"Just a second."

Rustling sounded. A breeze caressed her cheek.

"Okay. Take off your blindfold."

She did, and blinked. Where were—? "We're in Elvis Presley's backyard." Her heart pounded.

"We are indeed." Nick smiled as he sat on the bench beside her.

"But how—this isn't open to the—"

"Don't ask, just enjoy." He handed her a wrapped box about four inches by four inches. "For you."

Her fingers shook as she untied the bow. The

paper fell away to reveal a lovely jewelry box. Her breath caught in her throat. "It's beautiful."

"Open it." Nick's breath was warm against her face.

She eased it open. Sitting inside, atop red velvet, was a stunning marquise solitaire.

Her heart went into triple overdrive. She lifted her gaze to his.

"Madeline Baxter, you make me a better man. You fill my heart with a completeness I never knew existed. I've fallen in love with you, and if you'll do me the honor of agreeing to marry me sometime in the future, I'd be the happiest man alive."

She blinked the hot tears away. "Yes." She could barely speak.

Nick slipped the ring on her finger. When the weight of the ring was released, the box began to play.

With the slowest of movements, Nick lowered his head and kissed her. Soft, tender. She leaned into him, responding with all the love in her heart. He wrapped his arms around her and deepened the kiss. And the music box serenaded them . . .

Amazing Grace, how sweet the sound,
That saved a wretch like me.
I once was lost but now am found,
Was blind, but now I see.

'Twas Grace that taught my heart to fear.
And Grace, my fears relieved.
How precious did that Grace appear
The hour I first believed.

Through many dangers, toils and snares
I have already come.
'Tis Grace that brought me safe thus far
and Grace will lead me home.

The Lord has promised good to me.
His word my hope secures.
He will my shield and portion be,
As long as life endures.

Yea, when this flesh and heart shall fail,
And mortal life shall cease,
I shall possess within the veil,
A life of joy and peace.

When we've been here ten thousand years
Bright shining as the sun.
We've no less days to sing God's praise
Than when we've first begun.

Dear Reader,

Sharing this story with you was so much fun for me. Thank you for coming along and participating in the Justice Seekers series and getting to know the Baxter siblings.

So much of Maddie's struggles with "science doesn't lie" came from within my family. I'm grateful you've allowed me to share.

While familial DNA testing *is* being done, at the time of this novel's publishing, it is *not* being done in Tennessee. I took quite liberal literary rights in incorporating the guidelines and details from another state and applying them to Tennessee.

I hope you've enjoyed getting to know the last Baxter and see Nick find love. It's a bit bitter-sweet for me to say good-bye to this series and these characters. I hope the Justice Seekers series touched you in some way.

As an avid reader, I love to connect with other readers. Visit me on my website at www.robincaroll.com and sign up for my newsletter. You can connect with me on Facebook at www.facebook.com/robincaroll or write to me snail mail: PO Box 242091, Little Rock, AR, 72223. I can't wait to hear from you!

Blessings,

Robin Caroll

DISCUSSION QUESTIONS

1. By her own profession in the field of science, Maddie had trouble reconciling her faith with her job responsibilities. Have you ever had a conflict between your faith and ideals against your job duties? Discuss and explain how you felt and what you ultimately did.

2. Nick had his own ideas of justice and had difficulty with acceptance. What does Scripture say about our role in justice (see Leviticus 19:15 and Deuteronomy 16:20)?

3. Maddie built up a wall around her heart because of being hurt in the past. Have you ever done something similar? How? Discuss how you overcame, or if you are still dealing with the issue, how you are handling it.

4. Nick seemed to have survivor's guilt because his brother died and he didn't. Do you ever feel guilty for something that is beyond your control? Discuss how you can use Scripture to overcome this type of guilt.

5. Brody's pre-Christian past came back to haunt him. Everyone has a past. Are there pieces of

your pre-Christian lifestyle you wish never happened? What does Scripture tell us about taking responsibility for our actions (see Romans 3:19)?

6. David had ulterior motives when he met Gina, but he dropped them when he fell in love with her. Discuss ways the outcome could've been different for David had Gina not found the photos. One instance can change our lives. Discuss times in your life when one instance totally changed it.

7. Senator Ford had a lot of power, but that couldn't help him with the death of his daughter. Have you lost someone you loved? How did you handle the grief? Discuss John 16:19–21 and what it says about grief.

8. In the end, Nick realized he was wrong about his father and forgave him. Forgiveness is often something we Christians struggle with. What does Jesus tell us about forgiveness (discuss Matthew 6:14–15 and Matthew 18)?

9. Cynthia Mantle was quite the character. Have you ever met someone like her? Been a friend to someone like her? Discuss what friendship means to you.

10. Familial DNA testing is new and cutting-edge. Do you believe science doesn't lie? Discuss ways you can help improve our legal system.

References

The research for this novel was massive. Below are some of the sites where I've gleaned some information:

http://www.tbi.tn.gov
www.evidencemagazine.com
http://wapp.capitol.tn.gov/apps/BillInfo/Default.
aspx?BillNumber=HB1823
http://www.dna.gov/solving-crimes/cold-cases/
howdatabasesaid/
http://www.denverda.org/DNA_Documents/Forensic
%20DNA%20Testing%20Terminology.pdf
http://www.brighthub.com/science/genetics/
articles/18273.aspx
http://www.sorensonforensics.com
http://www.reuters.com/article/2011/03/30/
us-crime-dna-familial-idUSTRE72T2QS20110330
http://www.scientific.org/tutorials/articles/riley/
riley.html
http://www.mesaaz.gov/police/ForensicServices/
FAQs.aspx
http://www.fbi.gov/about-us/lab/codis/codis_
brochure
http://www.fbi.gov/about-us/lab/codis/familial-
searching
http://www.memphispolice.org/investigations.htm

Center Point Large Print
600 Brooks Road / PO Box 1
Thorndike ME 04986-0001 USA

(207) 568-3717

US & Canada:
1 800 929-9108
www.centerpointlargeprint.com